MARRIAGE LYNX

THE LYNX SERIES
BOOK 7

FIONA QUINN

Marriage

Lynx

Fiona Quinn

THE WORLD OF INIQUUS

Ubicumque, Quoties. Quidquid

Iniquus - /i'ni/kwus/ our strength is unequalled, our tactics unfair – we stretch the law to its breaking point. We do whatever is necessary to bring the enemy down.

The Lynx Series

Strike Force

In Too DEEP

JACK Be Quick

InstiGATOR

Fear The REAPER

Striker

Uncommon Enemies

Wasp

Relic

Deadlock

Thorn

FBI Joint Task Force

Open Secret

Cold Red

Even Odds

Kate Hamilton Mysteries

Mine

Yours

Ours

Cerberus Tactical K9 Team Alpha

Survival Instinct

Protective Instinct

Defender's Instinct

Delta Force Echo

Danger Signs

Danger Zone

Danger Close

Cerberus Tactical K9 Team Bravo

Warrior's Instinct

Rescue Instinct

Hero's Instinct

Cerberus Tactical K9 Team Charlie

Guardian's Instinct

Sheltering Instinct

Shielding Instinct

This list was created in 2023. For an up-to-date list, please visit FionaQuinnBooks.com

If you prefer to read the Iniquus World in chronological order you will find a full list at the end of this book.

To my dear readers,
Thank you for the encouragement you've given me
from the very first step I took on my writing journey,
which all started with Weakest Lynx
I so appreciate your kindness.

THE PLAYERS

The Hydra

The Mastermind—Indigo, deceased
The Moneybags—Sylanos, status unknown
The Private Army—Omega Defense International headed by Dillon Cartwright
The Legal and Political Cover—The Assembly

Iniquus

General Elliot
Leanne Burns
Spyder McGraw
Striker
Lexi

Galaxy

Herman Trudy
General Coleridge
Doc

THE PLAYERS(CONT.)

FBI Joint Task Force

Calvin Hock
Steve Finley
Damian Prescott

CIA Color Code

John Black
John Green

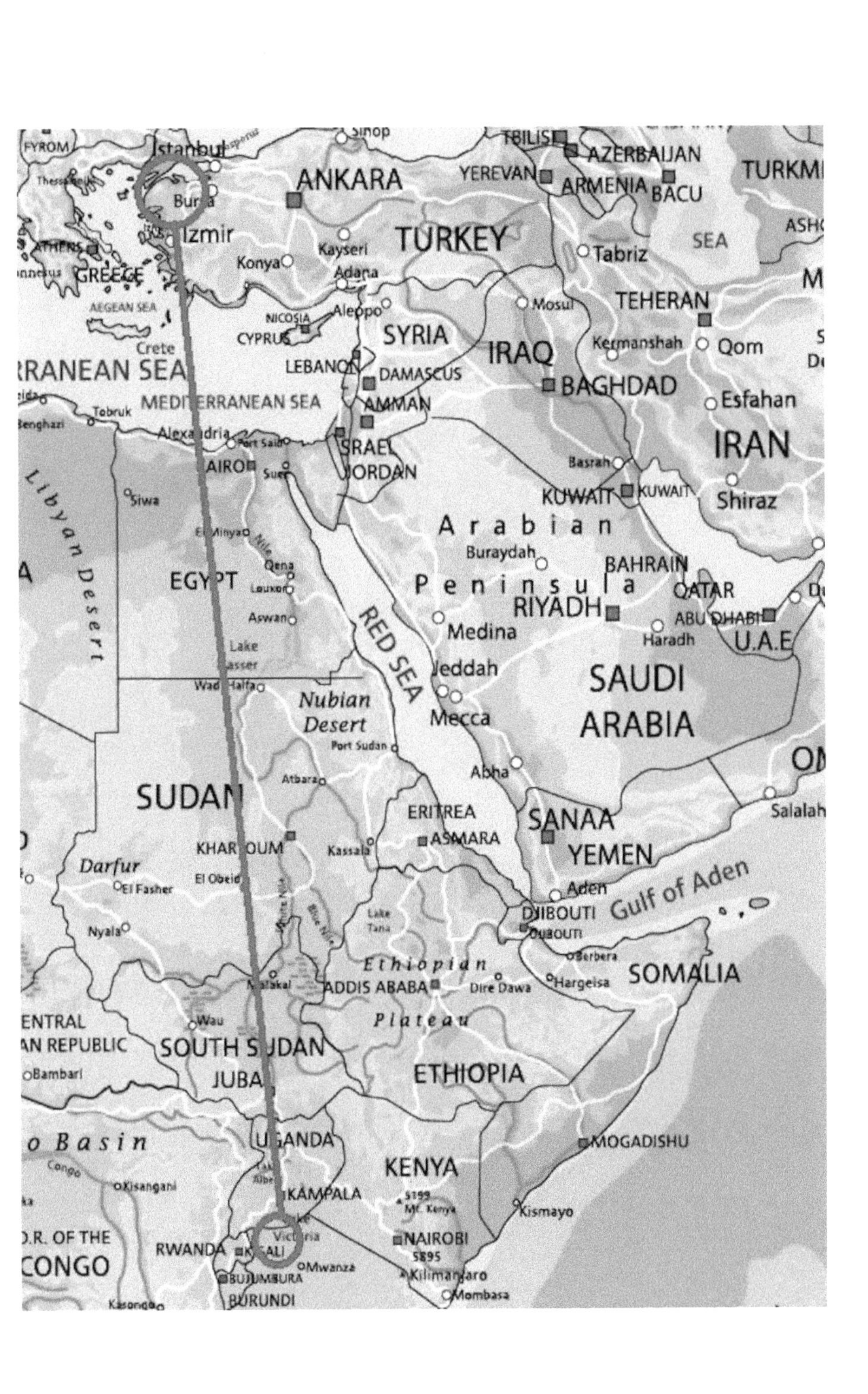

Istanbul
Sinop
TBILISI
AZERBAIJAN
ANKARA
YEREVAN
ARMENIA
BACU
TURKM
Izmir
TURKEY
Kayseri
Konya
Adana
Tabriz
SEA
GREECE
AEGEAN SEA
Aleppo
Mosul
TEHERAN
NICOSIA
CYPRUS
SYRIA
Crete
IRAQ
Kermanshah
Qom
LEBANON
DAMASCUS
BAGHDAD
MEDITERRANEAN SEA
AMMAN
Esfahan
Tobruk
Benghazi
Alexandria
Port Said
ISRAEL
JORDAN
IRAN
Suez
Basrah
Siwa
KUWAIT
Shiraz
Libyan Desert
El Minya
Nile
Arabian
Buraydah
Qena
BAHRAIN
EGYPT
Luxor
Peninsula
QATAR
RIYADH
Aswan
RED SEA
Medina
ABU DHABI
Haradh
U.A.E.
Lake Nasser
Jeddah
SAUDI ARABIA
Wadi Halfa
Nubian Desert
Mecca
Port Sudan
Abha
Atbara
SUDAN
Salalah
ERITREA
SANAA
KHARTOUM
Kassala
ASMARA
YEMEN
Darfur
El Obeid
Aden
Gulf of Aden
El Fasher
DJIBOUTI
Lake Tana
Nyala
Berbera
Ethiopian
Plateau
Malakal
ADDIS ABABA
Dire Dawa
Hargeisa
SOMALIA
Wau
SOUTH SUDAN
JUBA
Bambari
ETHIOPIA
UGANDA
MOGADISHU
Congo
Kisangani
KENYA
KAMPALA
Mt. Kenya
Kismayo
RWANDA
KIGALI
Victoria
NAIROBI
5895
CONGO
Mwanza
Kilimanjaro
BUJUMBURA
BURUNDI
Mombasa
Kasongo

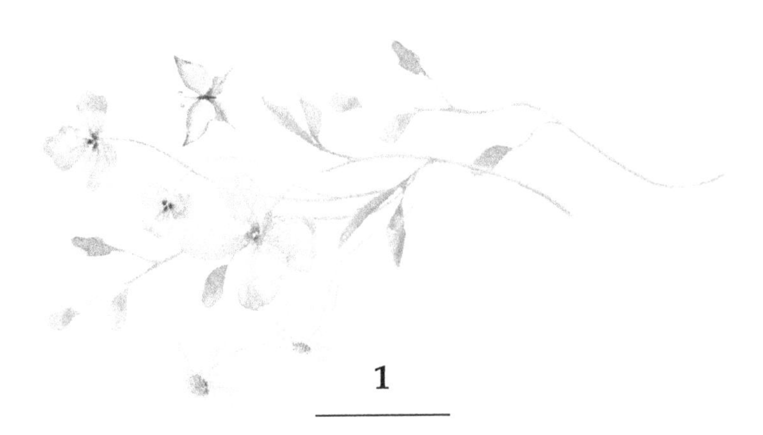

1

Early mornings were my most coveted moments of sleep. Throughout my nights, I tossed and turned and was startled by nightmares. Come morning, perhaps out of sheer exhaustion, I can dive deeper into the sleep cycle and glide beneath the tumult of my overactive brain.

Honestly, I don't know how Striker gets any rest coming to bed with me to sleep. I've suggested he make the guest bedroom his and that we visit back and forth. But he stops me mid-sentence, holding up a hand and saying, "No, I spent too many nights desperate for you to be in my arms. Sleep in the room next door? That's not happening."

And so he puts up with my nighttime internal fights.

Sometimes, in the mornings, Striker will hold me and gently comb his fingers through my hair. Those are the good dreams, the peaceful, "floating on the river in the August sun" dreams. And I loved the luxury of slowly surfacing into a new day. A blinking awareness. A moment when I can piece my world back together: I'm in my bed on Silver Lake. I'm safe.

On other mornings, like this morning, I sensed Striker quietly climbing from the bed, dragging on his running clothes in the bathroom, and tapping his thigh to let Beetle and Bella know that, yes, he was taking them for a run. They didn't have to stomp and clatter their nails on the hardwood floor in the hallway to make their point.

Waking up with a burst of go-juice was a Striker thing, *definitely* not a me thing.

After Striker set the coffee up to perk, there was a slide-tap of the shutting door and the *catchunk* of the lock tumbling into place.

The house settled into a deep stillness that became a weight, sinking me deeper into restorative sleep.

And that was exactly where I was, deep in the depths of my subconscious with an utter lack of awareness, when suddenly, a scream—a sustained high note of desperation, shrill and echoing—shattered the peace from the front of the house.

Lying cozy in bed one moment, sprung into midair, racing forward the next. Fists balled, face fierce, anything—and I mean *anything*—that was endangering my niece would feel the full explosion of my wrath.

Flicking on the light, head on a swivel, I found the soft pink walls and the gentle billow of white sheers dancing with the vented air conditioning.

There was no enemy to doom.

My heart pounded so hard in my chest that it threw me off balance, and I grabbed at the doorframe.

There, in the glare of the overhead light, Cammy knotted her thin limbs into her unicorn sheets, her long black curls damp around a sweating face. Beneath her lids, her eyeballs shot back and forth in REM. Her whole body shivered as she fought whatever demon was rearing its ugly head.

I had years of experience on the sleeping side of a nightmare. I can't say I've ever been around someone else's night terror. Though I wanted to shake her and snap her into the present, I knew how disorienting that could be.

I turned off the light and did what Striker did for me. I crawled into bed with her, wrapping my body around hers. And I chanted,

"You are not alone. I'm here, keeping you safe. You're safe. You are not alone."

I normally don't scream in my sleep. I talk and claw and cry. Striker won't tell me how many times in the night I wake him up with my night terrors, but I knew that when I was living in the safe house when he first came into my adult "Lexi" life, it was at least once or twice a night. The only time I screamed out as loudly as Cammy had just done was when I was psychically connected in my dream to a flailing, failing, dying Gator in desperate need of rescue. That scream had been loud enough that it pulled in the calvary, and sure enough—

"Lynx, it's Reaper and Houston. We're in your house." The call came up the stairs in a voice that would tell any intruder that boded poorly for their health and well-being.

Reaper was an ex-SEAL, now Cerberus K9 trainer. He and his family lived on the other side of my duplex. His house configuration was the flip of mine, so his master bedroom and Cammy's room shared a wall. Of course, he heard. And, of course, like me, he sprang awake and into go-mode with Houston, his tactically trained service dog extraordinaire, by his side.

Houston yipped and whined. I knew she wanted to race up the stairs, but Reaper was giving it a minute. Imagine him barging through a door to find me naked and screaming at a spider. Not that that was the kind of person I was, just a scenario that might occur to him and one that he would want to avoid.

I dragged my phone from my pajama bottom pocket. I had gotten in the habit of sleeping with it on me lately, though I didn't know why. Perhaps I found reassurance in sliding it into my pocket and feeling like I had a lifeline should a lifeline be needed.

Lexi: **Cammy's room**

When Houston's claws scrambled up the stairs, sleeping Cammy opened her arms wide, and a smile danced at the corners of her mouth. Cammy was nuts about dogs, all dogs, all the dogs. She couldn't get enough dogs.

Without waiting for a special invitation, Houston leaped onto Cammy's bed, which told me that was a place where Cammy had welcomed Houston many times before.

She turned a circle, then collapsed into a yin symbol, pushing backward just a bit so that Cammy curled around her furry back. Houston looked at me over her shoulder with a "you can go now, I've got this" glance.

Cammy wrapped an arm around Houston, dragging a sigh of contentment into stuffy nostrils, deeply asleep.

I gave Houston a scratch, then climbed out of Cammy's bed, making my way over to Reaper. His brows drew tightly together, not yet ready to release that warrior go-mode that I myself had experienced moments before.

Patting Reaper's shoulder as I moved past him into the hall, I tipped my ear toward the stairs. Silently, we slid through the darkened house, around the geometric shadows of my furniture, and into the kitchen where the light was still glowing from when Striker put the coffee pot on this morning and grabbed the girls' leads.

"We heard a scream," he said. "I came to see if I could help." Reaper was wearing a pair of blue gym shorts, and that was it. With tousled hair, he slicked his tongue over what were surely still-unbrushed teeth.

"Thank you. I'm really grateful." I opened a cabinet. "Can I pour you a cup of coffee?" Without his answering, I pulled two mugs from the shelf. "Nightmare. Cammy sprang me from my bed, too," I said, reaching for the pot.

"Poor little kid." Reaper dragged a chair from the table and plopped down on the seat. "She's seen entirely too much in her short life. I look at my own kid, and I sometimes picture—"

"Yeah, you need to stop that." I walked over to him and set the steaming yellow mug with a smiley face onto a napkin on the table. "Serves no purpose other than making you crazy." I kicked my chair out just enough to slide onto the seat, set my too-hot mug on the table, and shook my hand to cool it off. "Cammy talks about having bad dreams. That's the first screaming nightmare she's had since she's come to live with us. She didn't wake herself up. Hopefully, she'll forget all about it with a little Houston dog medicine." I rubbed my hand over the cotton fabric of my pajama bottoms. I was still sweaty from the adrenaline geyser. "Whew, Cammy scared the living daylights out of me with that scream. She's got a set of lungs on her for sure."

"Kate looked like she saw a ghost when I headed over."

"Kate!" I pulled my phone out again and tapped out a text: **Sorry, kiddo had a nightmare. Thank you for sending Reaper and mostly Houston. Dog medicine is being applied.**

"I'm letting Kate know everything's safe." After pressing send, I laid the phone on the table in front of me. "I can't imagine the level of vulnerability she's feeling in her third trimester. The sense of risk, knowing that you were housing your baby inside of you and not really being able to fend off any foe, must be so hard on a mother."

Reaper lifted his mug, blew on his coffee, and set it down without tasting it. "She loves that you've been letting Beetle and Bella spend their days with her. Thank you for that. She has her share of nightmares, too."

"I bet. Hey, my blood is still throbbing in my veins. Let's change the subject. What do you know that's good? How's Kate doing when her neighbors aren't exposing her to night terrors?"

"The doctor wants her off her feet as much as possible. Sarah is keeping Little Guy across the street when he's not napping. I'll bring Kate breakfast in bed when I get home." He blew and sipped. "Then I'm heading to Cerberus. We've got a guy coming in to interview for Team Charlie. Basil St. John code name Halo, and his K9 Max. I'm picking them up at the airport."

"Max! What kind of dog?"

"Malinois. Nose and a bite, training in tactical. If this team seems like a good fit, we'll work on building the necessary skill sets."

"Basil St. John isn't a name you hear every day."

"He's an Australian Commando brother of Ryder Kelly. They trained together in K9 handling."

"He's an Australian? An American?" I asked.

"Dual citizen. That's all I know of the situation. And you? What's going on with you?"

Me? Why, I had just threatened the Joint Special Operations Command that I was about to unmask their ongoing black ops unless they gave me what I wanted. And today, I would find out what they thought about my threat.

My gaze wandered to the bird that chirped outside my kitchen window. "As soon as Striker gets back from his run with Beetle and Bella and can take over Cammy's care, I'm heading to General Elliot's house. He has some information for me about a personal situation. I've got my fingers crossed that it's good news."

And that I hadn't made myself enemy number one of the men in charge of the most secretive, lethal forces in the world.

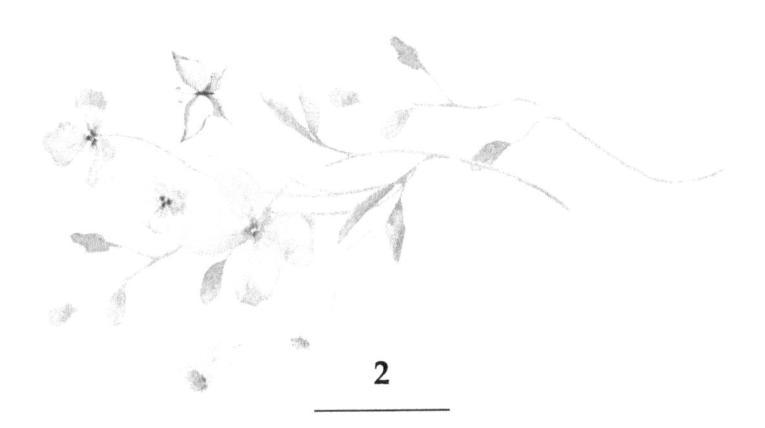

2

THE DAY'S HUMIDITY FOGGED THE GLASS STORM DOOR, HIDING THE decorative wreath with its red, white, and blue bunting left over from the Fourth of July.

I stood on the brick porch between the two cement urns of red geraniums, breathing in their heady scent, wiggling my knees back and forth nervously.

The corgis barked the alarm inside, and I could hear the whisper of Mrs. Elliot calling out for them to hush themselves as she tap-tap-tapped over the slate foyer to open the door. "Right on time," she called out, reaching for Petunia's collar and pressing the latch so the storm door cracked open.

Balancing my dessert offerings in one hand, I pulled the door open to a blast of arctic air. It was probably a reasonably set thermostat, but it was a hundred and five degrees of muggy heat outside.

"What have you got there?" Mrs. Elliot asked, reaching for the plate of key lime bars I had brought as her hostess gift. "My, my, look how pretty you made them with those little sugar-coated violets. Come on in. Follow me."

Turning, I shut both doors tightly behind me, tumbling the deadbolt, then trailing dutifully behind Mrs. Elliot. The dogs leaped onto their tiny legs, looking to see if the good thing on the platter would translate into treats for them.

"You must have done these candied violets up in the spring."

"They're my last ones for this year," I said as I found myself in the kitchen. The house felt still. No General Elliot. "They make me happy—the violet against the cool mint green of the key lime."

Mrs. Elliot put the platter on her countertop. "That's mighty generous of you." She reached out both hands and squeezed my arm. "You look nervous." She squeezed again. "Not that anyone else would see it. I've just been through the wringer a time or two with you, and I have a mother's eye." Her lips pressed into a little frown, and her brow had an empathetic crinkle.

"Yes, well…" I swiped my hands down the front of my blue dress. This was the first stressful step in a series of stressful steps I needed to take today.

"I don't know what all this is about," Mrs. Elliot said. "But I do know that the general has that look in his eye. Locked and loaded. He's going to see this through." She lifted her chin toward a tray set with two tall glasses and a clear pitcher of something pink over ice. "See there? Watermelon lemonade with mint. I'm going to set this on the table out on the veranda. The general decided to fire up the grill. In this blistering heat? I can't imagine the need, but there you have it. Least I can do is help to keep you two hydrated." She lifted the tray. "Listen to me babbling on." She chuckled. "I feel like a mother hen wanting to tuck you safely under my wing."

I opened the kitchen door and held it wide for her as Mrs. Elliot sidled past me and over to the table. She pressed her lips together in a tight smile as she set her tray down. "The general already apprised me the topic of today's little cookout is top secret, so I'll be in my sitting room upstairs." She caught my gaze. "I'm here. If you need anything at all, you just let me know, all right?"

I nodded. My mouth had gone dry enough that my lips caught on my teeth.

"All right then." Mrs. Elliot squared her shoulders, lifted her chin toward the general, sending him some wifely communication, then she turned and went back into the house.

By the time I got my lips pried loose to say, "Thank you, ma'am. It was nice to see you," the door had already thumped closed behind her.

I eyed the watermelon lemonade with longing.

Hot to cold did one thing to my system.

Cold to hot did another.

I turned my attention to General Elliot.

"Grab yourself a seat. I want to bring you up to date, Lexi."

I went ahead and poured out two lemonades and set one in front of General Elliot. Today, outside the Iniquus campus, the general was out of his typical gray bespoke suit. He could be on his way to the country club or a yachting event and fit comfortably into either venue. The general wore a navy blue golf shirt over a pair of pressed khakis. A pair of boat shoes protected his feet from the searing slate patio. A ball cap covered the vulnerable skin of his balding head and shielded his eyes from the sun's glare. It was just shy of noon, and he didn't look like this heat fazed him a bit.

I retreated with my drink to a chair in the depths of the veranda roof's shadow. The underside of the porch was painted the traditional blue to ward away the "haunts." Wide paddled ceiling fans above me wafted air over my glistening skin. I sank into the comfort of the padded chair, taking a sip of my lemonade to unstick my mouth before I set it down on the side table.

If the subject of today's meeting wasn't so replete with dangers, then I could imagine having a lovely visit.

I'd admit, my nerves were still jangled from the way I sprang awake this morning.

Giving the burgers a flip and pulling the lid down over the grill, General Elliot picked up his glass of lemonade and came to sit across from me.

"You're dressed for work," he observed.

And I may have to change if I keep sweating into my dress. "Yes, sir, I have a meeting at Langley."

"You give 'em hell." General Elliot's eyes glistened with grandfatherly affection. Mrs. Elliot was right; we had all been through the wringer together, and through the adversity, we had forged strong bonds.

"Let's talk about clearing a path to getting you and Striker married." He leaned forward, his elbows resting on his thighs, focused. "I understand that with some new personal issues, there is a concern about his niece."

"Cammy, yes, sir. Her mother is in rehab, and Cammy has come to live with us. Striker's sister, Lynda, is uncomfortable with the idea that—as she puts it—Striker and I are living in sin. Lynda thinks that we are poor role models for Cammy. This is, of course, out of our hands at the moment. But it makes us anxious for any decisions Lynda might make about where Cammy lives. Striker has always been Cammy's father figure, so this is extremely concerning."

"How old?"

"Cammy? She just started the school year as a first-grader, sir."

"So too little to have a say in the courts."

"That's right." I had thought that Striker's and my wedding would have happened fourteen months ago. It had been planned, the invitations sent and then snatched back. *Whoops, sorry, we'll keep you apprised.*

Everyone had expressed concern. And curiosity. What was happening between me and Striker?

What was happening?

My dead husband had come back to life; *that's what was happening.*

I ran into him on a mission in Syria—or, to be clear, I received information that he was alive in Syria. But he—Angel Sobado—had been captured, tortured, near death. And I ran into the fray to save him with my fiancé, Striker Rheas, and the Strike Force team at my side.

The person who confirmed that my husband was alive? John Grey of the CIA Color Code. Grey was the man who told me he had recruited Angel in the world of black ops.

And here, I felt some self-anger.

I had thought that because Grey was the guy who had moved Angel from the land of the living into the shadows of the black ops community, that meant that Angel was a CIA black ops operator.

My job for General Elliot was Iniquus Puzzler.

Puzzler.

The woman who figures things out when no one else can.

Why did it take me so long to figure out my own mystery?

Fourteen freaking months of being angry at the CIA for not giving me the divorce papers promised to me.

Fourteen months of having my eyes clouded.

Then someone who knew the story—when no one should know Angel's story—told a friend where Angel would be and when.

There were two bad parts to that scenario and one ah-ha!

Bad parts—Angel's job was to do good in a very dangerous part of the world. He was up against bad guys with terrible powers. Angel "died" to get his name off the books to protect me—his wife—as well as his other family members.

Cruel and courageous at the same time.

That so many people outside of his employer now knew about him being upright and breathing? Yeah, that was a very bad thing.

The second bad part was that when I hunted him down, he escaped back into the desert heat without signing the divorce papers I waved in his face.

General Elliot had warned me in no uncertain terms that he was done waiting for the powers that be to right that ship. It wasn't a matter of my inconvenience or "my man doing me wrong." It was that everyone who knew that Angel was alive became a liability.

So it could be that the bad guys could manipulate Angel by subjecting his loved ones to a long, painful captivity or maybe even death on one end of the spectrum or something as simple as extortion on the other. Of course, I couldn't see Angel caving to either; he'd assess the bigger picture and decide one life might need to be sacrificed for the good of hundreds or even thousands of others.

I was so glad it wasn't in my job description to weigh those moral and ethical issues.

Besides that, there were legal matters that put me at high risk for serious prison time once I knew without a doubt that Angel was alive. For example, I couldn't stop getting my widow's compensation, but that was stealing from the federal government.

"—morning," the general said, looping his half-drained glass in the air, making the ice cubes rattle.

"Sir, I am so sorry. My thoughts were so loud. I have no idea what you just said to me."

"I said that we are heading over to the Pentagon in the morning, you and me. We won't have a lawyer with us. It's a listening tour. We'll pull Sy Covington in if it looks like that's warranted. I've consulted him, of course, but it ups the posturing when a lawyer's in the room. So JSOC, after breakfast, zero eight hundred at the Atrium door, we'll have a car. Move everything off your calendar. This takes precedence."

I swallowed the lump of saliva in my throat. I wasn't going in alone. I'd have the general beside me. As one of the Iniquus commanders, it wasn't like he could go missing and the alphabet world in D.C. wouldn't light up brightly with concern. "Yes, sir."

"What's on your agenda today? Langley, you said?"

"Yes, sir."

"When I spoke to JSCOC, I asked for permission to contact Color Code over at the CIA and tell them to stand down when it comes to you. We understand that they are proximal to your personal situation. And I was granted that permission to use those words."

I leaned forward. Besides the personal issues that Angel's little ghost act caused, they had also caused me a heaping helping of career headaches, making those I worked with in the CIA Color Code eye me with suspicion. In our line of work, that could cause issues, and issues looked like lives on the line. I'm glad that this was getting cleared. "And their response?"

"Cordial, but I sensed relief. Hopefully, at least in terms of the Color Code operators, you'll meet with less friction over there. It should make your job easier."

"I hope so, sir. Thank you, sir."

"Now, in the meantime, I'm going to state my wish, beyond my wish, that you are as happy in your marriage as I am with Mrs. Elliot, that is." He leaned back in his chair, resting his glass on the arm. "I know that your life is filled with strong bonds. And you have many people that will participate in your wedding, but as your self-proclaimed grandfather, I'm going to make an ask. Once we get this mess cleared up, I hoped you and Striker would consider allowing me the honor of being your officiant."

"Oh!" Emotion gathered and crowded my senses. "I..." Pressing my hands to my chest, I tried to get my lips to smile, for my face to show pleasure. "Thank you," I managed.

"I know you're a duo. So there might be someone that Striker wants up there. If this doesn't work out, I'll find another role. I want you happy."

Striker and I had already talked about it. And General Elliot presiding over our vows was what we had hoped. But I wasn't ready to start putting the wedding into gear again.

Until some judge in some courtroom released me from my ties to Angel, any plans for my wedding to Striker had to be put on ice.

Reaching for my "happily ever after" too soon seemed like bad juju.

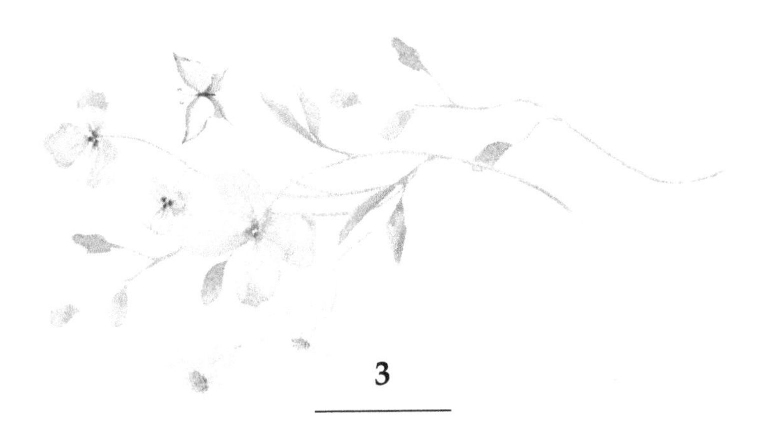

3

TYPICALLY, STRIKER LIKED TO BE HERE WHEN I CAME TO THE alphabets, like the CIA, to reveal a puzzle. He enjoyed seeing how I laid out my narrative, listening to my random stories, and watching the officers' faces as I revealed the palm-to-forehead thing right in front of their eyes.

Me too—if I'm being honest with myself.

My mentor, Spyder McGraw, had always said that my best disguise was a fluffy bunny, sweet and cute, with not much going on in my head. When I opened my purse and pulled out a can of whoop-ass, be it a fighting technique or the sharp weapon of my puzzling skills, it felt victorious. Though, in settings like the CIA, I tried to use my best sportsmanship.

Like in all games, sometimes you win, sometimes you lose, and sometimes it ends in a draw.

My best hope for today was leaving with a draw.

If the puzzle box needed five hundred pieces to form a complete picture, I needed enough pieces to predict the possible image. The CIA hadn't given me even the corner pieces to work with.

Puzzling had been my way of life since I was itty bitty.

One day, I was in my mom's bed, reading beside her as she drew.

Mom moved a piece of art, an ink drawing, off to the side with a huff. Picking it up, I looked at the intricacy of her work, the extraordinary details. It was an illustration of a scene Dad read as my bedtime story the night before. I always had my bedtime stories cozied up on my parents' bed, warm and safe.

"What's wrong with it?" I'd asked. "This is beautiful."

Mom said, "Once you know, you know, and you'll never be able to unsee it or unknow it. Do you really want to know?"

Of course, I did.

Mom leaned in and pointed to a huge splash of ink at the bottom.

I had looked right past it. And I had been searching the illustration to discover what had aggravated Mom. Even looking for the fault, I hadn't seen it. And she was right. There it was, right in front of me. My brain overlooked it for whatever reason brains do that kind of thing.

That was a big lesson for me when it came to puzzle-solving. It's important not to come at something straight on. At the time, I thought that if I had repositioned the ink drawing somehow—looked at it upside down or at an angle—that splotch might have jumped out at me. And so it was with all the puzzles from then on.

That journey of twisting the puzzle this way and that, filtering the light through literary stories or history, or science experiments, that mind map revealing the path that took me from mystery to solution, that's what Striker loved.

There was nothing for him to love in today's meeting. I was coming up with a goose egg. No need for him to be by my side as I told the table of men, salivating for their anticipated solution, that they would go hungry.

"Here we go," I said under my breath, "time to face the music." I pushed through the front door at Langley. High heels echoing over the white marble, I made my way through security.

Climbing into an empty elevator, I stretched my finger toward the panel when I heard, "Hold the elevator, please."

Who should walk into the car but John Black?

He stepped in with his gaze on his cell phone screen. As the doors slid shut, he looked up and caught my eye. Too late to escape, the doors closed.

I pressed the five button, then turned to Black to get his floor number.

"Casper?" he asked.

"That's where I'm heading. You?"

"Same."

Poo. It was bad enough that I had to show up and talk to Casper's crew, but now Color Code would be in on my failure, too. At least Black wasn't sprung on me as a surprise in the room. This might be my opportunity to cool the temperature between us a bit. "Black, I feel like we may need to lay some cards on the table." Surely, General Elliot hadn't had time yet to get the *stand-down* decree whispered into the right Color Code ear or for that information to filter its way to Black. "I'm wondering if your colleague discussed with you a recent interaction he and I had at the Dead Sea?"

"He did." He turned to face the closed doors as the elevator began its ascent.

"I want you to know that I don't hold your colleague responsible for my predicament," I said, referring to John Grey. "I'm handling it respectfully and carefully through the correct lines. I get that the CIA has an obligation to maintain State secrets. Your colleague is *not* obligated to correct the issues that came into his awareness while being read into a program by a different entity." Being plain and cryptic at the same time was always a bit of fancy footwork. I thought I got my point across, though.

"Oh." He angled his face toward me just enough that he could get me in his peripheral.

I watched his body language carefully. Even though the CIA officers were highly trained with biofeedback machines and practiced with lie detector apparatus to be able to lie effectively under the most difficult of circumstances, that didn't mean that distance from that training and years away from field work didn't let those skills atrophy a bit. Black's "Oh," while said in a neutral tone, seemed to exhale relief.

"Thank you for saying so." He pointed between us. It didn't seem to be a gesture he normally made. "We're good?" That phrase sat oddly on his tongue. Maybe he was trying to do "young-person communication?" I could appreciate the attempt.

"We're good," I agreed.

We walked side by side down the hall. Not companionably. But at least this time, he wasn't signaling the security guard to draw his weapon on me. That was progress.

I walked into a room filled with officers.

Casper sat at the head of the oval table. He pointed out a side seat to Black. The only seat left for me was at the other head of the table.

Casper stood, shut the door, and started by saying, "Iniquus Puzzler Lynx is here with what information she was able to cull from the tapes we've sent her." Casper didn't enjoy calling me in to offer my tidbits to his team. That was obvious in the bile color that he used to shade his words.

It wasn't my job to care about his feelings, though. The best I could do was channel my inner Striker and try to mask my discomfort with stoicism.

The men turned eager eyes on me. Better nip those expectations in the bud.

I could neither prove nor disprove the criminal theory that they had handed me.

Sweeping my hand down the back of my skirt, I sat and offered up a fluffy-bunny smile. Today, I had changed out of the earlier outfit I'd worn to see the general. Nerves and tropical conditions meant I wasn't professionally fresh. Now, I wore one of my favorite dresses. It was the usual nineteen-fifties-style form-fitting bodice with a skirt held wide with a crinoline petticoat. It had a modest boat neckline and three-quarters sleeves. The fabric pattern was created with overlapping sprays of what could be D.C. cherry blossoms in cream on navy. When I wore this dress, it made me feel oddly powerful, maybe regal. I needed to feel good in my skin today. Admitting that there was no rabbit for me to pull from my hat was tough.

"Gentlemen." I cast my gaze around the table.

"If we're ready," Casper said, tapping a command on his laptop that dimmed the lights. "Lynx, I'll start by showing my colleagues the film we sent you to analyze."

Now I knew why Casper gestured me to the end of the table. The video played on the screen over my head, and there were no additional chairs to relocate to.

Over my years working with Iniquus clients, I learned a lot about ego and pettiness.

I also learned how not to give it any energy.

I stood back up and walked halfway down the length of the table, put my shoulder to the wall, and turned to watch with the rest of the CIA officers.

My adjustment put Casper's move on full display. The officers were aware of the power grab. This really wasn't the way to treat someone who was there to help you—though, in this case, not so much. And I was beginning to feel a little better about that.

I could feel Black's eyes on me as I watched the film, and I felt his approval radiate across the table.

At least, I liked to imagine that I could.

I don't know why, but I wanted the Color Code's respect. I didn't always agree with their methods and tactics, but then again, I didn't do what they did. I didn't know what they knew.

It was probably better that way for my ability to sleep's sake.

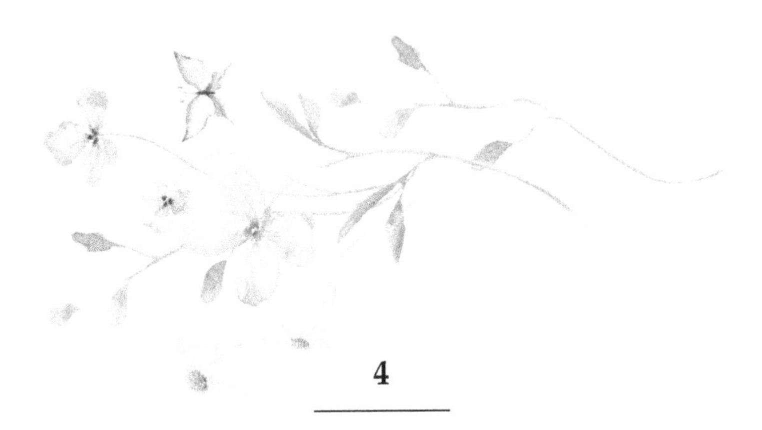

4

FOCUSING ON THE FOOTAGE, I WATCHED CAESAR IONA AT A BLACK-tie affair populated by international glitterati. Everyone there was dripping in wealth. And the CIA had landed on this man as the one who was obtaining above-top-secret classified materials and passing them to some unidentified receiver.

Why?

Not money. Iona had plenty. He was approaching billionaire status.

"All right, Lynx, we're ready to hear your presentation. How is Iona getting intelligence to the buyer?"

I looked around the table. *I dunno* seemed too weak. I'd tell them a story, make them feel like they'd got some bang for their buck. "In this case, I'm reminded of Benjamin Franklin." I smiled. "Did you all know that Ben Franklin used to live on Craven Street in London? Craven Street. The irony of that name strikes me. He lived there on Craven Street from 1757 until 1775, a good long while. Lucky for us, he was back in America before the Declaration of Independence. We needed him here." I walked back to the head of the table so I wasn't causing neck strains for the officers. "Did you know that about thirty years ago, they found a couple dozen bodies buried in that house?"

I was getting a lot of head tilts as the men tried to figure out why we were talking about Franklin.

"Yeah, crazy. Right? London police thought they had a new serial killer on their hands. But no." I shook my head. "No. Those bones dated back to the mid-1700s. In the mid-1700s, Founding Father Franklin lived in that house. But they don't think it was Franklin who was killing people and hiding them in the basement. There was another guy who lived there. His name was Hewson." I looked down at the floor. Was that right? "I think that was his name. Something-son, anyway. He was what they called an anatomist. He studied cadavers to learn what he could to improve our knowledge of how bodies worked. They weren't killed in medical experimentation. This wasn't a concentration camp type of scenario with a psychopathic surgeon. This was something that was going on in the era. The anatomists would get bodies where they could—unclaimed dead prisoners, for example. And sometimes, they'd pay grave robbers to dig up fresh corpses. Were these bodies legal? Illegal? It's hard to say two hundred years on. It's very hard to tell, once things are buried for that long, what actually happened. And, of course, even if you did know, Hewson, Franklin, and everyone else involved are long dead and will feel no repercussions. The point of this story? Just because you dig up bones, and just because someone lives in the house where the bones were buried, doesn't mean that your suspect has any knowledge of the bones or anything to do with them either."

Casper rolled his hand in the air as if wanting to speed me up to get to the punch line. "So you're saying?"

"There's a real possibility that Franklin was living his life upstairs while, unbeknownst to him, the knowledge-seeking doctor was carving cadavers stolen from the graveyard. Same thing with Iona in your video footage."

"Come *on*, Lynx." What a weird combination of emotions he was displaying—disappointed that I wasn't fixing their problem and pleased that he'd stumped me.

I reached down to my bag and pulled out my laptop. I plugged into the outlet on the table that would connect me to the screen and pulled out my own fob. I opened to a colonial-era painting.

Standing, I pointed up at the guy.

"There are other options for how to interpret these tapes. If Ben Franklin and innocent proximity don't work for you, let's try this one for size. Again, I'm going to frame it with a revolutionary personality. This guy was friends with Benjamin Franklin, actually." I pointed at the man dressed in an embroidered satin gentleman's finery, balanced on a wooden leg. "While Ben was known for his womanizing, his friend outdid him in that department. Let me tell you about one of our most important founding fathers, Gouverneur Morris. Do you know that name?" I looked around the table and was met with blank stares. "Yeah, not a lot of people have. Weird. He wrote the preamble of the Constitution. He spoke out against slavery. He was even predicting a future civil war based on the continuation of slavery. Maybe that's why his story isn't discussed in our textbooks. I mean, Jim Crow ended in my parents' lifetimes. So, between being an egalitarian and his lust for life, people of yore might not have seen him as textbook-worthy. I don't know, I don't choose curriculum." I turned to look at the picture and drew in a breath.

Turning back to my audience, I said, "Morris, who penned such words as 'We the People of the United States, in order to form a more perfect Union,' really, really liked to have sex. He liked to have sex in public spaces, the Louvre, for example." I stopped to offer one of my innocent bunny smiles. "He seemed to delight in having relations with other men's wives. In a story he wrote in his diary—a journal, I guess, would be a more manly term—he told about copulating with a woman in a public room while hubby was playing cards nearby. Morris got away with his fun and games that time but wasn't always so lucky. As it happens, Morris was getting it on with a married woman, the husband came upon them in the throes of passion, and the husband chased Morris through the streets. An accident ensued, and Morris lost his leg when a carriage ran him over."

I looked at the painting.

"That's how he got his peg leg, a sex accident. Eventually, his libido calmed down enough to get married. His bride had been his housekeeper and was about twenty years younger than he was. And again, Morris made interesting choices. Before the two met, it seems his future bride had an affair with her brother-in-law and became pregnant. She had the baby, and the baby died soon after birth. Not unusual for that period. But apparently, this seemed suspicious, so the authorities locked up both parents. It went to trial. Ugly trial. In the end, the judge dismissed the case for lack of evidence. Since she wasn't a convicted infanticidal criminal, Morris went ahead and married her. The takeaway from my story is that there are people in our past who did great things for our nation who were not shiny and golden in all aspects of their lives. Humans have their faults and weaknesses. Even with his wonderful contributions, Gouverneur Morris wasn't a beacon of propriety by the standards of his time or any period I've ever studied. But he was a person of great wisdom and intellect."

I flipped the picture on the screen to the CIA mark Caesar Iona, regal in his bespoke suit.

"Iona is such a man," I said. "With everything you've handed me to try and implicate him, all I can say is that he did or he did not do it. Just like with the trial over Mrs. Morris's baby who had died, there wasn't then, and there isn't now enough information to know what happened."

Casper tossed his pen, and it skipped over the table.

"You're a fan of this guy, Iona?" Cho asked, insinuating that I wasn't being forthcoming.

I planted my hands flat on the table, looking the guy in the eye. "If Iona was the most philanthropic person in the world, doing the best of things, I wouldn't hide the truth from you to protect him. I believe that no one is above the law and that justice should be blind. I would tell you if I saw an answer amongst the puzzle pieces. I just don't. If there's something there, you're going to have to provide more informative intelligence."

"But you want to put a thumb on the scale. I can see it in your eyes," Casper pushed.

"I want nothing to do with your team's inner decision-making. It is completely on you all to decide where to spend your manpower and your budget." I turned to look at Iona's picture, then back at the men. "He's not a beacon of good citizenry in terms of his promiscuity. He certainly has questionable friendships with our State enemies. In parallel to his risky behaviors, his contributions are extraordinary. His satellite communications system saves thousands of lives each day."

"This time, she told stories about randy forefathers." Cho leaned over to Black and said, "Last time, we learned about how Benedict Arnold was caught and techno art. I mean, her presentations are never boring." He didn't direct the comment to me, so I just kept going.

"Another brief piece of information, gentlemen, to leave you with a suggestion and some final thoughts. First, the suggestion. You are all men. There is a slight variety in cultural backgrounds, very slight. But you are all about the same age. Live the same lifestyles. And presumably share many of the same thoughts. Bias, gentlemen, can leave you blind to the thing that is right in front of your face. And worse? It can endanger you and those you care about, the things you want to keep precious." I lost them. They all tuned out to Charlie Brown's teacher's womp womp of unintelligible gibberish.

Tapping my fob, I brought up a picture of hurricane-force winds bending palm trees nearly in two.

"Let's leave Colonial America and move up to modern times for this next analogy. Did you all know that storms with female names are the most dangerous in a storm survival situation?"

"That can't possibly be statistically accurate." The guy at my left elbow said.

"On the surface, I would agree with you. How could it possibly be that the names of female storms happen to be the deadliest? It's because of gender bias. Males are big and strong. Females are weak.

You behave in one way if you hear Ivan roaring toward your town. You take it seriously and prepare. If it's Wilma, not so much. Researchers have looked at a half-century of storms and found that when the storms had female names, there were three times more deaths. *Three times the death*, that's an enormous number of impacted people."

"All right, people should listen to the data of the storm and not the name. What has that to do with this?"

"Gentlemen, you think that this man," I moved the image to a close-up of Iona's face, "is a storm that will uproot everything. You're busy battening down the hatches and nailing boards over the windows." I flipped to another picture. "Now, my question to you. Do you know this woman?"

"We believe the party coordinators hired her for the evening," the guy next to Black said. "The host often uses a high-level prostitution house to provide beautiful women as both decoration and stress relief."

"Mmm, and you don't have her name? Her background information? Did you see her arrive with the other sex workers?"

"The women arrived at various times. If they showed up in a bus all at once and converged on the party, the wives would grow suspicious and be angry."

"I see. Well, okay." I spun back nearly to the beginning of the tape. "I'm just going to give her a nickname then. I'll call her The Chameleon." I brought the focus down tight on her wrist where she had a tattoo of the Sephirot, just long enough for Casper to focus on it and see that I was correct, then I zoomed back out. "It seems that you're still working on the same case that you brought me in on before." I faced Casper. "The cigarette smoking twins case."

Three men in this meeting had been present when I'd pointed this woman out to them before. Her appearance on the screen had them squirming in their chairs.

Casper and Cho threw their hands in the air.

"Yup, she's back in your lives. And not a sex worker. Well,

maybe." I tilted my head and let a frown form between my brows. "I don't know. Maybe she uses sex in her work, but not in the way you described to me earlier. She is making me very curious, though. What is she up to? And why did she spend so much time with this guy?" I tapped the fob to move the film forward, then stopped on his face mid-funky dance move with The Chameleon smiling encouragement. "His name is Randolph Burke."

Casper stared me down. "Burke is solid. Patriotic."

"And a dear friend of the president's, move on," Cho said.

"Burke works with tippity top special sauce high security intelligence for the Pentagon. And he's thought to be unaffected by any of the typical red flag motivators: He has plenty of money. His publicly expressed beliefs are pretty mainstream." I leaned forward, elbows on the table. "He went upstairs to have his ego stroked in this video. Not as much stroking as Iona received at this party. Iona's conquests that evening were impressive, even Gouverneur Morris-like, wouldn't you agree?" I asked as I looked around the table.

The men leaned back, looking uncomfortable.

I sat down again, lifting my finger to point at the woman on the screen above my head. "This is a woman that you know is spying. This man, Burke, has all the things in his head worth spying about. But you followed Iona around, hoping it was him. You didn't hand me any intelligence that even remotely makes me think it was Iona."

I shut the lid of my laptop. The screen above me went black.

"To conclude, gentlemen, from what evidence you handed me, Iona might just be part Gouverneur Morris who enjoys his randy ways and slips into private rooms with...everyone. He might be like Ben Franklin's proximity without knowledge. To go any further with this, I need better intel. And the intel I would prefer would be on Burke. That concludes what I have to say. I'm open to questions."

Black ducked his head to hide the smile that wanted to curl his lips. I had never seen him happy before this. Generally, he was aggressive and hard-focused. Mirth? It was an unlikely emotion.

But, at least in regard to our relationship, I felt like I'd made progress.

That couldn't be a bad thing, right?

5

ALL THE WAY DOWN THE ELEVATOR, OUT THE AUTOMATIC DOORS, AND down the corridor, an earworm chanted, *"Birds of a feather flock together as do pigs and swine; rats and mice will have their choice, and so shall I have mine."*

It didn't surprise me at all as I moved through the doors into the steam-bath weather that I saw Calvin Hock and Rowan Kennedy walking in lockstep with a man that I didn't recognize. The FBI and the CIA didn't often hold hands, but in this case, Rowan Kennedy worked closely with his CIA counterparts as an FBI special agent, Eastern European legal attaché.

"Hey there." I lifted my hand to shield my eyes.

"Okay, here's a bright spot in my day." Kennedy sped up his pace to join me.

Two other members of the FBI Joint Task Force rounded into view, Prescott and Finley.

"You've got most of the crew here today." I nodded toward the man I didn't know. "Lynx Sobado, Iniquus," I said, extending my hand.

"John Green."

"CIA Color Code. I've heard your name so often, I feel that we should be friends." At the startled look in his eyes, I added. "Though I know absolutely nothing about you. It's nice to put a face together with a name." I turned to the others. "Prescott! Finley!" I smiled my greeting.

"I'm hoping that your standing here with Kennedy means he invited you to this meeting," Prescott said as he jogged up the steps to join us.

"No invite." I reached for his extended hand and gave it a friendly shake. "But I can stay if there's something I could be helpful with. I was going to call your office later today to see if I could swing by and pick your brains. I don't know—"

Prescott tugged my hand to turn me toward the front doors. "Black suit. Brutal sun. Let's go in. Yes, glad to help if we can. Thank you. We'd appreciate you in the room. Finley told me when we saw you come out the door that you had a connection to our topic, a distant one, but that you'd spent an evening with our subject."

"Interesting. A whole evening?"

Finley yanked the door open and held it wide as we entered the building.

Green badged us through security and led us to a room needing biometric data to unlock. Whenever I entered secure areas like this, I felt like an actress playing a role rather than a human having a real-world experience.

We arranged ourselves in the chairs, and I reached forward to snag a water bottle.

"Where were you coming from?" Green asked.

"A meeting that included John Black." I smiled.

Green shot a glance to Kennedy of confusion.

"Lynx is the Iniquus puzzler," Kennedy explained. "She's a mad genius."

"Stop," I said. Green was going to ask Black about me, and Black was going to say, "She had no answers, but she did talk about founding father libidos and storm names." I twisted the top off my bottle. "I was challenged to examine some party footage and make a case. I couldn't do that, not with the video they handed me, nor with the video that Iniquus had from an operator who filmed while at the same party."

The video had come from Command. They said I was free to share it with anyone I needed to. "Study it carefully," the message had said. And I did. And from it, I pulled very little, which I demonstrated at the CIA meeting earlier in the day.

Who knew? Maybe it was the FBI who could offer me an ah-ha here.

"I can't show you the CIA video," I continued. "I can show you mine. There are four people that I want to ask about, one in particular. Having said that, mine doesn't need immediate action. I can set another meeting with you if we run out of time. Do you want to go first? What did you want me to look at?"

Rowan Kennedy leaned forward. "You know my wife is a romance editor. And you know that she was able to help the FBI solve a crime because she understood something about grammar that we didn't pick up on at all."

"I heard. That was so much fun," I said with a smile. "She did a great job."

"I just handed her a letter to see if she noticed anything unusual. Care to take a stab at it?"

"Yes!" Under the table, I kicked off my shoes to get my feet on the ground so I could think clearly. I had worked with this team at Iniquus enough times that they'd seen me do this very thing. They'd understand that shoes off meant thinking cap on.

Kennedy pulled out his laptop and plugged it in. Now, the image of a piece of flowery stationery and an equally flowery script writing came up.

Dear One,

I had an issue at the house. The bolt. You know the one.

No matter what I do, it holds fast.

And before you ask, I know the righty-tighty rhyme, I was reminded by John, left.

One of our friends was bound to tell you about this at some point, anyways.

I'm at my wit's end; this needs to be fixed immediately.

With loving devotion,

Priscilla.

I READ it over and asked, "And you gave it to your wife because you saw how oddly it was worded and the bizarre punctuation?"

"Exactly, even with the loopy script and the name Priscilla, it just reads as an odd way to say something to anyone," Kennedy said.

"Well." This was child's play. I reached into my bag for a piece of paper and pen and copied the short letter down for myself. "The interesting things here are the oddity of the punctuation and that it's filled with contranyms." I circled them as I spoke, and then I looked up.

Kennedy was laughing. "So, for everyone who is not Lynx, a contranym is a word with two contradictory meanings. That is, they are their own opposites. Unlike homophones that messed me up throughout my elementary school days, this list is very short. There are ten of them, or so my wife Avery tells me."

"I've circled the contranyms, and I'm writing them out. As the opposing meaning." I got up and moved to the seat where the men could see my page. "Priscilla, that's a nice touch. That and the loving devotion. Here we go."

- Something bad happened at the house.
- (Bolt) I quickly ran away.
- (No matter what I do, it holds fast.) They tried to fix the problem but to no avail.
- (John, left. or something that would be interpreted correctly when they saw that name) ran

"Left is a contranym: he left the house, the key was left on the counter, but interestingly, this contranym is used as a third definition as a direction."

- (our friends were bound) He had been restrained.

"And not a contranym, but I'm writing it down here anyway."

- (I'm at my wit's end; this needs to be fixed immediately.) You need to step in.

"Now I'm correcting for sequence, and I get, 'I was at the safe house (or some secret place, but the recipient knows where). We were trying to fix a problem but weren't successful. John ran. I ran. A third person was captured. And you (the recipient) need to do something about it.'

The men laughed.

Kennedy tapped his computer, and there on the slide, almost the exact same message was written out.

"Brava to Avery." I grinned. "That was really well done. I enjoyed all of it. It would certainly be overlooked if this was just in a pile of papers. Looking at it here on the screen, it's obviously suspect. But yeah, fun. So is that it? Does anything else need to be figured out about the puzzle?"

"Well," Green said, "you have me intrigued by what you wanted to present to us. How about we take a look at your players and see if any of us can help you with your questions."

I plugged in my computer and attached the cord so my video would display on the screen. Scrolling forward to where I had bookmarked the spy with the Sephirot tattoo, I stopped. "Anyone know her?" I zoomed in on her face.

"Context?" Prescott asked.

I moved my cursor down to her left wrist and zoomed in there.

Prescott and Finley came out of their seats, leaning forward to get a better look.

Green shot a startled look over at the men.

"Where?" Prescott said.

"The Seychelles. It was a party of international powerhouses heavily populated with Russian glitterati. The Omega head honcho, Dillon Cartright, was there. And three other American men, whom I want to understand better, were there. But I'm going to hold that off for a moment."

"Which Sephirot is illuminated on her wrist? Have you been able to see it?" Prescott asked as he reclaimed his chair.

"Wisdom, understanding, and knowledge," I told him. "The same group that went after DARPA scientist Kealoha."

Green raised a brow, asking for context.

"There is a group of people that cross our paths from time to time," Prescott explained. "They are black ops associated with Israel. Their exact task is a little confusing. It seems to have something to do with which circle on their tattoo is illuminated with color."

"Examples?" Green asked.

"The FBI was pursuing a case of domestic terrorism," Finley said, "where we believed that an archaeologist might have been selling conflict relics to aid and abet ISIS. A man came into the picture who had the Sephirot. He had illuminated *tiferet*. His role seemed to be protecting those relics and, to some extent, the scientist."

"Science seems to be a common denominator," Prescott said. "I worked a case where a DARPA scientist was marked. We don't know to what end. They attempted to kidnap her when her then-boyfriend, a Marine, came home to find them in her bedroom. He killed them both. But there were a dozen involved, highly trained, lethal, and motivated."

"There was another case with the scientists where they showed up," I added. "The Tanzanian terror attack where the scientists were abducted. Iniquus operators spotted a Sephirot. Iniquus never determined his real name, the man who perished in that attack. We were able to give the location of his body to the Israeli government. We keep running into these tattoos. And Prescott, you're right. It seems to revolve around scientists."

I leaned back in my seat and looked up at the ceiling. I wasn't prepared to speak to them today. A bird in hand, though. "Here's the interesting thing about this woman. She's come up in a case I'm not at liberty to discuss. Prescott," I turned to catch his gaze, "at the time I puzzled that case, the client promised to pass the information to you. Did that happen?" I asked cryptically.

"It did. And I didn't recognize her face until I saw the tattoo. The context is so different."

"Agreed. Gentlemen." I directed this to everyone at the meeting. "I call her The Chameleon. She is a master at shapeshifting. I find her fascinating. When I worked the other case, I was able to follow her movements only because of the tattoo. I've never seen her operating on American soil. I did find her in another obscure scientific spot, though."

I scrolled through my files while I talked. "I was at Dr. Arya Khouri's house. You all know that name?" I knew the others had, but I was checking to see if Green was in the loop without singling him out.

"Sound scientist whose findings were used in attacks on various diplomatic buildings?" Green asked.

"Among other things, yes," I told Green. "Arya is a friend of mine and is receiving daily medical intervention for what happened to her. But she said I could come specifically to Calvin Hock and tell him about a memory that resurfaced for her." I focused on Hock. "Thank you, Calvin, for being so kind to her during the FBI interrogations. She is so fragile, and it means a lot to me that you've taken good care."

Calvin nodded. "Yes, of course."

"Now, before I get there, let me show you this." I found the picture I needed and posted it on the screen. "I realize I'm jumping around like a jackrabbit. I hadn't organized myself for a meeting with you all today. But I promise to thread it all together." I posted a picture on the screen. "I was looking through a book of Arya's pictures. This one is from a conference for the UN talking about sound pollution. Do you see this blonde who is reaching out to hug Arya?" I zoomed in on her wrist and the tattoo.

"It's the same woman?" Green asked, squinting at the screen.

"Our AI systems say it is. They looked like friends, so I asked Arya who she was. She said that it was a colleague, that much she remembered. She couldn't recall the woman's name. That's neither here nor there. Surely, The Chameleon would have used an alias, and Arya's memories are returning to her in sputters. Arya did, however, remember that this woman is a sound scientist and that they had had a project in common, which oddly had to do with the sound of hibernation."

"Hibernation," Green repeated, looking baffled. "Interesting. Did you figure out what it was by tracking down her publications?"

"I didn't. I went back and found a roster of the attendees. I looked up each one's bio and photograph. The Chameleon is nowhere in any of that. Our AI systems find her nowhere on the Internet. She's getting scrubbed somehow."

I took a big swig of my water.

"So now that I've exhausted what I have on The Chameleon," I said, setting my bottle back down, "I have a couple of science parallels pinging for me. I just wanted your take. First, this guy." I changed the photo. "Caesar Iona. He's big into satellites. As a matter of fact, he owns the satellites used by the space archaeologist Finley mentioned before. Very loose connection there." I flipped the picture. "And this guy is Randolph Burke."

"Also a billionaire. He plays a wide game," Finley said. "He's good friends with the president."

"Exactly," I said. "I just find it interesting that Iona is here at this particular party at the same time The Chameleon was. And I was particularly interested that Burke spends most of his evening with—" I now showed the whole picture of The Chameleon dancing in a very familiar way with my target. "The Chameleon."

I looked around at the scowls.

"Both Iona and Burke made their money through very generous government contracts that were part of The Assembly," I said. "Both of them, because of their importance to the world economy and their philanthropy, seemed to have dodged the fate of many of the other Assembly members when the whistleblower data was released to the public."

I flipped to another photo.

"And here's another Assemblyman who slipped past the repercussions, Griffin Babcock. Now, I have come across this man a few times. Once, on a mission, I spent the evening getting to know him. On that evening, I realized that he, though small in stature, was incredibly connected. He knew everyone and everything about everything. *Brilliant* mind. Awkward as a date. Finley, you'll appreciate this: Babcock is the owner of a painting created by Tsukamoto, and when your ex-girlfriend was trying to gather all the artwork in the D.C. area to send to what she thought was a museum show, she was not persuasive in getting Babcock to relinquish the painting in his office." Though Finley didn't understand the significance of the Tsukamoto artworks as doorknobs, a kind of protection against remote viewers, he would now have a personal connection to the man.

And that's when I recalled that Prescott, on the front steps, had said I'd spent a whole evening with their subject. They hadn't introduced a subject to me. Could it have been Babcock?

"Really? Small world." Finley obviously didn't like that connection.

I scrolled through a series of photos as I watched for body language tells from the men. "Here, Babcock is speaking to Iona." Click. "Here, Babcock is laughing it up with Burke." Click. "And here, Babcock is slow dancing with—"

"The Chameleon," Green said. "And yet, they're all at the same party." Yeah, something about this had them tensing up. The problem was that they weren't offering me data in exchange. Prescott didn't verify this was the guy he'd referred to outside or that he had anything to do with the cryptic Priscilla letter.

This was another example of the problem with need-to-know and, frankly, the problem with my curiosity.

But I bit my tongue other than to say, "About two hundred invitees, for context."

"But those three men were all in The Assembly, and they're in a foreign country amongst people speaking different languages."

"Yes, there's that. And I would have only given it a passing glance, except for the Sephirot. And the fact that these three men are involved in varying degrees with profound scientific applications."

"And The Chameleon has a Sephirot with the illumination that seems to mean that they will not allow science to be used for human destruction," Prescott reiterated.

"In my mind," I tapped the button on my computer, and the screen went blank, "I feel like it's their Oppenheimer response. Had spies prevented the science of a nuclear explosion, the world would not be terrorized by the chance of an apocalyptic bomb being set off. A world-wide fear. It is a threat, especially for a small country like Israel. That's pure speculation, gentlemen, but her presence at this party and attention to Babcock, along with Iona—who we know chats on the phone with the Russian president at the same time he runs his critical satellites—and then Babcock. I ask myself, why are they all out partying with Russian elites while the Russians are being heavily sanctioned? Yeah, way outside of my expertise, but I want those in intelligence to see what I'm seeing."

"That tattoo is always a concern," Prescott said. "Look, I don't have anything that I can hand you that I think would help you along about the lady with the tattoo or The Assembly men. But now that we know what you're looking for, if I can legally get that information to you, I will."

"Thank you." I smiled.

And I hoped he did because my gut was telling me something dangerous was afoot.

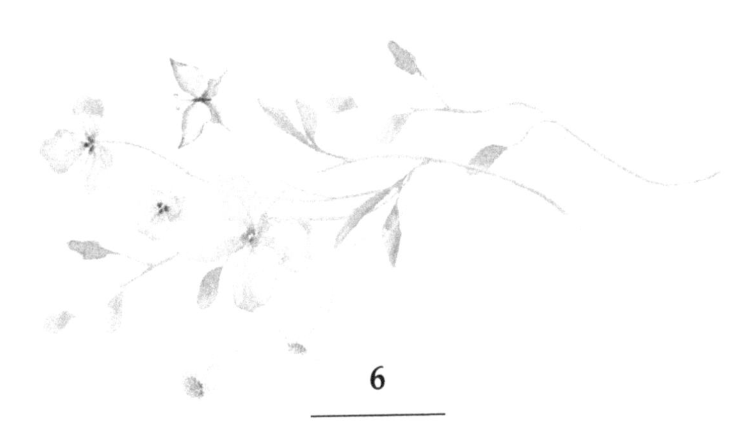

6

I STOOD IN FRONT OF THE MIRROR, TURNING MY BODY THIS WAY AND that. I thought this was probably the right choice for today's outfit. The black raw silk suit was somber but not funerary. The classic Jackie O cut harkened back to the days when society thought that women needed saving, especially among our warriors class. The generals I was going to meet with today would remember their better halves dressing like this to go to a luncheon for officers' wives or maybe a charity event.

Yes, that was what I wanted to elicit—the idea that I needed saving and protecting. It would give the senior officers a chance to ride to my rescue in today's face-to-face at the Pentagon.

And if they decided not to?

Well, then, I'd have to take matters into my own hands. There was too much at stake, especially when it came to Cammy's living arrangements. She needed to live in a stable home surrounded by people who could give her the support she needed.

Smoothing my hands down the jacket, I decided it needed something.

A brooch, maybe.

Downstairs, the door whined open. Bella and Beetle's paws

scampered across the wooden floors from living room to dining room, following Striker's directive to go get breakfast.

I had debated having Striker there beside me today, a show of aligned force. But I decided that having Striker there would be personal and emotional. I wanted this to be business and strategy. Better to keep my team as General Elliot.

Striker's feet were light on the treads as I dug through my jewelry box for my grandmother's wreath pin of gold lace leaves and flower clusters made of seed pearls. As Striker pushed through the door with a smile on his face, his skin glistened from working out. With my peripheral vision, I saw him tip an ear toward the bathroom. He was saying something to me.

"What?" I asked, pulling out the cream-colored satin bag from the corner of the jewelry box.

"Do you need anything before I shower?" he asked a little louder.

"Oh!" I gasped. "Wow."

Striker stepped further into the room. "What have you got there?"

I tugged at the ribbons to open it and tipped two rings onto my palm. "Whew, what an odd sensation." I looked up at Striker, my eyes wide with surprise. "But also a really good omen."

Striker waited patiently for an explanation.

I held out the two rings, three gold bands seemingly twisted together. "These are my parents' wedding rings. On the trip to Ireland—Dad's graduation gift to Mom when she finished university—he proposed to Mom. They bought the rings there. Wow, isn't that…curious?"

"May I?" Striker asked, and I held my palm closer to him. He lifted Dad's ring reverently. "And you're just now finding them?"

"I knew I had them. I just forgot. They were hiding from me." I stepped back until I felt the mattress press against my thighs, then sat, clenching Mom's ring in my fist, lifting my other hand to brush across my eyes. "Vibrationally hiding from me. It's happened to me before, but it's still a shock to the system when something resurfaces like this."

Striker leaned his shoulder into the high boy, crossing his arms over his chest.

"About the time Mom died, Spyder took me to a Chinese restaurant, opened a fortune cookie, and read it aloud. He said that fortune would be our super-secret signal."

"Say that again," Striker said, his eyes dancing, getting ready for whatever it was that I was about to surprise him with this time.

"Super-secret signal." I grinned then the smile fell off. "He told me that if I needed him, send those words to him. He'd drop everything and come to my side."

"You didn't use it when you were facing Travis Wilson?"

I brushed my hand in the air near my head. "That knowledge hid from me. I desperately wanted Spyder to be here with me, but I forgot I had a key to unlock that door until Indigo attacked Iniquus, General Elliot, and you. And suddenly, I remembered. I asked Leanne if she had a way to contact Spyder, and when she did, I asked her to read the sentence to him."

"It worked?"

"We were eating Mango sorbet on the shore about twenty-four hours later. No idea where he started from. But of course, at the time, Spyder was working on making sure that we could chop the heads off The Hydra. Omega tumbled, The Assembly exposed, Indigo died." I stopped and frowned. "We didn't kill it. We certainly didn't get Sylanos, and the other heads are regenerating."

Striker gave a little shake of his head, then redirected me. "You were saying that the rings were hiding?"

"I use my jewelry box every day. I don't remember seeing them until now." I opened my hand and picked up Mom's ring, sliding it onto my left ring finger. "Look, it fits." I caught Striker's gaze. "Try Dad's." I stood and stepped forward to see.

It slid right on. Of course, it did. The universe did crazy things like that, the things that make me think that the Heavens have a sense of humor. "Fits?"

"Yes, it does," he said. "Interesting day for these to find their way back into your awareness. I'm going to point out the significance of today."

"That I'm going to talk to the Joint Special Operations Command and tell them time is up?" I stepped forward and wrapped my hands around Striker's arms, looking up at him. "It *is* a good omen, right? This is going to work. We're going to get married."

"I hope so." Woo-woo omens were still a bridge too far for Striker, even after all he'd seen and heard in our lives together. And there was that little tickle in the back of my brain that said, "*You had these rings when you married Angel. And they hid from you.*" Yeah, that was interesting. Very interesting. This sudden appearance of my treasure felt like my parents' approval; I was on the right path. Finally.

"Are you nervous about today?" Striker asked.

"Me nervous? Psh. I mean, I'm going to the Pentagon for a meeting with the most powerful men in the United States. I'm going to confront them. I'm going to threaten to expose their black ops mission. What could possibly go wrong?"

Wolf-like emotions raced behind Striker's eyes. He rolled his lips in. I knew that he wanted to be there today. I knew that the possible danger to me brought out his inner caveman. That he'd like to stand between me and any threat and pound his chest. But he also knew, strategically, why that was a bad idea.

Personally, I thought General Elliot was a strong shield in the moment. Honestly, if I were to confront and threaten the CIA, I would be a lot more concerned. The Pentagon? Yes, they could order someone in special ops to cause a fatal accident. Not falling out of a fifth-floor window—that was too Russian for them—but there were other ways to affect an accident. It's in my memory bank that when we were going to expose Colonel Guthrie, who had targeted an Iniquus client, the colonel had a cement truck hit a witness's car, killing her instantly in the seeming accident. Even if I did drive a vehicle with bullet-resistant windows, that could easily be my fate. After all, I was the burr. I was the threat. And the leadership always looked at the whole rather than the parts. They were willing to sacrifice an individual for the goal. That was the structure of the military beast.

Was I scared?

Yeah, little bit.

But I wasn't going to say that out loud, so I went with, "What do you think? Should we use these as our wedding rings? Or do you think there's too much attached to them?"

"Too much attached, like memories and sentiment?" He took my hand and led me to the bed, where he sat facing me, so I wasn't straining to look up at him.

"Yeah, something like that. Yeah."

"I've only heard about the strength of your parents' marriage—faith, love, commitment, and care. I couldn't imagine a better legacy to carry into our married lives. It would be an honor to wear your dad's ring."

Stepping forward between his knees, I caught his face between my hands. Closing my eyes, I lowered my forehead until it rested against his. I stood there, breathing in the peace of our connection. His hands wrapped behind my thighs and held me in place.

When the alarm on his phone sounded, the spell was broken.

He tilted to brush his lips across mine. "I'm going to get Cammy up."

"I'll get us breakfast. A cup of coffee is calling to me." I moved back over to my jewelry case and found the brooch I had been searching for. I slid the pin into the jacket fabric right over my heart.

"This is an interesting configuration." Striker held up his hand to show me he was speaking of the wedding band.

I reached for a pearl earring and slid it into the hole in my lobe. "These are gimmel rings. From the Latin for twins, gemellus."

"Uh-huh." He pulled it off and held it up to examine.

"From the 16th century." I walked over and manipulated the ring until three separate rings looped together.

"Like a puzzle," he said.

"It's an engagement ring and a wedding band."

"And the third ring?" He tipped his head up to catch my gaze.

"Represents the milestones that the couple goes through together. Traditionally, a couple goes through a series of big, hairy, awful events together before celebrating their weathering life with the third ring. It's kind of a lovely tradition, isn't it? I mean, all this 'happily ever after' stuff from the fairytales that never really happens. There's no wedding magic that says you killed the dragon, and there are no more on your horizon."

"Wouldn't that be nice?" he asked.

"It would be nice to know that the bad stuff was behind us. But unrealistic. Knowing as a couple that when you get married, there's a third ring that will be earned through shared tribulation—"

He nodded. "Is a big dose of reality."

I tapped the ring. "Mom said the milestone she and Dad commemorated was my safe birth. At the time, Mom was telling me that story. I had no idea that she'd been attacked and that her survival and mine were at risk. My dad heaved up their entire way of life to best align it for Mom's safety."

"And yours."

"Yes." I rolled my lips in and nodded. "And mine. I bet it did feel like a major milestone to come through that together."

The alarm on Striker's phone jingled again. He tapped the snooze button a second time. "What do you want me to do with the ring right now?" he asked again.

I pulled off Mom's ring. I'd call it 'Mom's ring' until it became mine with legal vows I made to Striker; I decided on the spot. I slid the ring back on my right hand. "Let's wear them like this, and then in the ceremony, we just switch them over from right hand to left? What do you think?"

Striker slid the ring onto his right ring finger. "Good. I didn't like the idea that it would go back in your box and be lost in another wormhole." He stood, gave me another kiss, and headed out the door with a singsong. "Cammy, it's a bright new day. Time to wake up, buttercup."

My attention went back to the mirror, where I held my right hand up to my face. "Okay, Mom, first, thank you for this gift. It means a lot. And second, thank you for your affirmation that today will be a step forward. Things should hopefully go smoothly from here, don't you think?"

7

It was time.

I picked up my bag, headed out of the Puzzle Room, and walked toward the elevator where Deep stood waiting for a car, the down button already lit.

"Storm's brewing," he said as I approached.

"Bad?" I'd looked at the weather that morning and saw strong winds; that information had been part of my wardrobe choice. Typically, I like the comfort of full skirts, but not if I was battling to keep them from becoming sails and flying up. Today's suit had a pencil skirt style, not tight or sexy, more office-appropriate for the 50s and 60s. Nancy Drew would be comfortably modest wearing this.

"High winds, heavy rains, but it should move through the area quickly," Deep said as we stepped into the elevator car.

He tapped the lobby button. "Where are you heading?" he asked, eyeing my outfit.

Typically, I was in varying shades of pink at Iniquus, and today's black suit very *un*typically fit right in with the uniform that everyone else was required to wear.

"I have a field trip with General Elliot. You?"

"I'm going down to forensics to ask their opinion."

So, neither of us was willing to say what we were up to that day. Ah, the secretive world that was Iniquus security.

Out of the car, and a finger wave to Deep, I moved to the plate glass windows to watch for my ride.

Soon enough, the chauffeured car with General Elliot arrived. I was surprised to see Colonel Grant's profile in the window as the vehicle pulled to the curb.

As I left the Atrium, the winds were already rising, whipping at my outfit.

I'd gamed it all out in my head. I orchestrated and choreographed to the best of my ability before walking onto this improvisational theater stage with bright lights and an audience very different from what I typically dealt with.

I typically dealt with laying out the puzzle pieces and pushing them around until I could show a cohesive picture. Tada!

This time, I was one of those puzzle pieces. And it was someone else who had the power to shuffle me.

But *not* ignore me.

The problem would be solved.

I clattered down the steps as the driver rounded to open the back door. "Good morning," I said to him as I stepped in and found a seat next to the general. "Thank you," I told the driver as he shut my door. "Good morning, sirs." I pulled my seatbelt across my lap.

They offered brief nods in response.

Whew, the car was filled with testosterone.

This was a lot.

I unbuttoned my waist-length jacket and fluffed the sides a bit to cool the sudden heat that bloomed in my chest.

After greeting me, the men returned to their phones, reading and responding. I was an agenda item in their busy day.

As we drove, I looked out the window and thought about how nice it had been to have some peace between me and John Black over at Langley.

I had been so angry with the CIA.

And I never should have been.

Spyder would be so disappointed in me, jumping to conclusions.

I knew that John Grey from the CIA special Color Code division had recruited Angel to become a shadow in the black ops. They used the cover of Angel's team hitting an IED to stage his death and make me a seeming widow.

Once I found John Grey and discovered Angel was alive and needed rescue, that solidified the idea in my head. Angel was a CIA guy. And since this was a CIA scheme, and they had put me at risk of committing a crime by marrying Striker and being married to two men at once, it was their responsibility to back me out of that corner, free me, and let me lead my life. In my mind, it was a simple thing. "Here, Angel, we need you to sign these divorce papers you agreed to. We'll have the courts seal that file. You're good to go, and Lexi will be free to move on with her life."

Oh, the anger I have been simmering over the CIA—the seething infection of self-righteousness.

And I was wrong.

Completely wrong.

The CIA had no control.

And they could do nothing to help me.

Compartmentalized Top Secret.

So, any time I confronted them, they both knew the truth, understood the complexity of the issue, and had no agency to make things better.

Off I headed to the Dead Sea to confront my not-so-dead husband for the second time. "Angel, divorce papers?"

There was a whole story behind Angel's eyes. And also confusion when he responded, "Problematic."

"Let's take care of that problem," I'd said.

"I have superiors." Those superiors, I assumed, had been John Black and others in leadership. Poking my aggressive finger into John Grey's chest, I warned him that I was about to bring my wrath down on Langley. Grey very slowly and very cryptically said, "That's not going to help you."

"Care to expand on that?"

He could not. Nor could he answer my next question. "Not CIA?"

And there it was.

Not CIA.

There was only one other entity that it could possibly be. And it made all the sense in the world. There were known special operations forces, most of which were on the movie screen and part of our American iconography: SEALs, Green Berets, Delta Force. Few people knew that there was a secretive group within the military called The United States Army Intelligence Support Activity (USAISA), typically shortened to one of their nicknames, "The Activity." "Task Force Orange," or at the beginning of the Afghanistan war, "Gray Fox."

The Activity was tasked with collecting actionable HUMINT, human intelligence, for the JSOC special operations teams to act on.

I only knew about them because of a brush past on a mission I was puzzling. I had to do a little digging to find out anything at all. They were fairly new to the military scene. Sometime in the 1980s, same time frame as the Galaxy Project. A lot of innovation was being tried out at that time.

Back in the day, a brand-new special forces team called Delta Force was trying to effect a rescue of the American hostages in Tehran. A series of bad luck events made Operation Eagle Claw a failure. That wasn't to dump on Delta Force. They did what they could with what they had. They needed more. They needed not just actionable intelligence but pathfinding and operational support.

Hence, The Activity was developed.

And it was right up Angel's alley, all of it. Languages, cultural understanding, signals skills, hand-to-hand fighting skills, the ability to morph into various characters, to get people to like and trust you, the ability to think on your feet and strategize, the job was complex, dangerous, and terrifying.

Of course, The Activity would want Angel on their team.

The Activity had been the team searching for Saddam Hussein. They continued to work at stopping the most dangerous and evil people in the world.

Angel would want to be part of that. And, too, he'd want to protect his family from possible retribution.

Yes, Angel was the perfect candidate.

His recruitment came at a perfect inflection point.

It had to be that Angel was following his life's trajectory, his soul's path.

What he hadn't counted on was a madman with elite military etheric skills sewing his soul to a woman he'd never met. Nowhere in his life path was he supposed to meet me and marry me three weeks later as a manifestation of our psychic injuries.

No wonder he got drunk out of his mind on our wedding day.

We were forced upon each other in a way that was inconceivable.

Not even General Elliot knew about the psychic surgery that Indigo performed on Angel and me to free Striker to marry Indigo's daughter.

He certainly didn't know that surgery was performed by the Galaxy psychic physician and an African tribal chief I called Grandmother Sybil to separate us back apart.

I imagined it was like the case of conjoined twins surgically separated. Angel and I no longer had that soul connection like we'd had for so many years. It was disorienting and liberating at the same time.

To this day, though I have the concept clear in my mind, it still seemed like something out of a horror film.

Something out of a sci-fi nightmare.

I was done fighting for freedom from Angel in the ether.

But for now, I was sitting silently in the car with my bosses, heading to the Pentagon to try to get free in the physical world. Yup, just me, sitting in a car, heading to the Pentagon, ready to reveal that I am willing to expose The Activity if the military continued to put me—and, by extension, Iniquus—in the path of blackmail and extortion.

It was all too dangerous.

I didn't think they could summarily throw me into prison under the Espionage Act to keep me quiet. Or have me shipped to some black site prison somewhere.

Too many people knew about the circumstances—Color Code, my new besties, John Black, John Gray, and John Green.

All of Strike Force, and now Margot, from Panther Force, had seen Angel.

People knew.

And Command had a direct line to the president.

It was unlikely that I'd disappear. Right?

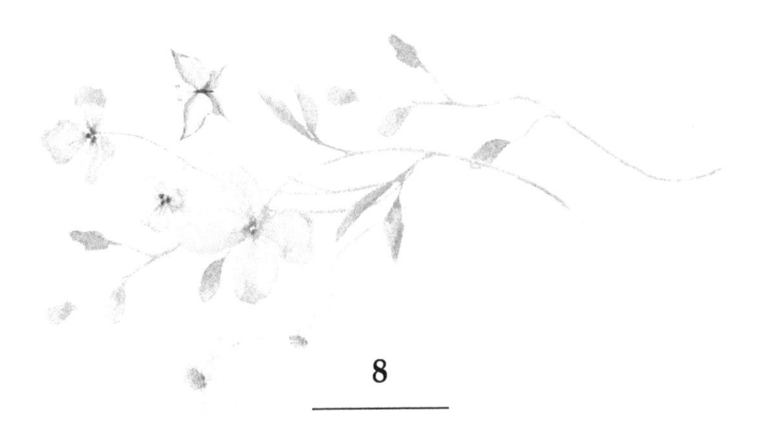

8

An escort met us at the VIP entrance of the Pentagon. From there, we were marched through the doors, escorted to a golf cart, and driven to a SCIF—Sensitive Compartmented Information Facility—a room where secret information could be securely handled.

It was all very crisp, clean, and dramatic.

Our escorts took the performance of their duties very seriously.

They made me itchy. I wanted to go.

Our phones stayed in a box outside the door, along with my handbag. The soldier on duty at the SCIF said, "I'll be guarding the area, miss."

I bit my tongue to keep myself from correcting his with a "Mrs. Sobado" since the reason I was here was to get rid of that name.

In we went.

"You know," I said, directing my comment to General Elliot, "it will forever amuse me that the Pentagon was built where they had a research farm and grew marijuana—well, hemp, really—and that they call the big wigs the *Joint* Special Operations Command."

I saw a puff of amusement exhaled by the general. I had to watch closely to see when I amused him.

As I took my place, I looked around the room. The only amenities inside the rather sterile room were water bottles, a pad, and a pen at each seat.

Both of my commanders pulled out their chairs and took advantage of the pen and paper to jot notes to themselves.

I just sat there, waiting.

Not long after I sat down, I felt a whisper cross over my skin. Tiny bubbles that seemed to effervesce. And I recognized the sensation instantly. I scratched my nails over my skin to make it stop. But there it was, buzzing around me—not me, the space—the sensation growing louder, more intense.

The last time I felt energy brush by me like this, Indigo was alive and in Iniquus Headquarters, roaming the halls looking for answers. Gator could feel him, too. At Iniquus, the sensation Indigo left was anger.

Right now, this bubbling energy felt curious.

It was me that was angry.

Indigo was the catalyst that brought me to this moment.

And Indigo was dead.

I sat very still as I let my mind ponder the possibilities. Here was one that I hadn't considered until now:

When Iniquus was failing, and General Elliot was comatose, I had first identified the Galaxy Remote Viewing Project—the military's psychic spies—as having a role to play in solving the criminal coalition attacking us. Spyder called that coalition The Hydra, which included Omega as brute force, Sylanos as shipping and logistics, The Assembly as control of government and judiciary, and Indigo as the brain.

Indigo was not a strategic genius. He was a highly trained remote viewer for the United States military. With those skills, he could gather data and answers out of thin air.

At that time, very shortly before his death, Indigo had two quests: One, destroy the United States government and all who supported it.

Two, give his daughter Scarlet her dearest wish, a happily ever after, married to Striker.

In Indigo's quest, Iniquus was a prime target because General Elliot oversaw Galaxy at its inception. Indigo (falsely) blamed General Elliot for all the truly catastrophic things that happened to Indigo and his family following the dismantling of their psychic efforts.

Trying to save Iniquus from Hydra, I discovered General Elliot's connection to the Galaxy remote viewers.

Galaxy was still at work in Wyoming. They just did their work for non-governmental entities, including my mentor, Spyder.

Spyder and I flew to Wyoming so I could meet the Grand Master of It All, General Coleridge, the founding commander of Galaxy.

The day I first met General Coleridge, Spyder and I flew far out, out into the middle of nowhere. I was swept up in a hug by the biggest man I'd ever met, with a silver braid down his back and dirt rubbed into his baggy jeans. General Coleridge greeted me with a "Lexi, awesome!" And from there forward, he continued to shift my worldview like a magnitude ten earthquake.

For example, I learned that in the ether, there is no past, no now, no future. You could be anywhere and everywhere. The concept of time or space did not exist.

Mind-blowing stuff.

It still made my stomach flip-flop when I thought about it.

As Spyder and I worked to save Iniquus, I learned that Indigo saw that Striker was going to marry me, not his beloved Scarlet.

Indigo had lost his moral compass and acted with impunity, no holds barred.

What's a guy to do?

Apply science. Experiment.

So, he just sewed me to another man, Angel, and watched us like a lab experiment. A prototype. If it worked for Angel and me, Indigo might sew Striker to Scarlet, too.

And with that in mind, the etheric effervescence I was experiencing here in the SCIF made all the sense in the world.

Surely, after Indigo sewed Angel and me together, he would have tasked remote viewing searches as something like: Go to the time and place where I can best understand what comes of Angel and Lexi's marriage.

And Indigo would show up here. Snooping around, trying to comprehend what was happening in this room with these players, in this context, at this time.

I was pretty sure that Indigo was both *dead* and *here*.

And there was no other word for it than that this was a mindfuck.

The door opened. "General Thomas," the guard announced.

A single elderly man in a pristine military uniform moved into the room, and the guard left, silently closing the door behind him. It wasn't the board of hard men that I had anticipated.

I sensed the effervescence rush over to Thomas, swirling around the briefcase he had brought in with him.

General Thomas walked over to where I sat, and I sprang to my feet. "General, I'm Mrs. Sobado." I thrust my hand out, and he shook it.

Then he turned his head to nod at Colonel Grant and then General Elliot. "Long time no see, Elliot. Grant. Glad we're here under happy circumstances."

Happy? Okay. I could go with happy.

"I had a look through my files. I found a tasking sheet that predicted that we'd be here in this meeting today," General Elliot said. "It also predicted that you'd be telling us the tale of how you used remote viewing to start this ball rolling."

Tasking sheet? *Remote viewing?* That vocabulary meant General Elliot had to have asked Galaxy for this information. Was that who I felt in the room? No, that couldn't be right. I had been the subject of a tasking sheet used by Galaxy dozens, if not hundreds of times, and I had never sensed the observation except for one specific remote viewer, Indigo.

This *had* to be Indigo trying to gather understanding.

General Thomas looked from General Elliot to me and back again.

"Her mentor is Spyder McGraw. Do you think she doesn't know about remote viewing?" General Elliot asked.

Thomas rested his elbow on the back of one of the captain's chairs and leaned on it for support. "All right. That's as good a place as any to kick this thing off." Thomas turned his focus on me. "When Galaxy got too much public scrutiny, we had to shut down that project. That doesn't mean we didn't understand the importance of their work. We just needed to be even more circumspect about using this tool."

I stood there awkwardly, not sure what to do. It felt like poor etiquette to sit while the General stood.

"We have a team of viewers that work on projects for us. They're pretty good, not as good as Galaxy was, but better than a coin toss, and often that's enough to tip the scales. Take a seat, Mrs. Sobado. I'm standing because I've got a leg spasm that jabs at me if I sit too long."

After I sat, he continued, "We had an eye on Angel Sobado for our intelligence group, The Activity—normally, we don't mention the group, but since you figured out that's what Angel is up to, I'll go ahead and acknowledge this fact. We here at JSOC had an eye on him from the time he started Ranger school. He was a standout, and we wondered about channeling him toward Delta Force once he had more field time under his belt."

"You task remote viewers to fill special operations slots?" I asked.

"I was on the fence between Delta Force and The Activity for Angel," General Thomas explained. "I tasked our viewers to see what they could tell me about him. They saw, quite accurately, that he would get out of a truck, and the truck would then explode. They were able to pinpoint the area. We concluded that that was a nice jumping-off point to move Angel into black ops."

My brows furrowed. "Sir, I was told I was a widow. The military conferred Gold Star status on me. It was a lie. Why would you consider doing this?"

"Because our viewers saw that Angel would die within the year. Again, they saw it very clearly. Captured, he was sick, tortured, and he died with a slashed throat."

"What?" The matter-of-factness of this conversation was mind-blowing.

"The viewers had trouble seeing Angel. There are people like that. The group calls them 'dense.' They can't see them, just the environment around them. We thought from the pictures that the viewer could somewhat see it was Angel at his death because he was in a weakened state."

"What?" I squeaked. I thought I was going to vomit. I scanned for and spotted a trash bin.

"As to our viewers' accuracy, the truck explosion was given a fifty-five percent chance."

"And yet you did nothing to save the Rangers?" Yes, I definitely needed to vomit.

"Remember, they were in a war zone. Can we stop a truck from moving down a road known for IEDs because there's about a fifty-fifty chance it will blow? That would grind our war effort to a stop. What we did with this information was to position a CIA representative who was working in that area on the spot where the explosion had a fifty-five percent chance it would occur."

That was John Grey.

"If the agent heard an explosion, then came across Angel, he was to hand Angel a satellite phone and walk away while we had a conversation."

"Angel didn't want to join you if you were going to lie to me." Of that, I was sure.

"Correct. So we told him we predicted he'd die within the year."

"You what? You told a man you believed he would die when he

had just seen his entire Ranger crew blown to bits and was in shock?"

General Thomas stalled. "Yes. That's correct."

"So your viewers were right about Angel joining. But the death within the year?"

"It was someone else," Elliot said dispassionately. "Angel was in the building but not that part of the building. Angel was fine and continued with his mission. He's an asset. And we were very glad, but that left us with a problem." Thomas shook his finger at me. "He always said that one day you would turn up in the desert looking for him, and by god, that is exactly what you did. Twice."

"If I'm the problem and Angel gets to stay alive, I'm fine with that. But I'm not fine with committing felonies under this farce. Do you have divorce papers for me?"

"It's not as easy as you might think," General Thomas said.

"Fuck." I skated out a hand. "Sorry, sir. It slipped out."

"Understandable. Angel is apoplectic. Especially after you showed up in Jordan. Chasing him down in dangerous areas of the world puts a lot at risk. Lives. Do you care to tell me how you found your way to the Dead Sea and into his hotel room?"

"I do not." I scowled. "Angel is angry that I want a divorce after he promised me?"

"He's not angry with you. He's furious with the situation and himself for putting you into an unlawful position. He demands that we right this. And has offered to step out of the shadows. We need him there. He's built too many outstanding relationships that serve the greater good."

"And yet," I countered, "too many people know about this. My team notwithstanding. Others have crossed his path. This puts me at risk of extortion or, worse—Iniquus—Abuela Rosa. You have lawyers. How are you going to fix this?" I asked.

General Elliot was silent as this played out. I saw his eyes glittering as if it was fun to watch me spar with Thomas. Still, I knew my commanders had my back if the dynamic shifted.

"It's hard to put things on the book and keep them off the book at the same time." Thomas scratched his nose. "Just so you're aware, Angel signed the divorce papers already."

"When?" I asked.

"While he was still in the hospital recovering from your mission with Grey. He thought it was a done deal, and you were moving on with your life."

Horror washed through my body. I'd been sending him daggers of razor-sharp anger thoughts for years. No wonder he looked at me like he did in Jordan. No wonder he acted the way he did. "*Fuck.*" I clapped a hand over my mouth. "Sorry, it slipped out again. I don't like to use that word."

"Understandable." A smile tickled the corner of his lips, and I resented it. "That you showed up asking for a divorce in Jordan, listen young lady—"

"*Mrs.* Sobado," I said sternly.

"Mrs. Sobado, we're going to get this done. We need to do it delicately."

"You've had years for delicacy." The more he talked, the angrier I grew. I didn't want to be the hothead here. I tried to channel my inner Striker.

"Here's the problem," Thomas explained. "You think we can go to the judge—which we will do today—and get this divorce signed by all necessary parties and have it sealed again? This will happen today as soon as we're done here." He checked his watch. "But then you want to get married to Striker."

"Correct."

"In the United States, when you fill out a marriage application, you must designate your status: single, widowed, divorced. If you lie on the application, it can make the marriage license void."

Shit.

"If you don't lie on your application, you can put lives in danger."

"That's what's been holding this up?"

"Yes. It's a felony to lie on a federal document. And you have pointed out that you don't wish to break the law."

"Especially when it comes to marrying Striker. Yes, sir, that's correct." My mind began to tumble this information around. He was absolutely right. I could get divorced. That would go the way I had hoped. The problem was, under these circumstances, I absolutely could *not* marry Striker.

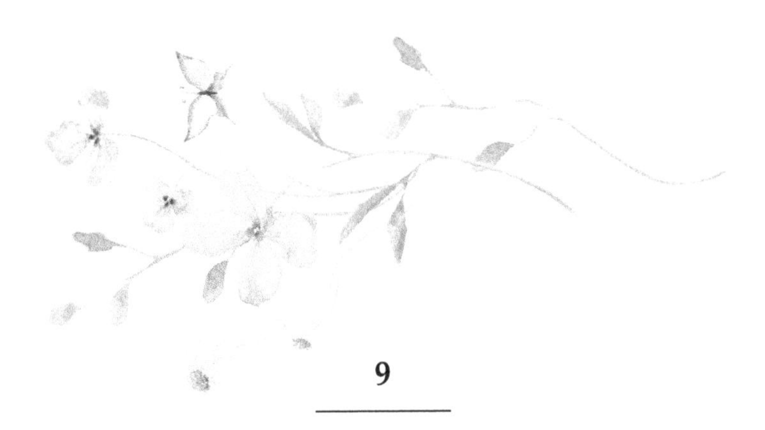

9

"IT TOOK US A WHILE, BUT WE'VE COME UP WITH A SOLUTION." Thomas looked pleased with himself. "We have a plan."

I leaned forward.

"You need to get married to Striker in Uganda."

I collapsed back in my chair. "Okay, that's out of left field."

"Striker was in a cooperative mission in Uganda many years ago along with your mentor Spyder McGraw. We know that Striker recently returned to one area where he served on that special mission to deliver humanitarian aid."

"Yes." He had gone just last year to take solar panels, lamps, and stoves to Grandmother Sybil and her village of round huts.

"That tribal chief can perform your wedding," General Thomas said.

I waited for more. That seemed to be it. I shook my head.

"Striker already knows the tribal chief, Mirembe Okello. She can perform a *tribal* unity ceremony."

Mirembe (which meant peace) Okello was Grandmother Sybil's given name. She asked me to continue calling her Grandmother Sybil so I would. I loved the idea of my grandmother marrying us. She was the reason I was alive. And Lynda. And Cammy. It would be an honor for her to bless us, and I was absolutely sure that Striker would feel the same. But still, I had questions like, "Is this something your viewers saw as a plan that works to keep everyone secure?"

"I didn't have it tasked with our viewers if that's what you're asking me. There are no sureties, young—" He cleared his throat. "Mrs. Sobado. But it is the option that we have devised to keep everyone as safe and as legal as possible. Let me explain." He stepped wider and leaned both elbows on the back of his chair. "We wish for you to fly into Tanzania as tourists. There is an animal habitat in the north."

I shook my head. *What?*

"From there, you will drive into Uganda and to Okello's village, where you and Striker will be united in marriage. You take the paperwork to the magistrate in the nearest town and register your union."

Again, I shook my head. *What?*

"In Uganda, with a chief performing a tribal ritual, you need not declare anything other than that you were married and receive your marriage certificate. You have no marriage license with data about your past relationships that needs to be signed. Under these circumstances, you would have a Ugandan marriage certificate, and you can tell no one that this is the case. You would simply drive back to Tanzania and fly home, married."

I shot a look toward General Elliot to see how he was receiving this information. But General Elliot was as stoic as Striker. He rarely showed a tell.

"How will people know we're married if Uganda is a secret? I'm not going to lie about my marriage."

"General Elliot can perform a ceremony in front of your friends and family. He knows there will be no marriage license to sign at the end of the ceremony. We'd like this to be well attended so that it is generally known and witnessed that the ceremony took place. We don't want anyone looking around to the origin of your union and the why of it."

It occurred to me, as that effervescence seemed to settle on the glass with the prismed bottom, that this scheme would be very hard to unravel, for most people, that is.

Striker and I didn't fit into that category.

Our relationship had been of intense interest to a dead man. A man with the ability to see without the boundaries of time, and he had a scheming, vengeful mind.

I had a terrible feeling that Indigo didn't ever want Striker to marry anyone but his daughter. She was dead now, too. I killed Scarlet with my bare hands. Though, I did it in a location with enough etheric clutter that Indigo could not possibly have seen.

"All right," I whispered. "Let's move forward. Divorce, then Uganda."

With that, everyone moved toward the SCIF door. We retraced our way out to the car that waited right where we exited, the door held wide by our driver.

General Thomas climbed in with General Elliot, Colonel Grant, and me. He leaned forward and rattled off an address for the driver. Then he slid the privacy window closed.

"The timing of your finding and saving Angel was problematic," General Thomas threw out.

"Oh?" I asked. I didn't care what we talked about; I just wanted to not sit and stew in my apprehension. This should be joyful. I was on my way to sever my last tie with Angel. I was wearing Mom's good-omen ring. Still. "Tell me about that."

"There was the change of administration, and therefore, a change in priorities and personnel. More importantly, we had a group of judges we worked with regularly years ago that made things work seamlessly. When the whistleblower released The Assembly papers, many of the systems that we had put into place—"

"The Assembly affiliated judges?" I asked. The Hydra kept rearing its head over the last few days. Coincidence? Spyder told me that there was no such thing. He always cautioned me to pay careful attention to what events converged, just like yesterday—the CIA and FBI, the tattooed spy, and Iona, Burke, and Babcock.

"Exactly." General Thomas stretched out his leg with a wince. "We needed to identify the right judge to handle this situation."

"Within a military court because Angel is still in the military, right?"

"Yes, we're heading over to the Federal Courthouse."

That seemed to end the conversation because Thomas turned to look out the window, massaging the back of his thigh.

My mind went back to the hotel room at the Dead Sea, where I confronted Angel. What did I say to him? It was a question and a statement from me, "Divorce papers?" And in return, he said, "Problematic." But he didn't. No, he said, "Problematic?" It was a question. I missed the tone.

"When I was at the Dead Sea, General Thomas, Angel didn't know he was still married."

He turned my way. "We were actively trying to work this out in a way that everyone stayed safe."

"Safe, sane, and legal." My voice trailed off. "After Syria, you knew I knew. Why didn't you just pull me into a room and tell me what was happening?"

He shifted his shoulders back to make the ribbons on his chest stand out. "Because that's not how we operate."

"You took an enormous risk that I wouldn't go to the press." I pushed. I got that this was tiny in the grand scheme of things he dealt with, but it upended my world.

"We profiled you."

Profiled, not tasked, well, that was better, perhaps. "And discovered?"

"One of your dominant traits is loyalty. We believed you would be loyal to your country and to Angel's safety."

"You all suck. It's inappropriate to say, but honestly, those are the tamest words I can find."

Fortunately, we had pulled up to the side of the federal building. We slid into a side door, where a Marine saluted and ushered us to the correct courtroom.

In we went.

Papers were handed over.

I signed the form that said we had irreconcilable differences. Stamps were applied.

"I declare this matter sealed for fifty years." That, too, was stamped.

And just like that, I was no longer married to my dead husband.

Though there was no drumbeat or fanfare, there was a tickle of purple effervescence sparkling just behind the judge as if peeking over his shoulder.

"Can I have a copy of the paperwork?" I asked.

"They are under seal for fifty years," the judge repeated.

I felt the effervescence become violent with rage. It was as painful here as back at Iniquus when the protective Tsukamoto art had been removed.

I glanced around, desperate to find anything that might work as a doorknob to bring me respite. Thunder boomed outside with energy that shook the building.

The lights flickered, and everything went dark. There was a growing growling hum, and the lights flickered back on.

And the effervescence of a remote viewer was gone.

Or maybe I had had so many brain injuries and had become so paranoid about anything good happening to me that I made up the whole thing.

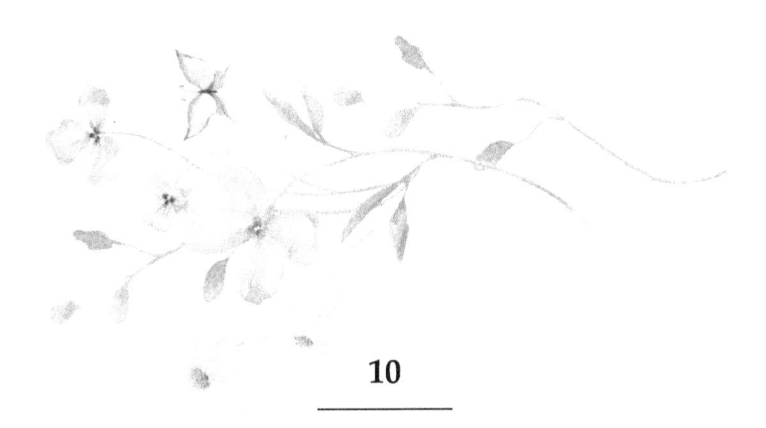

10

We pulled through the guard station at Iniquus.

I was finding it hard to sit still. My hand swept over my face, where a strand of hair became a tickling irritant. Then my eye twitched and needed a rub. My cheek needed a scratch. My hair needed patting into place. The collar of my suit jacket was strangling me. The fabric wrapped too tightly around my legs.

As I shifted to smooth my skirt beneath me, the general waited until I was sitting flat again, and then he reached his hand out and covered mine. "Big day. Big doings."

"Yes, sir. Thank you, sir." I looked past him to Colonel Grant. "Thank you, sirs." I licked my lips and swallowed.

"My weekend calendar can accommodate any day you choose next month for your ceremony," the general said. "I suggest you don't shillyshally. Get this taken care of so you can get on with things."

"No, sir." My throat gurgled, and I coughed. "I mean, yes, sir. No shillyshallying. Getting on."

His leathered face was set with his typical gruffness, but his eyes showed a glimmer of amusement.

The driver eased the car smoothly to the curve, put us in park, then rounded to open the entrance-side door. He pulled it wide, angling in such a way that he could extend his other hand to assist people from the back.

"Why don't you jump out, Lynx," the general said. "Get back to me when you have a date."

Holding steady, I reached for the white cotton-gloved hand, stepping into the lung-crushing humidity.

Crossing the sidewalk, I aimed for the blast of arctic air on the other side of the glass doors. When I went in, it was a great relief, and then it turned uncomfortable as the moisture in my clothes wicked away my body heat. I'd change as soon as I got up to my office. And I'd call Striker. And I'd tell him about everything that had happened with General Thomas. Now that I was out from under the buzzing energy, I wasn't sure that that had happened. I had to think about whether I was going to broach that subject.

There have been many times in my life when I was doing something, and I had no idea that it would change the trajectory of my life, I thought as I made my way to the elevators.

There was the time when I saw a piece of paper that someone had slid under my door, picked it up, and discovered I had a stalker.

There was the time when I got a call that little Ruby had stopped breathing, and I raced across the street to help, not knowing it was a ploy to kidnap me.

There was the time that I walked into this very atrium and felt etheric electricity dance over my skin, and I discovered that Iniquus and Striker were under attack.

This time was different; I knew exactly what life-changing thing would happen next. I would go upstairs, announce my freedom, and the next steps would make me Mrs. Gavin Michael Rheas.

Married to the man I had been destined to marry.

Reclaiming the life that I wanted.

Free.

I had been tied for so long to a manipulation that the new reality hadn't settled into my gut.

When I opened the door to my office, Striker stood up from behind my desk, papers in hand, gaze hard on me—warrior mode.

I'm just going to admit it to myself: when Striker looked at me that way, whew! It did all kinds of good things for my libido.

I stood there, blinking at him.

Finally, Striker broke the spell. "You were gone a long time."

I shut the door behind me. "Yes, it took some time to get to the courthouse and sign my divorce papers in front of the judge."

"Done deal." His eyes opened wide. "You're a free woman?"

I shook my head. "Not really."

The energy dropped off Striker. "What now? Why aren't you free?"

"Well, I am free-ish. But you see," I held up my right hand, "my wearing this ring says that I'm also a woman who has made ties to a man. So, freed from my past, but I'll be tying the knot again shortly."

Striker threw his head back and whole body laughed. Joy just flowed from him. It was overwhelming to see someone so invested in *us*. It felt so good.

He strode forward, bending to wrap his arms around my thighs. He lifted me and spun. "God, this feels so good." He let me slide down his body until my heels reached the ground.

"Yes, well. All that glitters isn't gold."

"Shit." He stepped back, and I curled my finger in a follow-me gesture as I headed toward my closet to gather more comfortable clothes, then moved across the hall to my bathroom to change.

Striker sat on the toilet lid as I unbuttoned my suit jacket and put it on the hanger. "We can't get married in the United States," I said, stepping closer to him and swinging my hair out of the way.

He pulled the zipper slowly down. "Where can we get married?"

"Uganda."

Striker wrapped his hands around my hips and turned me to him. "Uga—what?"

I quickly explained the felony involved in incorrectly filling out my marital paperwork. His felony as well if he signed those papers knowing they were incorrect.

"But the file is sealed," Striker pointed out.

"It's not worth the risk. Angel can show up alive at any point. Or his body shows up, for that matter." I stepped out of my dress.

"But there's some trick to Uganda? Did they know that you had a connection there?"

"They knew about *your* connection and that you traveled there to see Grandmother Sybil—though they used her given name." I reached up on the shelf to retrieve an outfit. "How would they know about that?"

"Before I went, I made some phone calls to find out about the activity in the area and to let them know I was going and why."

"You wanted their permission?" I dropped the shirt onto the floor and shook out my yoga pants.

"I don't know what I don't know. I wanted to ensure I wasn't doing anything to endanger Grandmother Sybil and her people, dragging unwanted eyes back to the area."

"That was very conscientious of you, thank you." I stepped into the legs of the stretchy pants. "So JSOC agreed?"

"They agreed when I told them I listed the trip as a humanitarian mission to deliver the solar panels and well water apparatus to a village. What's the magic of getting married in Uganda? It seems remote? Not many people would think to look there? Lying on that paperwork wouldn't have ramifications here at home?"

"It would, though." I dragged the waistband up over my hips and reached for my shirt. "It might nullify our marriage, and that could have legal implications. If we were married with falsified documents, and then we told people here in the United States that we were legitimately married—"

"You're making this very complicated."

"Luckily, the powers that be figured out this workaround." I dragged the T-shirt over my head and tugged it down. "If a tribal leader performs a traditional ceremony, we just need to register it.

We don't sign paperwork that stipulates our former status. Multiple wives are legal. Multiple husbands are not."

"Anywhere?" Striker asked.

"I think two places." I plopped down onto my butt to pull on my socks. "The Plateau of Tibet and the Marquesas Islands down in the South Pacific."

Striker grinned. "Would you rather go there?"

"No need, I'm divorced. But is it okay with you that Grandmother Sybil does the wedding ceremony?"

"It's wonderful." He grinned. "We'll just arrange for our—"

I reached around for my tennis shoes. "No."

He stilled.

"You were about to say our wedding party to come with us?"

"Cammy, at least."

"No. *No one*." I shoved my foot in and yanked at the laces. "That was part of the deal I agreed to before they took me to the judge."

"Listening."

"We have to get married secretly in Uganda and tell no one."

"So no one goes fishing for a reason and turns up Angel?"

"I think this one also has to do with you and the black ops." After tying the bow, I pulled on my left shoe. "But yeah, why would we go to Uganda to have this elder marry us? What is the connection? I could see you going over to deliver the solar panels, which is easily overlooked. A wedding is an extremely personal thing. I don't want anyone to know what's happened. I don't want their tribe to be targeted in any way."

"Got it. Go on with your agreement."

"Then we have a ceremony here." I paused to finish the bow, then reached for Striker's hand. He gave it a little tug to help me stand up. "I told them I wouldn't lie to those I loved and call it a wedding. I would call it a marriage celebration instead, and they were down with that."

"All right." He stood and followed me back out to my office area.

"They want us to set a date and do this as soon as possible.

General Elliot said we should do it next month." I rested my thigh on the table and shifted my weight to half-stand as Striker pulled out the chair in front of me. "They didn't say why. I think it's about tying up loose ends and moving on. While appreciated, I also got the impression that our saving Angel was concerning. And one more thing, they want General Elliot to perform the ceremony because a different officiant would know there was no American marriage license to sign."

"We were going to ask him anyway. So this is all working out. Let's look at a calendar."

"Striker, I want to wait until we get home from Uganda. I don't want to jump the gun. I need to know that each step is taken individually."

"There's more to this. I've been waiting for you to spill the beans."

"I think, whew!" I stood to smooth my hands down my sides, and then I put my hands on my bent knees to pant. I didn't want to say this out loud; it threw me into a full-blown anxiety attack.

"Lexi." Striker was using his commander's voice. He gripped my shoulders. "Tell me. What?"

"I think Indigo is watching this unfold," I whispered. "And I'm terrified of what he might have done about it."

11

In the dim morning light, I focused on the sensation of Striker's arms wrapping me tight. With my head pillowed on his chest, the steady beat of his heart was soothingly meditative in my still groggy state. My right hand extended out and draped over the coffee mug Striker had set on the bedside table. The steam rose, dampening my palm, hot, moist, and fragrant. Mom's ring had twisted and was trapped between my fingers with a little bite. Not enough that I wanted to move.

This was the way I liked to start my mornings, slowly.

Striker was a jackrabbit this morning, springing from the bed and into his day.

Already, Beetle and Bella had had their run. Downstairs, the girls' kibble rattled and pinged in their bowls as they scarfed down their food.

It was nice that Striker could shift gears, bringing the energy down and climbing, freshly showered, into bed with me.

I turned my head to kiss his warm skin.

"What are you up to today?" Striker's voice was melted butter, rich and delicious.

"After we get Cammy on the bus." I glanced at the clock, six.

Cammy still had a half hour of sleep. "I'm going to the office. I have a puzzle sitting on my table."

"Do you have a direction?"

"Right now, it's like that cooking show where they hand you a basket of things that should not go together. And yet, they need to. So it takes some creativity. But in my case, it might need some quiet and some tree time. I may take the girls hiking near Jack and Suz's place. If you haven't worn them out for the day, that is." I leaned my head back. "They're getting older. It seems just yesterday that I was moving them into this house as mere pups, just a year and a half old. And now—" I stopped and shook my head. "Well, that was a punch in the chest."

Striker slid a finger under my chin to tip my head up to where he could look me in the eyes. "Dobermans live ten to thirteen years. You give them excellent care. They don't have any health issues. Cerberus's training exercises keep them sharp and interested in life."

He was right, but the ache from my thoughts hadn't lifted. "They were my family when I lost my family. They are such a big part of my heart, and they're sisters. When I say goodbye to one, I'm afraid it will be about the same time as I say goodbye to both. As painful as that will be for me, they have been together since they were in the womb. I can't imagine how hard that mourning will be if one leaves without the other."

"These are bleak thoughts. Anything behind them?" Striker asked, unwinding from me so he could sit with his back against the headboard. He tugged my hand to help me pull my legs around and sit up. "Some holdovers from last night's dreams?"

"No nightmares last night that I can remember, but…" I lifted my nose to inhale as if I could sniff out a problem. There was nothing readily there. "Distress," I concluded. "Something's buzzing the air." And I stopped with that thought. Buzzing in the air. Was Indigo here? I stared down at my lap and tried to calm my beating heart and sense if there was an effervescence. Paranoia can do wicked things to the brain.

"Distress," Striker repeated.

It gave me a moment to sit with that word, distress. It was the wrong word.

The word I wanted had more power and danger—a thunderstorm with whipping winds.

"No. Not distress. Destruction."

"Destruc—" he began, but that single word snapped in two with the high-pitched wail of an ambulance rocketing along the highway that was down below the retaining wall across the street.

With the slightest shift of his shoulders, Striker seemed to expand against the headboard. To broaden his muscles. To grow in power and strength. Striker always wanted to stand in the way of my monsters. The universe had a different idea of how things should unfold. Typically, my path became dangerous when I was on my own. He slowed his breathing, forcing his body to relax.

Questions twitched at the corner of his mouth.

I felt guilty for doing that to him, dangling danger when I had nothing to back it up. My suspicions about Indigo yesterday were doing a job on me still. "Let me mull those thoughts. I'll get back to you. I need to get myself into gear. While you get Cammy up, I'll make breakfast."

Climbing from the bed, I lifted the mug of coffee, now cool enough to enjoy that first bitter taste. I drank enough that I wasn't worried about sloshing it on the stairs as I went to the kitchen.

After giving Beetle and Bella extra belly rubs and hugs, I let them play in the backyard. They'd be staying with Kate again today. It was interesting to see how protective they were of her, how they'd lay their graying muzzles on Kate's expansive belly. One always kept an eye on the front door, and the other watched the back. And both were rewarded by ear scritches and love from Kate and Little Guy all day.

Closing the door behind Bella as she leaped toward her ball, I scooped the neck strap of my apron over my head and opened the fridge. Tying the ribbons around my waist, I looked over the ingredients on the shelves, looking for inspiration.

Today was Wednesday, Nana Kate.

Nana Kate's husband, Bill, was a crew worker fixing the city's public infrastructure. He ate a big breakfast to fuel his day, what Nana Kate would term a farm breakfast: eggs, potatoes, bacon, toast slathered in butter, a vegetable of some kind, usually broiled tomatoes. By today's standards, we might look at that breakfast and decide that he was a coronary waiting to happen. But that wasn't how Bill died. He died a hero. A flashflood swept a car toward the river. Bill shucked his tool belt as he ran to them. He rescued the family—a young mother and two toddlers strapped in their car seats. When he went after the family dog, the car rolled in the current, trapping him.

I remembered his funeral, but I was very young.

In the retelling of the story, Nana Kate was pragmatic about it. She said it was absolutely the way Bill would have wanted to go, doing a service for others.

Still, I've always thought about the abruptness of that story. How he went off to work with his lunch pail, probably filled with meatloaf sandwiches, and that last goodbye was a final goodbye.

Same with my dad.

We were there singing together as we always had, laughing.

Boom. Gone.

Dead on the side of the road.

Mom was the opposite. She lingered and suffered.

Which was a better parting?

Like Bill, Dad would have wanted to be laughing and loving life and then onward bound. He watched Mom's suffering, how she couldn't get out of bed for a decade except to make it to the bathroom. Dad wouldn't have handled that the same as my mom. She did her art on a table that she could use propped up on pillows, imagine, read, and love. Dad would have slipped into a depression.

How do I want to die?

Old, loved, and peacefully sleeping.

Do I get the choice?

No.

But I did have a choice about breakfast. Scrambled eggs, toast, and I could repurpose the extra baked potatoes from the other night into a hash with some peppers and onions.

The sounds of Striker coaxing a sleepy Cammy to get out of bed and get dressed wafted down the stairs. It was so domestic. He was such a natural father figure.

After prepping the food and heating it on the stove, I set Cammy's book bag on the table to check her class folder and add her lunch.

When I opened it, there was a picture with a sticky note attached.

I LIFTED THE NOTE, and my blood iced.

CAMMY

An invisible hand clawed at my throat. My lungs tightened. And in my mind, all I could think was, No! No, no, no!

And I forced myself to switch it to an okay. Okay good. It's like going to the doctor and getting bad news. The bad thing was happening in the body all along. Left undiscovered, it could manifest into something that wasn't fixable. But with information, steps could be taken. *Would be taken.*

What steps?

First, show it to Striker and see what his gut says. I might still be seeing things through Indigo-colored glasses.

Who can I talk to about this, Miriam?

Not her bailiwick.

Doc. Doc was the psychic physician assigned to the Galaxy Project. And she had been so helpful to me in the past; maybe she will have insights.

Phone?

Probably not good enough. Probably, I needed to head up to Wyoming.

I finished reading the teacher's note.

Often, a child her age will land on a picture and repeat it as they figure out how the lines and shapes work together. Typical pictures that we see at her stage of development have to do with families and family pets. I wanted to bring this to your attention because these themes might need further consideration if you don't have a pet rat in her sphere or a tarantula. I thought I'd check in to see if this pertained to a book she loves or some other easy explanation. If not, we do have resources to provide

Cammy with psychological support. Please send me a note on the class page if you want me to pursue this for Cammy.

With kind regards,

Jennifer Grafe

THE SMELL of breakfast tickled my nostrils, and I hustled over to the stove to turn the food, sliding the picture into the cutlery drawer to protect it.

My mind raced.

Spyder, where are you? What are you up to? You're in danger.

Spyder was right there, dangling into the mouth of the rat. Wyoming and Galaxy. The remote viewers could take a look at the art, and we could discuss the ramifications.

I portioned the eggs onto three plates.

Spyder was a spider. His job was to build a web and catch the prey. Did catching the prey mean that he was dangling in clear sight so that he could lure them in?

No one believed that Sylanos—the rat—was still alive.

He could be dead, and the rat could be his organization that continues. After all, Spyder was chasing down Sylanos's cartel last year when he asked me to befriend Destiny. The investigators believed that when she fled the cult compound, she had taken files that were irrefutable evidence against not only the cult leaders but also Sylanos. She was murdered. No documents were discovered. Had I heard wrong? Was I jumping to conclusions? Sylanos? Or was Sylanos synonymous with Sylanos Cartel?

I frowned over my skillet.

As Striker and Cammy entered the kitchen, the noise and movement shook me from my inner dialogue. I plated the rest of the food and brought it to the table.

Striker shot me a look as I set a plate in front of him. "Everything okay?"

I gave him a flat-lipped smile. "Breakfast is a little overcooked. Sorry, I got distracted."

"I think it's good, Aunty Chica," Cammy said as she shoveled a forkful of eggs into her mouth.

"Well, thank you, sweetheart, that's very kind of you." I smoothed a hand over her hair and dropped a kiss on top of her head.

I turned back to the counter, straightening up my prep mess.

"You gobbled yours right up. You must have been hungry," Striker said. "Do you need more food?"

"Nu-uh."

I turned to Cammy, tipping my ear toward the sink. "Can you bus your plate, then run upstairs and brush your teeth? Uncle Gavin will help you fix your hair in just a minute."

Without saying anything else, Cammy did as asked, then pounded up the stairs.

Striker turned his gaze on me. "Okay, Chica, you've never burned breakfast before. What gives?"

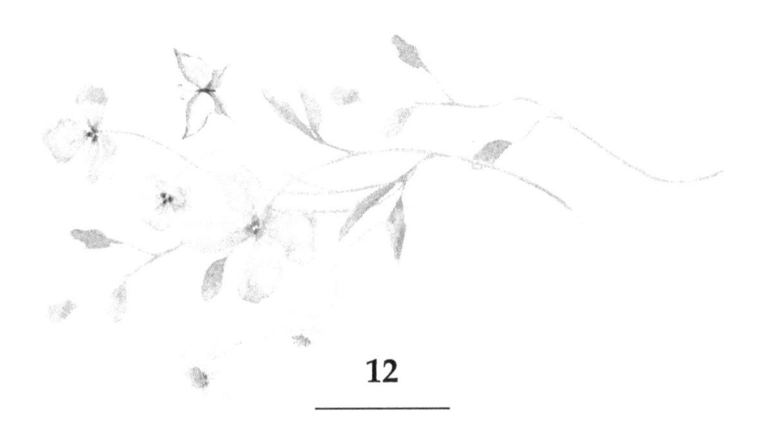

12

"I NEED TO SHOW YOU SOMETHING." I OPENED THE DRAWER, PULLING out the picture and the teacher's letter.

He read it over, then lifted the sticky note. His face hardened. When he brought his gaze up to meet mine, he asked, "Does this mean what I think it means?"

"I'm not a mind reader."

He popped his eyebrows at me.

"I'm a lot of things, Striker. I'm not a mind reader. I wanted to hear what you thought you saw in this picture."

"That looks like a rat. And the rat looks like it's wearing a tracking collar. That rat looks like it's positioned under a spider. And that the spider might be lowering itself into the mouth of the rat. The rat looks like the dreams you've had since you worked with Iniquus on solving the Sylanos case." He rattled off his observations like he was at a hotwash after a mission. "The person working on that case is Spyder McGraw. The reason he's working on it is that Sylanos was one of the heads of The Hydra that he has been trying to stop for the protection of democracy in the United States. The last we heard about that effort was over a year ago when you were playing roommate with a witness, and she was killed while you stood on the stoop outside the door."

"She was killed before I got there."

"*Don't* split hairs with me." Fierce Striker. Yeah, I got that same emotion when seeing the picture, too.

"Fine," I modulated my tone to sound practical. "But Spyder never asked me to room with Destiny. That was my idea—a shortcut to grow closer faster. No one had any idea that she was followed to D.C."

"Exactly. How was Destiny followed? How did they find her in D.C.? You told me she did it right when you looked at her strategies for getting to the apartment where you all lived. She was very savvy," Striker said. "They *shouldn't* have been able to follow her."

I shrugged. "Destiny could have made a mistake we don't know about."

"Like what?" he asked. "You would have found that slip and moved her."

"I can make mistakes too." My voice dropped, and I sounded childlike to my own ears.

"Not very likely. Not with this," Striker insisted. "Not when you were trying to keep her safe. How did they find her? Do you have a hypothesis?"

"A concern."

"Okay." He crossed his arms over his chest and slipped down in his chair. His feet spread wide, boulder style.

"Could Sylanos's people have used someone trained like Galaxy?" Indigo. Could Indigo, in the past, have tasked himself to look for someone that would lead to Sylanos's capture? Could Indigo have found Destiny? Or me? He could have seen either of us and handed that information to the cartel with a date in the future. I blinked. I was probably filtering my thoughts through that weird energy I experienced in the SCIF yesterday. It was too frightening that Indigo could still be a catalyst for other people to die even after his death. "Not Galaxy." I licked my lips. "Indigo surely told the other heads of Hydra about his skills. Sylanos would know remote viewing was possible. And Sylanos would have learned that he could get a percentage of trust when using the woo-woo stuff."

"Mmm." Striker shook his head.

"It wouldn't have to be a remote viewer. Someone could have hired a skilled practitioner—a psychic, like Miriam."

"She works cold cases. Destiny was still alive." Striker might wish we were sitting here making up fantasy stories. But he knew better. He'd lived through the ramifications of things happening outside the physical plane. And I knew he was trying to meet me where I was when he added, "Someone who specializes in psychically finding missing persons. The family makes up a story, or maybe it is truthful, 'Our daughter was getting ready for her wedding day, and she disappeared. The whole family is frantic'."

"They were frantic but not for her safety, for their own. If someone had the skills, they could look at them and see that fear-energy was predominant, and that might convince them it was a legitimate search. That person might have been able to put a pin on a map. Maybe not an exact pin, but enough clues: She's in D.C., a waitress at a diner, and the diner looks like this. It's not outside the realm of possibility for someone with etheric-seeking skills. But you said Sylanos. Do *you* think he's alive, Striker?"

"I get that you do. Me? With any level of conviction? Not really. The rat having a tracker in Cammy's drawing is the biggest significance to me. It puts me instantly in mind of what you described to me. The rat you dream about tells me—when I drop my need for facts and let myself believe in the inexplicable—that some aspect of Sylanos is at work. Is it the man himself, the way you believe? Is it the infrastructure that he created? I don't know. But when I refer to Sylanos, I guess I'm referring to all levels of possibility. When Cammy comes down, we should ask her about the picture. It might be we're seeing something that's not there. For her, this might be like a dog shock collar. Or it might be a translator so we can understand what the squeaks mean when the rat speaks."

"But you think this picture is about the images of Spyder and Sylanos?" I pressed.

"The teacher flagged this as concerning. It tells me that the themes didn't come up in class and that the images aren't from a popular TV show or book, and it was just some crazy coincidence."

"Uncle Gavin, you were supposed to help me with my hair!" Cammy scolded.

I spun toward the kitchen entry, wondering how long Cammy had been there, but fortunately, she was still making her way through the dining room, hairbrush in hand.

Striker stood up and walked to the dining table, pulling out a chair. "I apologize, buttercup. Aunty Chica was showing me a picture you drew in class. It was in your school folder."

I held the picture up to my chest. "A purple rat!" I tried to sound enthusiastic.

Cammy stood between Striker's knees, and he began sectioning off her long black hair.

I dragged a chair in front of her so we were eye to eye. "This looks like there's a story here. Will you tell me about your art?"

"So this is a good spider," she started.

"What makes him good?" Striker asked.

"I don't know. I think he's a protecto-spider. He scares the bad things away. I like him."

"How wonderful," I said. "Can you tell me what kinds of things he's scared away?"

She looked off for a minute, then shook her head. "No."

Striker moved his finger down the silk thread to the spider. "Is that what he's doing here? Scaring the bad things away?"

"That's a science rat," Cammy said.

"He has something around his neck. Is that part of the science?" I asked.

"Like wolves."

"Wolf science?" Striker asked.

"They put a tracker on the wolves, and they can see how far they run and when they play with their friends in the pack."

"That's fun," I said. "Does the rat have a pack like the wolf?"

Cammy squished her lids down tight as Striker worked at a snarl. "Ow! Mommy calls those rat's nests. They hurt."

I tapped the paper to keep her talking.

"My hair's not got the same kind of rat's nest like he has. That rat's nest is filled up."

"With other rats?" Striker asked.

"Lots and lots and lots of rats."

"Do other rats have trackers so the scientists can tell where they run and when they play with their family?" I asked, perspiration dampening my armpits.

"No, just this one. He's the king rat. I was going to draw a crown on his head, but the bell rang, and we had to go get on the bus."

"Do you still like riding the bus?" Striker asked.

"I sit next to Ruby because she's little. Ouch, Uncle Gavin, that's a rat's nest!"

"Sorry, sweetheart. I'm trying to be gentle."

It flashed into my mind that I'd get better data if I hypnotized her, but then I rejected the idea. Striker would nix it anyway. "Hey, this spider here, he's hanging over that rat's mouth. Is the rat hungry?"

"Rats are always hungry like Gator is. Did you see last night that Gator ate a whole pizza, and then he ate some of mine?"

While an impromptu gathering of friends last night was usually relaxing, last night, for me, had felt a little overwhelming. Imagine being overwhelmed by pizza and laughter. "That was nice of you to share." I smiled.

"Miss Alice says that Gator has a tapeworm."

Striker laughed.

Cammy turned her big black eyes on Striker. "Miss Alice said a tapeworm can live in your belly and eat your food. If Gator has a tapeworm, someone should help him get it out, so he doesn't have to chew so much."

"I'll ask him about it. Promise." Striker rubbed her arms. "Is there anything else about this story of the rat and spider you'd like to tell me? In your imagination, what happens next?"

"I don't know." She stomped her foot. "Uncle Gavin, the bus is going to be here. I don't want to be late. I sit next to Ruby."

"Okay, let me put in your bow." He turned her to face me.

"I once had a spider bite," Cammy said. "It was big and fat, and my mommy didn't like that I was scratching it. Then it turned red, and we had to go to the doctor for medicine."

"I'm glad that your mommy took such good care of you. I know what, how about today in school, you draw a pretty picture for Mommy?" I suggested. "Something that will make her smile. And then we'll put it in the mailbox. The postal workers will drive it down to your mommy. What do you think would make Mommy smile?"

"I could draw a picture of Beetle and Bella."

"Yes. What else?" I set the rat picture down. That conversation was over, and now I needed to seed other ideas so Cammy didn't keep drawing purple king rats at school, raising warning flags.

"I could draw a picture of me playing on the swing at the park."

"Yes. You could draw that, too!" I smiled as Striker pulled Cammy's hair back with a bright yellow ribbon clip. "Tell me some other pictures you could draw."

"I could do one of me and Ruby holding hands. And I could make flowers and a rainbow and a sun, and the sun could have a big smile as it shines down on Ruby and me."

"Oh, all those pictures sound like grin-makers."

Striker's phone alarm sounded. "That's it, Cammy. Time to get to the bus stop. How about you give Aunty Chica a big hug? She's going to the office now."

Reaching out wide arms, Cammy leaned forward to squeeze me tightly, then bolted for the door.

I swung into the kitchen to shove her folder back into her pack and to make sure that I had put her lunch sack inside. As I zipped it up and pressed it toward Striker, Striker asked under his breath, "Next steps?"

I shook my head. I had absolutely no idea what to do. "I don't know. Something."

"Uncle Gavin, come on!" Cammy called.

Striker leaned in with a big smacking kiss. "You'll figure it out!" he said confidently as he jogged toward the front of the house.

Yeah, well, I wasn't so sure.

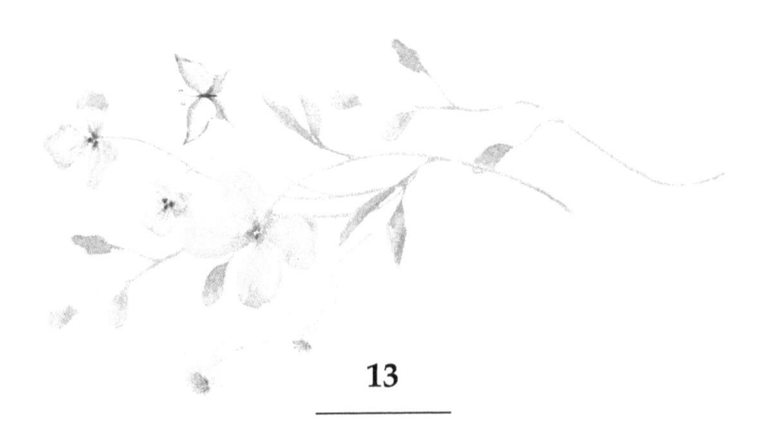

13

Sometimes, time does a funny little thing. Routes that take me thirty minutes somehow only take me fifteen. It wasn't my driving speed that made the difference; I was always careful with my driving for oh so many reasons, not the least of which was that I'd had my share of head trauma, and I was still symptomatic from my last concussion, though that had happened years ago. And it didn't have anything to do with traffic. The roads in Northern Virginia had a predictably dense population of aggressive drivers.

No, it was a weird flex in the time-space continuum that I had no explanation for today other than that the Universe wanted to get me into the office and on the phone with Doc.

It was two hours earlier in Wyoming, I calculated as I looked at my watch. Early, but not pants-on-fire emergency early, cup-of-coffee in pajamas early.

I put my thumb on the biometrics lock on the Puzzle Room door. The internal mechanism ground as the bolt retracted.

I had to force my feet forward.

I have learned that being scared for loved ones feels so much more frightening than fear for myself. I was terrified about that picture that Cammy drew—frightened of the ramifications for a little girl. Frightened for my second-dad, Spyder.

With the door shut and locked, I quick dialed Doc.

No answer.

I dialed again.

No answer.

I dialed a third time.

"Lexi, this must be a big damned deal for you to pull me out of the shower like this."

"Sorry. I'd hoped you were having coffee." I tried to make my voice sound light and friendly. "I had a situation come up today. I think it will intrigue you."

"It's not something intriguing. Just go ahead and spit it out. You wouldn't ring my phone three times in a row if you weren't freaked out about something. And as long as I've known you, you don't freak when a normal human being would or should."

"All right, agreed. I'm freaked out and hoped you all were around so I could fly up and pick your brains."

"When's this you want to come?"

"Tonight? Tomorrow?"

"Yup, you're freaked out. Well, come on then, let's get you sorted. Tomorrow's best, Trudy will be in the city picking up some supplies, and he can gather you at the airport. When you have your travel information, let us know."

"I can get a rental car if it's easier. I mean, if he picks me up, it's a long round trip to take me back to the city again."

"Nah. The rental cars all have GPS units that aren't particularly secure. We'd rather not chance anyone knowing there's anything out here. We'll come. Just call with the information."

"K, thanks."

I moved back out to the hall, pulled the door, and headed to the executive wing of the Iniquus Headquarters building. There were some names that I didn't like to say on the phone. And Spyder's was top of that list.

I tapped on the open door before moving into General Elliot's suite.

In the reception room, Leanne was hanging up the desk phone. "Hey." She smiled and then frowned, looking down as her gaze landed on her appointment book.

"Impromptu popping in," I said.

"I'm sorry, the general isn't here. He, Mr. Spencer, and Colonel Grant are consulting with Sy Covington over in the legal wing."

"Thank you." I scooted closer to her desk and crouched down so we were eye to eye.

Her gaze held mine unblinking. Yeah, this behavior was odd. But somehow, I felt like—I didn't know, like I had to be super secretive, that the mere name, the mere ask put out into the ether would disturb that time continuum that I seemed to breach on my way here today.

"Leanne," I whispered. "Do you still have a communication channel to Spyder McGraw?" What was I even going to tell him, 'Striker's niece drew a rat eating a spider as it descended from its web. Beware!' That was *so* stupid.

"Yes." Her face compressed into an array of worry lines on her otherwise perfectly complected face.

"I need to get some information to him." Shit. What? What was I going to say here?

I knew the phrase to offer up if I wanted Spyder to drop whatever he was doing, no matter whose life or how many lives were on the line. If I used that phrase, Spyder would be here tomorrow. That wasn't what I wanted to happen. I had no "I need to tell you something" code. We needed to figure one out. Probably, not having a code wasn't an oversight on Spyder's part. Indeed, it was a decision—leave him to his work unless there were no other options. Still, I was going to try.

"I…uhm." Leanne shook her head, obviously not wanting this ask to go any further forward.

"You did this once before, do you remember?" I put my hands on the floor to steady myself in my stooped position.

She reluctantly nodded.

"And that was a good thing, right?"

"Yes," she said as an exhale.

What? What do I say? "I have an Aristotle quote to share with him."

Leanne picked up her pen and let her hand hover over her pad.

"'The aim of art is to represent not the outward appearance of things, but their inward significance.'"

Leanne read it back, then scratched Aristotle underneath.

"Can you get that to him today?" I pressed. "Now?"

She blinked at the paper and then back at me. She offered me a tight nod. And I knew she was breaking some kind of rule to help me. Leanne hated the idea of rule-breaking. It was anathema to her very being. I reached up and squeezed her knee. "It's important. Thank you."

"You're welcome," Leanne said.

I could tell from the lack of oxygen rounding her words that she was having a panic attack. I was sorry to cause her pain, but I was more interested in keeping Spyder safe.

My hands were sweaty. "And Leanne, I need to get in and access the Indigo collection to do some research on a mission I'm working on."

She shot an eye at the file room with its high-tech security system and back at me.

I had a medical reaction in there once, and since the security system only lets one person in there at a time, if you couldn't get yourself out, you were pretty much shit out of luck until the emergency protocols could be applied. Which, I later learned, was a timed sequence that took about twelve hours to accomplish. Striker had used his commander's voice to rouse me enough to stumble out of there. Ever since, Leanne wasn't jazzed about opening the door for me.

We went through the steps: she put in the codes, and my biometrics were analyzed—three-sixty body imaging, iris scans, my full handprint—all while being observed by security personnel in some remote location.

Once all hoops were jumped, I was in, sitting at the desk, opening the laptop that held all of the tasking sheets that I had been able to photograph at Indigo's penthouse on top of the Omega Security building.

Those notebooks were all that existed of Indigo's private work.

After I had grabbed what images I could of his remote viewer tasking logs, I escaped the building. Moments later, a fire broke out. The Omega building burned to a hollow shell.

It was a shame that I couldn't get it all. I had focused on grabbing what specific information I could to find and save Striker after Scarlet kidnapped him. Anything else in these files were tasks that happened around that time. With the fear of imminent capture, I wasn't reading the notebooks but turning pages and clicking pictures as fast as I could.

Here I went, back into the land of obsession and crazy.

I let my pen settle on the pad of paper that always sat ready on the file room desk. I thought of various searches I could task the AI system to undertake.

Spyder. Of course.

Rats. Sure, why not?

Cammy

Lynda

Uganda, though, why would he search for that country?

Lexi. Too broad, I scratched it out.

Lexi, wedding. Hmmm. Indigo wasn't particularly interested in my wedding. He was interested in Scarlet's wedding, Striker's wedding, and their possible married life. I scratched through my name and wrote:

Striker, wedding.

I looked at those two words for a moment. Did I want to know? Was this a whole kettle of worms? Certainly, Striker didn't marry

Scarlet. She was dead. Any remote viewing information would probably/possibly be about *our* wedding.

It might be nice to know about that. Maybe even a date when it was supposed to happen.

And with that thought, I wrote on the next page: **Kitchen Grandmothers.**

If the general wanted the marriage ceremony to be next month, Striker and I needed to be headed to Uganda via Tanzania ASAP. We also needed to make travel arrangements for my Kitchen Grandmothers since they were coming in from far-flung places. Biji was back in Punjab, India.

When my Kitchen Grandmother Biji was married, she'd only met her husband once. Where she came from, marriages were arranged, and her intended lived in the city where he was working on his college degree. They met once so they could take a look at each other. I assumed that meeting was to ensure they found each other attractive enough to imagine a sexual relationship. Biji said they wrote once a week to get to know each other. I asked Biji if she was scared to commit to a man she didn't know. She said no, they'd had their horoscope charts done and everything aligned.

As far as I could tell, they'd had a lovely life together.

Yes, I wondered if there were any task sheets with the date of Striker's marriage and the projected life path that followed, like what Biji had in hand when she agreed to take her vows.

Here I was, going into the tasking sheets to see what Indigo and Scarlet saw.

Grain of salt, they were both *insane*.

I started broadly—Assembly, Sylanos, Omega, seeding dreams, dreaming, dreams. The number of tasking files that came up on each of those parameters was unmanageable, given the time I had to expend on this search.

Then I remembered that when Indigo kidnapped Lynda, he asked her about the man with blackberry skin. And yes, there it was. A very clear task, given a high probability of gathering essential information. But like all tasks, etheric information needed a physical affirmation. "The man with blackberry skin was too dense to see."

What happened next was a known. Indigo had Lynda kidnapped and interrogated. She knew nothing about a man with blackberry skin taking her necklace. But Indigo revealed he knew something: I had helped save Lynda and Cammy one horrific night. And he knew that I had done it with psychic skills. In the interrogation, he was asking her what my psychic skills entailed. He also knew that I was able to leave my body. Herman Trudy was paired with Indigo when Trudy saw my energy in a meeting of The Assembly where they talked about remote viewers. And Trudy had tried to understand what my skills were then, too.

Not helpful in the now.

I drummed my fingers on the table.

I tried searching: **Delay, Striker marriage**.

Interestingly, Indigo had tasked that in various ways.

There were three pictures of what might be bears. Indigo was no Herman Trudy when it came to drawing. He landed somewhere in the spectrum between Cammy and Trudy. Yeah, I thought they were bears.

I pulled out my phone and took a picture of each.

One bear was dancing on a hill with a meteor shower overhead. The "come back and report" part of that report was a description of the picture. So were the other two bear pictures—a bear with an open mouth with winged notes coming out. One bear leaned back against a rock. He looked drunk or in a stupor, maybe falling over laughing, maybe he had a stomachache. Hard to tell from the poor renderings. And there was nothing in his description that gave the images any context. It was as if Indigo was bored and just let the scientific reporting consistency fall off.

There were other pictures the search engine found, some nonsensical geometry. A judge was in one.

None of it meant anything to Indigo.

Only the judge meant anything to me.

I did find one slightly more interesting search: Striker's wedding. Where does he travel next?

I assumed Indigo wanted to find Scarlet's honeymoon spot.

He got a blob.

There was no specific description of the blob other than. "Oh ho ho. Look what I found. An alien. Reminds me of—" I took a picture of that task, curious because Indigo didn't seem to take the time to describe this one or write his conclusions. Highlighting the tasking number, I copied it and pasted it into the search bar.

The task was from the same year that Scarlet and Striker had broken up.

Searching for that tasking number, I found a cryptic task dated a year earlier: Based on previous, take me to a time and place where I can best understand that trajectory.

The same blob came up, the smile, crooked and much smaller. The alien's eyes seemed to be open. There was the head of a cartoon-like queen with a stick in her hand.

The write-up was simply a description of what Indigo had drawn.

The conclusions said: Interesting. Try that one again with a tweak.

Honestly, Indigo had, on many of his tasking sheets, been hyper-scientific. There were others, like this series, that seemed like a hobby, like fishing around.

I copied that tasking number and put it into the AI search. That linked to another task that had been done the next day.

Task: The last task with a tweak.

Here again, the alien, the eyes, the queen's stick now looked like a phallus. There was now a helicopter dangling a net toward her. When I widened that part, I saw it was a spider.

Spyder?

If this had to do with Spyder McGraw, I would think that Indigo would get excited and put something about that in the notes. But there seemed to be no interest in the dangling spider. It wasn't even mentioned in the description of what Indigo had seen.

When I first saw that blob and thought it was a net, my inclination was that it was there to help the drowning queen and not to trap her. But what do I know?

I took pictures of both of those tasks. They were the clearest pictures associated with **Striker, wedding**. I'd show them to Galaxy and see if they contained some of their iconography.

Nothing I found in the files showed me anything about Striker's wedding or marriage that was concrete and actionable. Indigo's pictures mainly included trees and leaves and how sunlight filtered through.

Well, this wasn't helping anything. No, "Striker will get married at his bay home in September amongst the late summer roses."

I looked at my watch. Keep looking?

Did I really want to see all this? Especially when there was only about a sixty percent chance of it being right, if understandable? I mean, bears and aliens. It was as hard to interpret as one of my *knowings*.

And when I thought that, I stilled. Reflexively, I held my breath.

What was that?

There was a tiny tickle at the back of my brain, back where I had heard what I thought was a *knowing* about birds of a feather flocking together.

I sought out the Tsukamoto that hung overhead, the design that kept viewers like Indigo from seeing anything happening in the room.

There was a flash of red behind my eyes. A rhythmic whisper. A pounding beat.

What was that?

There was nothing to grab onto and pull closer for examination.

The experience left me off-kilter. I didn't like how my soul felt like an unruly passerby had jostled it. I thought about my morning ritual practices, meditation, a thinking run, then breakfast. Cammy's arrival had shifted how Striker and I moved about our day. Okay, as thrilled as I was that she was here, I needed to get back to my practices. They were essential to keeping me whole and healthy.

I stood up, and still, *something* inside my brain said, "Hey, look over here!"

I lay on the ground under the Tsukamoto mobile. With my eyes closed, I reviewed each of the pictures I'd looked at from the Indigo files. Nothing lit me up any brighter.

Still, my soul was ruffled. I wanted to tuck my hips against the wall with my legs straight up at a right angle. *Viparita Karani*, Biji taught me to do that when I wanted to clear my thoughts. But the last time I was in here and laid on the floor, I fell asleep, and everyone panicked.

And just as I thought that, I heard Leanne call, "Lynx?"

"Yup."

"You're on the floor again. Are you all right? Do you need me to get Striker?"

"I'm fine. This is my thinking position." I didn't think I was visible to Leanne, so I hadn't wrapped my skirt around my thighs, just lay there with the fabric swirling around me and my panties. Maybe she could see my head. "Ha. Time flies, doesn't it? I'm coming out now."

I sat up and stilled. A humming. A heartbeat.

What *was* that?

14

"ANOTHER NIGHTMARE?" I ASKED, CLICKING ON MY BEDSIDE LAMP. A warm glow lit Striker's path as he made his way back to our bed. "Poor kid."

"Yeah." Striker lifted the summer duvet and crawled under. Instead of lying back down with me, he put his back against the headboard. "I'm going to talk to the pediatrician that Sarah suggested. Get this on their radar. Ask if they have a therapist who has experience with children of addicts who've had violence in their lives. Do you mind leaving the light on for a few minutes? I want to be awake to hear if Cammy is falling into another nightmare."

I squirmed until I sat with my back resting against him, my head lolling back on his shoulder. I pulled his arms around me, and he cradled me there. I liked it when we sat like this and talked in the wee hours of the night. "Did I tell you about the CIA the other day?" I murmured.

"Nope." He petted his hand down my hair, then dropped a kiss. "How'd it go?"

"I tried to puzzle through the data they handed me. They wanted me to prove a theory. I saw nothing that did, so I told them a story about Benjamin Franklin and one about Gouverneur Morris."

"Morris the Constitution guy? Preamble?"

"That's the one." It tickled me that Striker knew who the guy was without a prompt.

"Yeah? Did you tell them Morris lost his leg because he was boffing some woman, and her husband came home?"

"Morris was as tall as Jack. It's hard to imagine he was scared and running for his life. But yes, actually, that is the story I told them. Hey, do you know that Morris both lived and died by his penis?"

"A penis death?" I could feel the chuckle rumble Striker's chest. "Another husband walked in with a knife?"

"Morris was married when he died and seemed content with just boffing his wife."

"Good woman. But your penis can kill you?"

"Not mine. I don't have penile parts, and one would hope this story wouldn't happen in modern-day medicine. So the story goes, Morris died because he had a urethral stricture. Had to be painful. So he took a whale bone from his wife's corset and shoved it up his urethra to fix it, killing himself in the process."

Striker's entire body braced down. "That makes my everything clench. That's ghastly. I'm assuming that you held back that part of his story?"

"I was trying to be demure." I looked up and was rewarded with a kiss.

"Hey, have you heard from Spyder recently?" Striker asked. "We need to tell him about the wedding."

"Agreed. I told Leanne an Aristotle quote at the office yesterday, so I'm hopeful he'll be in contact soon."

"I thought it was Confucious you used to reel him in last time." He rubbed a soothing hand slowly up and down my arm. "You said it was in a fortune cookie?"

"I don't need him physically here. I just wanted to let Spyder know that he should reach out to me when it was safe to do so."

"And you think that's what it will signal to him?" Striker asked.

"We'll see. Cryptic and clear at the same time."

"So, is that why you're so tense?" He lifted my hand to kiss me, and I assumed it was to alleviate any sense that he was rebuking me.

"To be honest, it's just that so many players' names and even faces from the last few years of crippity crap have been showing up in my work over the last week. It feels like they're crowding into me. That picture Cammy drew makes me feel like Spyder might be poking the bear."

The bear? Could Spyder poking the bear be what I was seeing in those pictures? I tried it on for size, and it didn't seem to fit.

"After Spyder et al. shut down their multi-million-dollar oil scam last year," I continued, "I'm not sure but that The Hydra players might be motivated to seek some kind of retribution."

"Against you?" Striker jostled me, so I had to face him. "Has something happened to you that I don't know about?"

"Me exactly? No. It's that the wind is picking up. The storm clouds are forming overhead. It's a sensation without fact."

"Okay, let's be pragmatic. How would anyone in Hydra know you were involved with stopping the oil scam? And also, let me point out, that Destiny's death meant you had nothing to do with the collapse of that scheme and the people who are now in prison."

"The two goons who killed Destiny saw me," I pointed out.

"There's seeing someone, and there's *seeing* someone."

"Okay." I turned around to sit cross-legged, my elbows on my knees, my chin resting on clasped hands. "I can't follow that."

"One goon found you standing on the stoop in the dark of night. The guy grabbed you and dragged you into the apartment. You were fighting the one guy, right?"

"Yes."

"He'd be watching your hands and feet, not memorizing the shape of your nose."

"They were both fighting me," I corrected. "And what you said is not true, and it might even be the opposite."

"Explain that to me."

"Two things. The most obvious one is that when the limbic system is lit up, the brain dumps chemicals and pulls in all the information it can to assess and act. Under the cloud of adrenaline, one might forget everything that happened, like accident amnesia. Or, one might remember every minute detail. Second, there is a cadre of people out there who are called super-recognizers. Granted, they make up less than two percent of the population. But they will remember you forever once they've seen your face, even for a microflash."

"This is true, but equally viable are those with prosopagnosia, or face blindness. They can't remember anyone. Surely Spyder had you tested. Where do you land on that spectrum?" he asked.

"Before Spyder trained me, top fifteen percent. After training, I was in the top ten. So certainly not among the super-recognizers, but high enough that it is a major tool in my puzzling toolbox." I reached for a pillow and hugged it to me. "My ability is to find a weird thing about them and follow it. I remember one case had me following a man with a hangnail at noon and two and five o'clock, but he didn't have that same hangnail at one, three, or six o'clock."

"Impossible," Striker said.

"Exactly."

"And the face?" he asked. "Five o'clock shadow?"

I glanced at the clock; it was not quite four—no point in going back to sleep. The alarm would be sounding soon. "I don't pay much attention to faces, to be perfectly honest. Mannerisms, gaits, things like that. You do it, too."

"And how do you know that?" he asked.

"Because I was fully undercover at the Smithsonian ball, I was wearing everything that belonged to Celia, so nothing from my closet. I had different everything. I even used makeup to give myself a different bone structure, and you still recognized me. I believe the quote was, "I would recognize you anywhere by your aura, your walk, and gesture."

He pulled his brows together. "*I* said aura?"

"Weird, right? And then, you quoted Byron's poem, 'She walks in beauty like the night, of cloudless climbs, and starry skies, Like a lady—graceful, and pure of heart.'"

"I only vaguely recognize that poem from AP English class," Striker said. "I can't imagine quoting it."

"You were under a psychic attack by Scarlet. You had a headache pounding between your brows. I can imagine she was trying to force those words into your brain, thinking of her at the ball, but instead, you saw me and applied them to me."

"Always. I remember that Smithsonian ball," he said. "She was all dressed up in a Jessica Rabbit red dress?"

I sighed. "Yeah, that's the night."

"Thankfully for me, that's all a blur."

"She and her dad were both working on influencing you like they had General Elliot. Luckily, you love me deeply, and as Spyder puts it, you're dense."

His lips slid into that sexy smile of his, a little crooked, a touch of dimple, warmth shining his eyes. "I'll take that as a compliment."

"Which is the way I meant it. See, there it is again—this weird convergence of these players and stories all of a sudden. The night of the red dress at the Smithsonian Ball, Babcock was there, too. And today, Babcock came up in a discussion at Langley."

"Why would the CIA care about Babcock?" Striker asked.

"After my CIA meeting, I ran into the FBI Joint Task Force and asked them to look at the tattoo gal to see if they could tell me anything. Which they could *not*. But it did freak them out a bit. Also, just an FYI, I went over to talk to Titus Kane and put the tattoo gal on their radar. Arya, Sophia, and Zoe all need to be kept safe."

"This is from the video of the Seychelles' party?"

"Exactly. Oh." I reached out and patted Striker's thigh. "I met John Green."

"Interesting."

"Isn't it? They're working on one of our open files. Guess."

"Zorics?"

"Nope." I shook my head. "Guess again."

"You said Panther Force just before you brought this up."

"Here's your next hint. Calvin Hock was there."

"The sound engineer who tried to figure out how our comms got jammed up when Scarlet had me shot?" he asked.

"It wasn't a hollow point bullet. Scarlet meant it as Cupid's arrow. It was supposed to remind you of her love." I made a little heart with my fingers. But whew, yeah, I was making light, but it was definitely gallows humor.

"Sounds like the King George song in Hamilton. I don't find that a fun subject. Let's move on. So sound plus Panther Force equals Arya."

"Bing-ish," I said.

"There is no *ish*. It's either Bingo or it isn't."

"You decide," I told him. "They're picking up some chatter on the Darknet about neuroweapons and sound waves that somehow have something to do with satellite communications and the Russian war effort. But as to Arya, did you know she was working on a project for something with the application of sound waves and has pictures of her with the tattoo lady at a UN conference on sound pollution? Arya can't remember her name, but she believes they were working together to solve some future survival issue."

"Of the whales?" Striker asked.

"She can't remember. She remembers the tattoo chick's face from before she was kidnapped but nothing else." I stretched my eyes wide. "Crazy, right?"

"Not red blood cells exploding, though."

"Arya wouldn't do that. That was a George Matthews initiative. No… Okay, listen, I need to switch gears on you. You got in late, so I was going to tell you in the morning." I glanced at the clock again. "But I guess it's morning."

Striker went stoic.

"I'm flying up to Wyoming today. I have an appointment to talk to Doc."

"Why? What's going on?" Warrior mode.

"Doc and the others." I reached for his hand. "A couple things. First, I want to talk to her about the possibilities around how Cammy drew that picture. I have some theories, but I'd rather talk them out with her. Second, I went into the Indigo files at Iniquus and was taking a look to see if he did any tasks that might give us information about our trip to Uganda."

"Why?" Nope, still in warrior mode. I pulled my hand back.

"Because I got spooked."

"Care to expand?" He crossed his arms over his chest.

"Nope. Because I can't frame it in a way that will have any meaning for you. I want to ask Galaxy their take."

"Fine. Good. Glad you made that call. I'm going with you."

I shook my head. "No. And thank you. I thought about that, but no. Cammy needs to be here in school. We're about to take off for Uganda. She doesn't need any upheaval. Right now, she needs to depend on you, and you can trust that I am doing my best on my end to keep everyone safe from the woo-woo."

"Chica, what did you see in the files?"

"Indigo did tasks dozens of times about your wedding. When he got nothing of clarity, he started tasking what happened right after your wedding." I leaned over to pull my phone from the pocket of my sleep shorts. "Oddly, bear pictures. And there was this one picture he drew that was bizarre."

I opened my encrypted photo file and handed it to Striker.

Leaning in to point, I said, "So there was this alien-looking thing with a bunch of eyes. And there was the queen. And she's holding onto—"

"Looks like a giant vibrator. This drawing looks like an acid trip."

I spread my fingers on the screen to enlarge the image and scrolled to show the top. "And then there was a helicopter." I drew my finger down the rope dangling from the helicopter and showed Striker that a spider was hanging there over the queen.

"Spyder dropping into the fight," Striker muttered. "Two woo-woo spider pictures in two days."

"Exactly where my mind went." I sat back again and let Striker explore the picture on his own. "The write-up had no conclusions. It simply described what he had seen in the ether. Indigo said, 'Alien.' He said, 'Queen' with a question mark. And 'vibrator-shaped object.' So, nothing helpful by way of explanation. This alien picture happened the year you and Scarlet broke up. Now, to be sure, Indigo had tasked: 'Show me Striker's wedding' a bunch of times. For those, Indigo basically drew things like sun rays and leaves over and over and over. He never got anything more. I thought it was interesting that he used the word 'wedding,' not 'marriage' for those tasks because you will have both a wedding ceremony and a marriage ceremony. And that might have confused him."

"Confused him enough to imagine dildo queens and alien beings?"

"The alien task started as a blob with: 'Striker's wedding, where does he travel next?'"

He looked up from the phone. "That's odd wording for a task."

"It is, and it isn't. When I was first looking through this mess, trying to figure out where Scarlet had taken you in your drugged stupor, I remember reading how she had planned your wedding and honeymoon. When you were in the hospital after she had you shot, you were wearing a wedding ring, and she—announcing herself as Mrs. Rheas—was also wearing a wedding ring and engagement ring. She had had them made and at the ready."

Striker shifted around uncomfortably.

"She had also said she wanted a honeymoon in Bora Bora, staying in an over-water hut. I hypothesized that if Indigo were tasking, 'Where did you travel after the wedding?' I assumed he hoped to see a honeymoon destination."

"If Scarlet wanted to go to the Bora Bora hut, that would probably be a fairly easy shape for a master viewer to make out." Striker returned to the phone, looking at the picture for a long moment. "Do you think you're the queen with the vibrator, and that's what you're going to use to fight this thing?"

"Since I've never needed a vibrator and don't even own one, that would be a stretch. Nope, not even I can make up a plausible explanation for what Indigo was seeing. Why have you said twice that you have to fight this thing?"

"It doesn't look friendly. I don't know." He handed my phone back to me. "The helicopter and the spider dropping in might give this a combat mission feel."

"Don't jump to conclusions. Just because it's a spider doesn't mean it's *our* Spyder," I whispered, hoping not to give those words any bad juju.

"Agreed." He chuckled, leaning forward to brush the hair from my face and offering me a delicious kiss.

"Well, one thing is pretty clear," I whispered. "That picture isn't a honeymoon hut in Bora Bora."

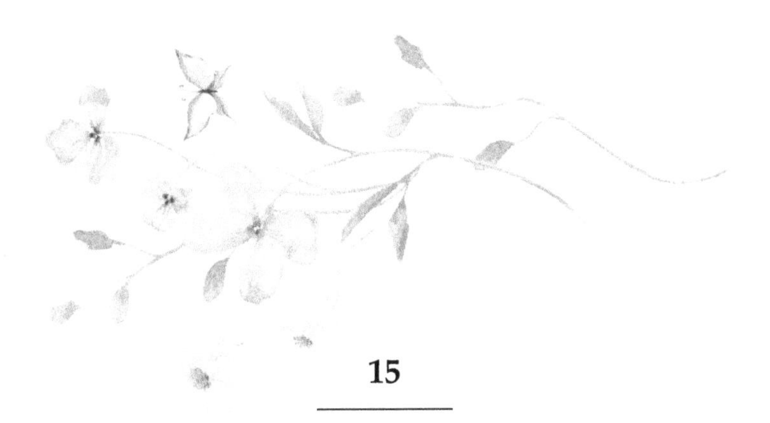

15

Since we were both wide awake, Striker had taken Beetle and Bella for a pre-dawn run, and I sat on my meditation mat in front of my altar. The last few days have reminded me of the importance of my practice to clear energetic clutter and to make myself dense.

Typically, I was good about my daily practice. But I realized with Cammy in the house, we had a new rhythm to our mornings, and I had pushed meditation to the side as I helped to get her settled into a routine.

When Striker returned, I made breakfast as he got Cammy up.

As she ate her meal—which I managed not to burn this time—I got her lunch together and checked the school file. Today, there were no examples of artwork and concerned teacher's notes. I zipped it back together and set the bag by the front door.

The morning flowed smoothly. Cammy was on the bus headed to school.

When Striker returned to the house, I was hefting my carry-on case down the stairs.

"You all set for Wyoming?" he asked. "What time are you going?"

"An Iniquus car is picking me up in about an hour."

"When you get home, we need to arrange our flight to Tanzania," Striker said, rifling through the mail stack. "Then we need to get rolling with the marriage ceremony if the general wants to do it next month."

"Once we have our marriage certificate, I'll reach out to Celia and Alice." I moved over to flop on the couch. I felt sleepy around the edges of my awareness. I'd try to get some rest on the plane. "They did all the planning the last time we were getting married, and I'm sure they have everything in a binder somewhere. And, of course, you already had the venue built at the bay house."

"Yeah, I'll call the landscaper and have him go over and start sprucing that up."

"Just a matter of flipping the switch." I hugged my knee to my chest. "Before we reach our plans out too far, let me take this first step: visiting Doc and see what they think happened that Cammy's drawing king rats with trackers on their necks. Figure out what needs to happen next for Cammy's well-being."

"Like psychic lessons you had with Miriam growing up?" Striker asked, setting the envelopes down and angling toward me.

"I hope not. I hope there's a simple explanation. I don't wish a sixth sense on Cammy or anyone else, for that matter."

"What in the world would constitute a simple explanation in this context?" He leaned back in the chair, stretching his long legs out in front of him, crossing them at the ankles.

"I was talking in my sleep," I shrugged, "and she heard me in her sleep?"

"You know what? That actually would be a simple explanation. You always talk in your sleep, and you can be loud."

"Sorry," I whispered.

"That's the simple explanation." He lifted his chin. "Tell me the complex one."

"I've felt Indigo in my sphere starting at the meeting with General Thomas."

"Has that sensation been in our house?" He went stoic on me.

"No, but that doesn't mean he isn't coming in and seeding these images to Cammy. He's an influencer."

Striker pulled his legs back in and jutted forward. "Indigo is *dead*."

"Dead *now*," I agreed. "Indigo was alive when he was tasking himself to go to a time—"

Striker held up his hands. "I… I can't."

"I know, it's really hard to wrap my mind around this, too."

"But why would Indigo look for Cammy and seed dreams about rats and spiders? That makes little to no sense. Did you see anything in the tasking sheets?"

"Mentioning Cammy specifically? No. Not *Cammy*, not *niece* either. I specifically looked up the time that he had Lynda captured so he could interrogate her. There were no notes about Lynda either. I did find the task data where he mentioned a tall, thin man with blackberry skin."

"From when Spyder was in Lynda's house collecting the evidence against The Assembly," he asked.

"Yes, the task was: *Go to a time when the viability of The Assembly is at risk.* After his henchmen kidnapped Lynda, Indigo, of course, figured out the connection. Surely, Scarlet knew the names of your family members from the time you were dating."

Striker nodded. "You thought that there might be a task like that leading to Destiny's death. Were you able to find anything like that?"

"I checked on both of her names and saw nothing. Zooming out, Indigo did task a *Go to a time when the viability of* adding each iteration—Omega, Sylanos, and The Assembly—hundreds of times. I didn't try to weed through all of them. Interestingly, he never tasked himself. That's probably how I was able to slip in and gather that data in the first place. God complex, no one was going to go after him." I reached for my mug of tea and took a sip. "Going back to when he had Lynda kidnapped, I found that specific task because I knew that he used the words *blackberry skin,* and that would be a standout in the files. Indigo knew someone had taken Lynda's necklace. Indigo knew that it would put The Assembly at risk. What he didn't know was *who* that was or *why* that was. That's why he had Lynda kidnapped, to try to fill in the blanks. From the AI search, Indigo didn't task anything to do with either Lynda or Cammy, your dad or Mimi, moving forward from that day." I tried to reassure Striker.

Striker nodded. He was pretty intense right now. "How'd he find Lynda's house?" he asked.

"He rose above and worked off the landmarks. It was the same technique that Herman Trudy used to find my prison."

"Okay," Striker said as a vehicle to move the conversation forward.

Obviously, none of this was okay. It was well outside of even my etheric comfort zone. "As to the dreams, could it be that Indigo is setting some kind of future trap?" I ventured. "He may want to hurt Spyder and maybe even you and me. I have no idea. He was crazy."

"Retribution for my not loving his daughter?" Striker asked, confusion clouding his eyes.

"We have to consider it. Your marrying Scarlet was one of his two goals. Huge goals: take down the US government and make you love a woman that you didn't love."

"Those two things shouldn't be put into the same sentence."

"For a sane person, I'd agree. But first, he was driven mad, and second, they had equal weight in his mind." I took a breath. "There's something more that I need to tell you."

Striker looked at me, and I could see him shift into combat mode. He must have read something in my body posture.

"*Birds of a feather flock together as do pigs and swine. Rats and mice will have their choice, and so shall I have mine.*" My voice was almost inaudible. I didn't want to give this thing any energy.

"A *knowing*." He breathed in. With the exhale, he hissed, "Shit." He pursed his lips and returned to stoic. "All of it? That whole phrase?"

"No. Just the first part, the bird part. And the rat part. It skips the pigs and swine part. The first time I found myself saying those words, I ran into the FBI Joint Task Force at the CIA, and they invited me into their meeting."

His eyes turned from soft moss green to the sharp green of a broken bottle. "It looked like a *knowing*?"

"It didn't at that time. It was just a thought. A precognition or incantation that manifested immediately."

"You do incantations?" he asked. "Like a spell?"

"No," I said. "I was trying to give the flavor of my experience."

"But since you went to that meeting, you've heard it again, only this time as a *knowing*?"

I brushed my hand through the air just behind my head. "Just a whisper of one."

He leaned forward, his elbows resting on his knees, his hands clasped, looking down at the floor.

I sat quietly as his mind churned.

When he looked up, he asked, "You bring up your *knowings* at times of great danger."

"True."

"Have any of them whispered to you before?" he asked. "You usually describe them as flashing red, oscillating light. I imagine them as sirens on the top of an emergency vehicle."

"That's a fair way to describe it, I guess. This one?" I brushed again. "It's too far away to tell if it's roaring up the road to overtake me or just a shadow walking back there."

"Have they ever been peaceful?"

"Sure, when I was growing up, I knew simple things like if I'd have a snow day and could play with the other kids living at my apartment building who had to go to school during the week. Or I'd know my dad was coming home with ice cream."

"And you categorize that as a *knowing* and not a precognition or something of a different name?" He held up a hand. "I'm trying to figure out what you could do before Indigo cut you."

Yeah, that had been on my mind, too. When Indigo first got the idea to sew me and Angel together in the ether, he had sliced into my aura to see what would happen next.

At the time, I was training with Miriam to send my awareness out at a distance, much like the Galaxy viewers did, to gather information. As far as I could tell, just after Indigo sliced me, I not only went out into the ether to find a victim the police were searching for, but I melded with her. The physical abuse she was enduring, I endured it, too. I could keep enough awareness to feed Miriam the information, and the police saved the girl.

After that, I said no thank you to purposefully heading out into the ether.

Then, Grandmother Sybil showed up and asked me to use that specific tool to save Cammy and Lynda.

Was it the slice that made that possible?

I have gone that route again and again to save people I loved. *Maybe* to save them. Who knew what would have happened had I not intervened? That Grandmother Sybil and her tribe were pulling me into the ether to assist them the day Lynda and Cammy were captured told me that I had been the vehicle for their survival.

One interesting thing from that time—that I found out months later—was that Cammy saw me in the ether. When I met her in physical form, she recognized me instantly and could even tell me that I had my hair styled differently.

I had never understood how that could happen.

When Grandmother Sybil and Doc performed psychic surgery to separate Angel and me, they saw the open slice and asked me if they should repair it.

Making the connection in my own mind, without any facts to lean on, that that slice was what had allowed me to connect in the ether and save my loved ones, I had said that I wanted to leave it alone for the time being.

I was suddenly wondering if Cammy's and my connection the night of her kidnapping meant she could still connect with me in the ether and whether that connection was made available because of the open wound in etheric me.

Yet another thing to discuss with Doc today.

"Chica?"

"I'm sorry?" I snapped my focus back to Striker.

He had moved his chair forward and leaned in so we were face to face. "Did you have *knowings* about danger when you were younger before Indigo assaulted you?"

When I didn't answer, Striker moved to the couch. Reaching for my hand, he pulled me onto his lap. "Your whole body feels afraid to me," he whispered.

He pressed my hips to move me farther down his body as he swung his legs onto the sofa. I rested my head on his chest, listening to the soothing sound of his steady heartbeat.

He wrapped me in his arms and legs. A cocoon of love, a shield.

Holding me tightly to him, cheek snuggled down against my hair, he whispered in my ear, "We've got this. We'll handle it."

I crossed my fingers hard to give that sentiment some extra juju.

Man, I hoped he was right.

16

HERMAN TRUDY, DRESSED HEAD TO TOE IN GRAY, STOOD NEXT TO AN equally gray column, waiting as I dragged my carry-on out of the secured area. I grinned and lifted a hand.

"Yeah, no. I'm not interested in that. I'm not happy with you."

I chuckled.

"You can stop laughing, or I'm not giving you a ride."

"I'm just glad to see you and see you haven't changed." I reached my arm around his waist and gave him a sideways hug.

He took my bag from me, pulling it along on its roller wheels with one hand and holding my hand with the other. "This it?" he asked, tipping his ear toward my carry-on as we passed under the baggage claim sign.

"It is. I'm traveling light."

"Yeah, just the one night," he said, turning toward an empty corridor.

"One?" I hadn't set an agenda.

"You need to be back in D.C. tomorrow." He pushed through the door, and we were outside. A golf cart was parked in the shadow of the building. "That's Jeb. He's going to drive us over to the private hangar.

I had no idea what was going on, so I just flowed with Trudy's forward momentum.

Again, we were silent until Jeb dropped us off in front of a little four-seater.

"You flew," I said, using my crack puzzling skills to piece this all together.

"Course I did. Do you know how long it would take me to drive all the way out here?" He put my bag in the back, and I took my seat next to his.

Soon, we were out on the runway, waiting for the tower to tell us it was our turn to take off.

"Is this why you're mad at me?" I asked. "From what Doc said on the phone, I was fitting in with your day. I didn't mean to inconvenience you."

"No inconvenience. I was picking up our groceries. They're packed into the luggage compartment. Nah, I got pissed because I was doing a quick task to check on your flight when I got sucked down into Never Never Land, and I didn't think I'd make it out again. Craziest damned doorknob I've ever experienced. You'll have to tell me what the heck it was—reminded me of an old MTV video I watched back in the day when music videos were a thing. Band by the name of A-ha. It was some regular chick who got sucked into a comic book."

"I know what you're talking about. The name of the song was 'Take On Me.' My mom loved that song. She said it reminded her of dating my dad, though she would never tell me why." I looked over at Trudy. "So you were in a pen and ink drawing?"

"I was *lost* in a pen and ink drawing and couldn't find my damned way out. I thought you might have invented some kind of viewer jail somehow. Worst doorknob I've ever experienced."

The tower cleared us for takeoff.

"Interesting," I said as we rolled forward, gaining speed. "Yeah, I'll show you what I was looking at on the plane. It might come in handy along the way."

On my flight from D.C. to Wyoming, I used my tablet to pull up a piece of art that I found intriguing. The artist used computer technology to make these fascinating drawings, which was an exploration. When I spread my fingers on the screen to enlarge an element, that detail became a journey. The first picture I saw was of a window. Spreading that wider, there was a trail. And at the suggestion of a head, I enlarged the hat, extending my fingers to get a closeup of all the details of a flower shoved into the brim's ribbon. There, I could see a leaf with a ladybug next to a raindrop. The raindrop had a reflection. I spread my fingers wider to see the details of that reflection, and I found a city. I spread my fingers, which brought me to a window, into a room, over to a snow globe. The snow globe held another town and on and on and on.

I have no idea how long it would have taken this woman to create this work or how long someone could continue to unfold more of the story.

It reminded me of the Dr. Seuss book "Horton Hears a Who." If I think of that book for too long, it makes me feel like there is no such thing as reality. It was a similar sensation in my gut when I thought of Indigo as being actively etherically present and simultaneously moldering in his grave.

I hadn't felt Herman in the ether on the plane ride.

I wondered if that was because he was a good person who used his skills to bring about positive outcomes or maybe because his consciousness found his way into that art piece I had in my lap.

It amused me to no end that "doorknobbing" became a remote viewer vocabulary word after General Coleridge got stuck drawing each facet of a crystal doorknob, and all along, he thought that was the best viewing session he'd ever had. That he was getting every detail and was able to render it perfectly. When his support called him back, General Coleridge looked down at the doorknob he'd drawn and was both bemused and highly disappointed.

Doorknobs were the first defense against remote viewers.

It explains the Tsukamoto art all over Iniquus and why Russians have their most secretive meetings on the top floor of brothels—talk about a distraction.

As we flew out over the great expanse of wilderness, I turned to Trudy. "We're flying really low. Under the radar?"

"That's how we like it." He looked down at his gauges.

"You said that I needed to fly home tomorrow?"

"Yep." He scanned the horizon. "We'll head back out after breakfast."

I looked at my watch. "That's not much time. I wanted to talk—"

"Mrph!"

"I—"

"Mrph," he said louder.

"Mrph?" I repeated.

"Absolutely no," Trudy said. "You're going to sit over there and be quiet. I don't want to know a damned thing, or you'll mess me up when I get your task sheets and go take a look. We've already done a bunch of tasks since you seemed to have done something to kick up a swarm."

"I—"

"Mrph!" He held up a finger.

And I slid down in my seat to keep my mouth shut for the rest of the flight. I'd kicked up a swarm?

TRUDY DIDN'T FOLLOW me into the house. "I'll be out back if anyone has an envelope with a task. If not, I'll be watching the game.

"Okay, thank you." I figured I couldn't get into trouble with basic politeness.

Doc held the door wide. "There you are. You sure do know how to get things hopping."

I walked in, bewildered.

General Coleridge walked over to me, finger in the air.

"I'm not saying anything." I mimed zipping my lips like I did as a child to protect a secret.

"My missus is up the street helping a friend who just had surgery," General Coleridge said. "My host skills aren't up to her standards. So pretty much, if you want something, you should go forage. And having said that, I'm going over to the office to watch the game with Trudy. Doc can bring us envelopes if they'll be helpful." And just like that, he sauntered away.

"Thank you," I called to his back.

"Things are hopping?" I repeated her words as I settled my bag beside the door and moved to the sofa.

"We got a message from a man who enjoys a good Aristotle quote. 'The aim of art is to represent not the outward appearance of things, but their inward significance.'"

Spyder.

"Uganda is an interesting place to meet up. That's not information from a tasking sheet, by the way."

I could hear Spyder asking me, "What would a good operator do once they received an emergency summons?" The answer was: obtain intelligence, make a plan, find alternatives, actuate.

"He must have spoken with General Elliot," I ventured.

"No clue," Doc said. "But once you quoted Aristotle, we got a call from Spyder that we should take a look-see. We went to the place and time where we could gather information about what's going on in your life that made you feel philosophical." Doc gathered a manilla folder from the counter and made her way over to the rocking chair she preferred. She wore her ubiquitous jean coveralls. Today, she had on a sunflower yellow T-shirt. She'd gathered her salt and pepper curls into a messy bun on top of her head, and the piece of straw sticking out of the tangle told me Doc hadn't seen her reflection since she'd gathered eggs that morning.

"What did they find?" I followed her into the den.

Doc opened the folder and produced a picture of a cartoon queen with earmuffs on her ears under her broken crown. There was a calendar at the bottom and a circle around the date.

"Four days from now?" I stared at the picture. Could that be the same queen sitting on the alien's face on the Indigo task sheet? That picture was associated with the smiling blob when Indigo tasked the place Striker traveled after his wedding.

I pulled a notepad from my purse and wrote the task: Are those the same queens?

Out loud, I said, "Trudy said I had to go home tomorrow. Striker and I didn't have a travel day. But if we're going to be here for this date," I tapped the circled date on the tasking sheet, "I guess we need to make some travel arrangements."

"Grandmother Sybil's granddaughter, Denbe, called me," was Doc's non-sequitur.

"Really?" I stilled. "We were going to call her to check on timing from their end." This must be what Doc meant by *things are hopping*. "What did she say?"

"That Grandmother Sybil says the time is nigh for your wedding —the granddaughter's words, not mine. And that you need to be there three days from now."

"Home tomorrow, on the plane to Tanzania the next day, a day to travel to Uganda, and another day until Spyder gets there?"

"That I can't tell you. But your timing sounds about right to me. Spyder says he'll find you at Grandmother Sybil's."

"That's the plan then, okay." Whew! It was as if the dam burst, and now everything flowed…not as a gentle stream. It felt more like a flashflood, and I couldn't get my feet under me.

One thing I had learned was that when this happened, it was better to aim my toes downstream, lift my knees to my chest, and bob along. Fighting the current was exhausting and meritless.

I pulled out my phone, looked at it, and shoved it back in my pocket—no cell phone connection here to send Striker a quick logistics text. Communication was via satellite link.

"We already called Striker and told him to get going on whatever needs to happen so you can leave," Doc said. "And we also got your tickets arranged for the morning.

Flashflood. "Thank you so much."

"Now that's settled. What got your knickers in a twist that you wanted to have a face-to-face?"

I pulled my phone back out of my pocket, scrolled to Cammy's picture of the purple rat, and then wordlessly handed the phone over to Doc.

She studied it for a good long while, with her face pulled into a tight concentration scowl. She leaned her head forward and scratched the edge of her hairline. "Well," she said, handing it back to me. "Isn't that interesting?"

I said nothing.

"Cammy?" she asked.

"Yes." The word rode my exhale.

"I see." Doc chewed on the inside of her cheek, looking out the window for a long time.

I let her have the space to mull.

Finally, she turned to catch my gaze. "That's problematic."

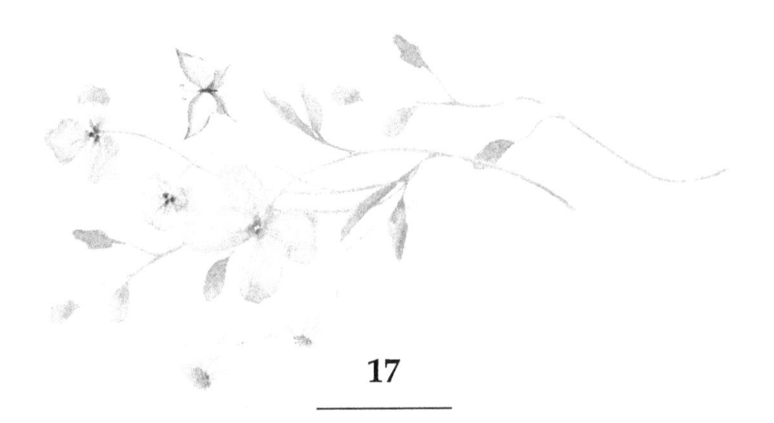

17

Doc wrapped her fingers around the smooth curve at the ends of the rocking chair armrests. She rocked back and forth, her bottom lip pressed tightly up under her top lip, wrinkling her chin as she processed.

Finally, she asked, "Have you been messing around in the ether?"

"I've not, no. But I've had some strange things happen to me in the last couple of days. When I saw the picture Cammy drew at school—the picture I just showed you—I did go look at the Indigo files."

"Why?"

"There's a lot of—" I shifted uncomfortably. "I looked to see if he had mentioned Cammy, and he had not. Then there was my curiosity. I understand that my soul decided to marry Striker in this lifetime. And I have been fighting the forces to accomplish that goal. I was just curious about what Indigo found as he was searching the idea of wedding and marriage in terms of his daughter, Scarlet. I thought it might give me a clue about when to plan the ceremony." I sent her a sarcastic expression to let her know I knew that wasn't a particularly cool thing to do.

"What did you discover?" Doc asked.

"Not much, bears, an alien. But here's the thing: I felt something when I was in there with me despite Tsukamoto's mobile."

Doc furrowed her brow. "I need more to work with than that. You said *alien*, correct?"

I pulled out my phone and scrolled to the last iteration, the one with the eyes open and included the helicopter and spider.

She looked at it for an overlong time. "That's very interesting." She handed my phone back. "When Denbe called to say that you were coming for your wedding this week, she also mentioned that you had been looking at a picture that caught the attention of the tribe. From Denbe's description, it sounded a lot like the alien picture. She said they stood in the way of the picture to protect you."

I remembered the sound of distant chanting and drumbeats just before Leanne called me out. Now, my experience in the file room made perfect sense. I had heard it as pounding like the beat of a heart.

Grandmother Sybil had been protecting Striker and, by extension, me for years now. The drumbeats and chanting were the vehicle that I had taken to save Lynda and Cammy when I was sequestered in the safe house.

If they were protecting me from the Indigo drawing, what was coming our way?

Doc sniffed, then opened the folder and handed a sheet to me solemnly.

I forced my eyes down. And there, neatly rendered by Herman Trudy, was the same picture the teacher had sent home in Cammy's school folder—a rat with a tracking collar, a web, and a dangling spider. This rat had a crown on it, just like Cammy had said she'd planned to draw.

"What was the task?" I asked as I turned the sheet over to read it for myself. "What dangers surround Lexi at this time?"

"Surround *me*?" My voice wavered off. I hadn't considered that Cammy's picture was a warning for me. I had thought it was a warning for Spyder. "Could it be the danger of the pain I'd have if something were to happen to Spyder?" A chill washed over my body, leaving me with goose bumps.

"Say those thoughts out loud," Doc encouraged.

"A rat with a tracker is the symbol I have for Sylanos. If he's alive, he—or his cartel—might be endangering me, I guess. I mean, it's always been at the back of my mind that they know the power and the efficacy of learning things in the ether. I don't think they know what my skills are or what they are not. I'm certainly not a remote viewer by any stretch of anyone's imagination. But they probably don't know that. They might find my existence to be a threat. They might equally wish they could capture me and use my skills to meet their ends, whatever they may be." I held up the rendering and pointed at the spider descending toward the rat's open mouth. "In my mind, this symbolizes Spyder McGraw. Possibly, he's trying to protect me if I'm in danger." I looked over to catch Doc's eye. "I called Spyder in with my Aristotle quote. If something happens to him, it will be my fault."

Doc sat back in her chair. "Now, come on, you know that's not how things work."

"What do you think it means?" I waggled the paper, then handed it back to her for the file.

As she slid it between the manilla folds, she shook her head to indicate she had no answers.

"Do you have the rest of it?" I asked. "There was no conclusion written on that page."

"What Trudy wrote: *This was planned. How did Cammy find out about it?*" Doc opened the folder again, pulled out a second tasking sheet, and handed it over to me.

On the bottom half of the page, a seed lay dormant in the ground next to a tiny oak sapling. On the top half, the seed was a seedling emerging from the ground. Where there had been an oak sapling, there was now a stump. Five rings traced over the severed trunk.

I flipped it over. The task was: More?

This time, Trudy had written the conclusion on the same paper: This was seeded five years ago. It's time.

"*It's time*." My heart thumped against my sternum. "That's ominous as hell."

"If you're of the mind that the seed is growing something dangerous. What if it's a medicinal plant, and it's time for you to heal?" Doc ventured.

I shook my head. Whenever the wheel turned, I got smooshed by it. Good wasn't something I looked for on my horizon, just survivability.

"I'm not a viewer," Doc reminded me, "and I have no answers. But it occurred to me that the first time Indigo tried psychic surgery and slit into your spirit, it was around about five years ago. Then he sewed you to Angel. Denbe said the village was preparing for your unity ceremony with Striker. That must mean you're free of that entanglement on the etheric and physical planes. This could be a good thing."

I hadn't reached out to Grandmother Sybil yet. And yet she knew. Even with my experience dealing with woo-woo, things like this set me back on my heels. I couldn't imagine how hard these concepts were for Striker.

"No," I told Doc. "It isn't something beneficial. And I'll tell you why." I held up the page for her to see. "This seed answers the question, *More?* and the 'more' was Cammy's drawing of what I interpret as Sylanos getting ready to eat Spyder McGraw."

"Or…" Doc held up a finger. "There's the spider web. Maybe he's luring the rat in?"

"When you look at this, is that what you pick up? Sunshine and buttercups?" Yeah, my voice was gruff with a raspy shade of irritation.

"I try not to overlay my fears or desires onto any of it. I'm pointing out that when we see things, we filter them through our experiences. We may not be able to see something clearly until we have passed through the event. You realize this. You've said it enough times about your *knowings*."

She was right, of course.

"The interesting part," Doc laced her hands and laid them on her copious bosom, "and the reason you are rightly concerned, is the question of why Cammy would pick up on any of this with her purple rat picture."

I sat perfectly still, holding my breath.

"That child has always intrigued me," Doc said. "We discussed this, Grandmother Sybil and I, your trip to Miami, and how Cammy recognized you."

"Yes?" Yes, that had freaked me out for sure.

"You were never in her presence. She had no way of seeing your photo?"

"Striker and I were colleagues. No one knew about us as a couple because we weren't officially in a relationship at that point. Cammy's mom asked me to go down to Miami so Cammy could see I was a real person and not a fairy godmother."

"That's an interesting way to perceive you. Let's think about this. There is a child without an adult's brain maturity and ethical training. Forced out of her body through drugs, wanting to survive, terrified, and then unconscious. What would a scared child's soul do, trying to survive?" Doc asked.

"I… I'm not following your question. She tried to fight."

"Okay, let me jump to Miami," Doc said. "When Cammy saw you for the first time in the flesh, what did she do? Tell me about that meeting."

"Striker was carrying her toward me. He was telling her that he'd brought her a present, a surprise. She was supposed to cover her eyes, but she peeked through her fingers, and when she saw me, she reached out for me."

"Immediate recognition. No need for an introduction. Instantly feeling a sense of safety. She reached for you, and then?"

I shrugged. "She snuggled into my lap."

"Burrowed in is how I remember picturing it when I heard this story before."

"I guess." Where was Doc going with this?

"She was four?"

"Yes. Striker and I went to Miami to celebrate her birthday."

"She was three when this event happened?"

I blew out. These details had to mean something to Doc. I wished she'd get to the point. "Yes."

"And what does a frightened three-year-old do?" Doc asked rhetorically. "They burrow into a place of safety."

Oh, shit.

Doc was entirely too calm about all this.

"Grandmother Sybil told me that when she and her acolytes sought a vehicle to send help to Striker, his sister, and niece, they discovered you in the safe house," Doc said. "That you had flexibility in the ether and, more importantly, an open wound in your soul—the first practice slice that Indigo took before he attempted to sew your soul and future to Angel. It was that tear that Grandmother Sybil exploited to help Striker save his sister and niece. We spoke about that tear being the way she found you without any difficulty and then used you."

"Grandmother Sybil would never do anything unethical. She spoke with my higher self. She had permission." Yeah, that was one of the hardest days of my life and one of the biggest honors. "I felt like we were cooperating on a mission. I wasn't fighting her."

"Yes, Grandmother said that she had very clearly listed the rules out loud and made sure Jack and Striker both understood and swore to abide by them to protect you. She would go no further, no matter the consequences to Striker, unless first, you were a willing participant, and second, no one on the physical plane would accidentally snag the opening that she was using and rip your soul while her acolytes held the slice wide with their chants."

That was exactly what I'd experienced. Without any context for what was happening to me, all I had was a solid conviction that I could do whatever was necessary to save the people Striker loved. I blew out the air trapped in my lungs and tried to force myself to breathe in again.

"Crazy brave what you did." Doc steepled her fingers and thrust them under her chin, considering me before she continued. "There was a lot of energy required to do what Grandmother did. She couldn't do it alone. Her people drummed and chanted to hold the cut open for her."

I focused out the window. The green of the trees helped. "Yes. I heard the drums all day. They vibrated my bones and made me feel otherworldly. I remember wanting to peel away my skin."

"Exactly," Doc said. "If you peeled away your skin, you too could be in the spirit world where there is no pain."

I paused with that thought, then whispered, "I was in a state of torment. I was terrified and physically assaulted. Emotionally drained. Out of my element. The drums, it was all too much."

"But you felt the level of sustained concentration it took for the village to convey Grandmother Sybil through the ether to you and to Lynda, to Cammy, and on to the various locations, to the car, to the evil doers."

"Yes." I exhaled.

"Again, the opening that Indigo made was held wide to allow all of that."

"And Cammy's spirit nestled in?" I asked.

Doc lifted her palms. "It's a theory. When we removed Angel and closed both your wounds and his, we all agreed to put off decision-making about that cut until a future date. Grandmother Sybil and I believe it has both done you personal harm and served you well."

"In protecting my loved ones." I nodded my agreement.

"Nope," Doc said, pulling her ankle up and crossing it over her knee. Today, she was wearing pineapple socks. "You, personally. Grandmother says it allowed your parents to communicate with you and help you find a truth. To solve a question. And it potentially allowed them to save your life."

My parents. Yes, that was true. "Last year, there was a terrorist attack. I felt them over my shoulder for days. I could hear their voices whispering to me to pay attention. At the last moment, just before the terrorists entered the ballroom, something shoved me, and I stumbled forward. It's the only reason I wasn't in that room but in the actor's staging hallway when the gunmen came through the doors. I was at the wall, trying to figure out how to help my team. The terrorist called my name off the top of their list. I was supposed to be on the dais next to London Davidson. The gunman shot her in the head, and she was in a coma for a long time. London is a shell of her former self. That could *easily* have been me. Or I could be dead. Or captured and taken somewhere against my will. All kinds of possibilities, absolutely none of them to my liking."

I shifted, pulling the throw pillow over, and then I hugged it in front of me like a shield. My own body language tell that I knew I wasn't going to like where this conversation was going.

"Good and bad, just like we predicted," Doc said. "Part of the bad? Cammy sees your dreams."

"Apparently." A frown tugged hard at the corners of my mouth.

"Not apparently," Doc said. "The iconography is too exact. You looked at it, I presume Striker looked at it."

"Of course."

She lifted her brows. "He saw what you saw?"

"Immediately."

"She has no frame of reference, no reason to think about spiders or rats? No stories about Anansi from the library? No movie about Charlotte's Web?"

Those were the genre of questions that Cammy's teacher asked. "Not that I'm aware of."

"You would be aware." It was a simple statement.

"Not necessarily. Cammy hasn't been with us that long."

"Would either be something she would have heard or picked up on in her previous environment?" Doc asked.

I kneaded the pillow. "No," I whispered.

"So she's in your head at night sharing your dreams. Is that a good place for a young girl to be?"

"Absolutely not." I pulled in a breath. "Could we just gently show her the way out?" I asked, hopefully.

Doc reached for the mug on the floor next to her chair. She lifted it and took a slow, thoughtful sip. "I have another concern, and you're going to like it even less. But you should have the resources for verification, pro or con."

My blood iced.

Doc read from the back, "Task: Edify the Lexi question." Doc caught my eye. "Did Cammy have a whale of a nightmare?"

"Yes," I whispered.

"This was what she saw in her nightmare." Doc leaned forward, thrusting the drawing toward me. It dangled out there in the space between us.

I pulled my lips in and was back into my frozen position of a wild rabbit, trying not to bring the fox's attention around.

Doc nodded. "I know. This is tough. Loved ones in potential danger is hard."

I took the page from her extended hand and scanned through all the scientific protocols to get to the conclusion: When Lexi understands this picture, it is time for the next steps.

"I looked at the time stamp on your phone when you showed me the picture with the queen and the spider," Doc said. "You had seen that picture in the files."

I turned the sheet over to find almost exactly the same picture—the alien and the queen with a very large dildo that I had seen in the Indigo files. This one had energy vibration squiggles around it.

"A six-year-old child wouldn't or shouldn't know about such things," she said.

I swallowed hard.

Trudy concluded: I found this in Cammy's dreams. For Lexi, it's time for next steps.

Problem was, I hadn't a clue what that picture could mean. Next steps in closing the slice so Cammy doesn't experience my dreams? Or next steps, as in this picture was about to unfold, and I was going to have to act on it. If I based it on the three iterations I saw in Indigo's tasking sheets, it might very well be both.

18

The following day, as predicted, Trudy flew me back to the city. He said my plane would be delayed, but he had a dental appointment. So he left me off on the tarmac, and a guy in a golf cart took me to the main airport.

Sure enough, there was a delay.

Iniquus switchboard patched me into a line encrypted end to end to talk with Striker. If we were going to be in Uganda on the day that Galaxy said we *must* be there, we needed to leave by tomorrow evening and take a night flight.

Striker said Doc had already called and he'd arrange everything as I was flying in.

And he had.

By the time I got home that night, a bag sat by my bedroom door, all packed up for me. There were three bags in Striker's pile. When I sent him a lift of the eyebrow, he just said, "I handed this to logistics, and they prepped us."

Interesting. I guess it would be a surprise when I arrived, but logistics was thorough and highly competent. The logistics folks would have researched everything and ticked every box.

I was winging this, and quite frankly, as long as I had clean underwear, I didn't care about anything other than getting there and getting home.

Faith was on her way over to get Cammy off the bus. She and Blaze would hold down the home front until we returned.

Striker had called Reaper to see if it was best for Kate that Beetle and Bella stay with her, or should we take the dogs to the Cerberus Kennel. "I assumed you'd want me to do that."

"You assumed correctly. Let me take the doggos' things over," I said with a smacking kiss. I was trying on my fluffy bunny costume to power through my apprehensions.

I stood in front of the Hamilton's door with a bag of my girls' food under one arm and a bag with their sleep blankets and toys in the other. I got my index finger out far enough to ring the bell, waiting for the "Come in!" and punched in the lock code so Kate didn't have to get up.

"You're back." Kate smiled. She had a mug resting on top of her belly as she stretched out on the sofa. "Striker said you had a meeting out of town and wasn't sure how long it would take."

"Yeah, research trip." I hefted a bag up a bit. "Kitchen?"

"Just anywhere. Reaper will deal with it when he gets home. Did you find what you needed with the research?"

After plopping the things down in the corner, I settled myself on the floor with a chair to my back so I could love on Beetle and Bella a bit before I had to go. "I have a plan for next steps."

"Ah, I see this is a cloak-and-dagger assignment. 'Need to know' stuff." She put her hands over her ears. "Lalalalala." She pulled her hands away. "And I have no need to know and no desire to know. Don't let my bored curiosity wriggle anything loose. Don't say another word about it. I have enough experience with Reaper and his SEAL brothers that I've learned to neither be curious nor take offense."

Kate was heading for the finish line with her pregnancy and toughing it out. Her feet were so swollen from the heat and humidity it hurt to look at them. I just couldn't imagine what she was going through.

As I scrubbed behind Bella's ears, I said, "I wonder what would happen if you called the Iniquus Support Office and asked them to come rub your ankles." ISO was a perk offered by Iniquus that oiled the cogs of the machine. When families lived on a military base, and their soldiers had shipped off somewhere else, the family was cared for with maintenance assistance, the yards mowed, and the flower beds tended. Iniquus took it another step. Any operator, whether it was the tactical forces or a branch of the charitable arm like the Cerberus Search and Rescue folks, their families fell under the ISO umbrella of care. If a spouse would do it while at home, the ISO would do it while the operators worked—long hours at the office or away on assignment. That meant food would show up, rides, and even the ISO that went to sports events to hold up cheerleading signs for a child and record it for the spouse who was in a meeting themselves. No child's event should go unattended. Family was primary. I had never heard of someone calling for a foot rub. But I'm sure there were any number of things that were phoned in. All the requests were privileged information, so, yeah, who knew?

"I'll fill your freezer with ready-to-bake casseroles if you make the 'I need a foot rub' call."

"I assumed you were going to do that anyway." Kate laughed.

"Still…" I lifted my brows and canted my head.

"Yeah," Kate said wryly. "I'll let you know if that ever goes down."

"Now wait, I never said anything about going down."

Kate's snort-laugh. "Stop! You're going to make me pee. And besides, I have something very serious to ask you before I forget. I can hold a thought for about a half a second unless it's about peanut butter and sardines, and then that's all I think about all day long."

"So gross."

"You think? So anyway, Reaper and I have been working on a

name for this little one." She rubbed her hands over her ginormous belly. "And we think it would be nice to call her India Katherine."

"India like the ink?"

"India as in indelible," she said. "Reaper and I wanted to know if it's okay with you."

"More than okay, an honor." I had to work to keep my chin from wobbling. Whew, that was unexpected. In the last few days, I felt like evil was pushing itself into my space. This was a beam of light.

"And with that name comes the expectation that you and Striker would be her godparents. We are going to ask you when we're all together, but I didn't want to officially launch the question on you without a forewarning."

"An honor. I, of course, can't speak for Striker, but I can't imagine…and from me, it's a totally enthusiastic yes. What are you going to call her?"

"Indie Kate."

"Hey, Indie Kate, we are going to have wonderful adventures together." I laughed. "Can I tell you how much her nickname cracks me up? In my mind, it sounds like 'Indicate.'"

"Oh yeah, I guess it does. You know there are no names that someone can't turn into some kind of tease. "What does that Indicate?' is pretty benign. When I was a teen, I babysat for this woman up the road. Her father had been Dick—back when Dick wasn't a…"

"Dick."

"Exactly. And she had a lot of people give her a hard time about it."

"A hard time?" I grinned. "Really?"

"Oh, ha! Yeah, uhm, teased her. So she was looking for a tease-free name for her new daughter, and they decided on Fatima. When the parents brought the baby home to meet her three-year-old brother, they said, 'This is your new sister, Fatima.' And he said, 'Glad to meet you, Fat Mama.' And that is what he has always called her no matter what."

"That's adorable." I lay on the ground to hug Beetle to me. "I wanted to let you know a couple of things. I'm inviting my Kitchen Grandmothers to come for a reunion. We're hoping sometime at the end of September."

"My due date is September 29th."

"You will take precedence. No worries," I reassured Kate.

Kate's brow drew together just a bit as she tipped her head. "Okay. And what else?"

"While Striker and I are flying all of my Kitchen Grandmothers in. There's one grandmother who isn't going to be able to do that." I waggled a hand in the air. "She hasn't got a passport, and she won't be able to get it in time. Striker and I are flying over to see her and offer our respects."

"Uh-huh." She chewed on her upper lip and considered me. "Where is 'over'?"

"Africa."

"Africa is big." Kate was good at fishing for information. All those years of teaching gave her the reflexes to draw information from students' mouths, and now she was doing the same to me. I needed to pay attention and not put this conversation on autopilot.

"This is kind of last minute." I pointed at the dog stuff. "Reaper asked that the girls stay with you all. Faith and Blaze are coming to care for Cammy in our house. I wanted to let you know we aren't abandoning you. We just needed reinforcements."

"I would never even consider you abandoning me. It's not your nature. So when are you going to the massive continent of Africa?"

"Tonight."

"And you'll be back…"

"Yes."

"Haha, funny girl. *When* will you be back?" Kate asked. "Man, I feel like I'm in some spy film, and you're only giving me need-to-know and think there are bugs in the walls. There are no electronics bugs. Iniquus scrubbed the place clean of any added apparatus. And there are no pest bugs because if there were, Reaper and I would complain to our landlady. Since that happens to be you, you would be the first to know. So what's going on here?"

"Striker and I are going out of town to pay our respects to a dear mentor. Faith and Blaze will be in our house caring for Cammy and available to help you with anything.

I could see that she knew there was more to this than met the eye and that whatever it entailed had some danger attached.

She was wrong, of course. This was a simple journey to Uganda, a tribal ceremony, a day in the town to file the paperwork and get the certificate, and a flight home. The path to this point was what had been harrowing.

We might see Spyder. We might not.

We might visit with an alien being and a masturbatory queen, or not.

Okay, maybe Kate was right to be a little worried. After all, I was about to ask Grandmother Sybil the best way to protect Cammy from a world of crazy that went along with having a strong sixth sense. And that might just mean psychic surgery for me. That slice into my aura was a tool I used to keep my loved ones safe.

Doc was right, though.

This wasn't something my soul had planned for. It was like going back in a time machine—all the warnings that authors and script writers offered, anything you change could change everything. There are some things I felt perfectly ethical about intervening—if it weren't for Indigo's craziness upending Striker's and my life trajectories, the team wouldn't have been set up in the D.O.A. debacle at the Fuller Mine event where Scarlet and her guards wouldn't have been killed in their crimes.

Gator would, for sure, have been in the water with D-Day, but as long as she didn't say the fateful words, they shouldn't have died. Someone would have crossed their path, I felt sure. So, maybe I messed up with that.

The truth was that I would never know what had changed because Indigo was insane.

I didn't know what fates I might mess with by staying open the way I was.

Doc was right about the questionable ethics of it all.

But now that Cammy was etherically involved, Grandmother Sybil could best advise me.

And I had no idea what was coming next.

19

HAVING CHARTERED A FLIGHT TO THE GAME RESERVE IN NORTHERN Tanzania, a tourist outfit provided us with a vehicle for our "personal exploration of the area." It had all gone smoothly.

Now, we were driving north to Uganda.

It was hard to imagine that I was married to one man until a few days ago, and now, I was heading to meet Grandmother Sybil for the first time. There, we would have a unity ceremony that would tie me to Striker, as it should be, and I would be married to two different men in the same week.

Life was a whirlwind.

And while it seemed that the universe heaved to make everything happen in quick succession. There was that whisper in the back of my mind, as if an old memory, a past thought, "*Birds of a feather flock together.*" It was the one I had been chanting when I left Langley and ran into the FBI Joint Task Force and John Green.

Interestingly, while that rhyme hummed behind me, I had another one that swirled in front of me in a sort of harmonious duet of children's verses.

I couldn't imagine what either could mean.

Hopefully, Grandmother Sybil would.

Doc said that before Grandmother Sybil would unite Striker and me, we would discuss my psychic health and do what needed to be done. I'd have to make a decision in everyone's best interest. Right now, I tried very hard not to ponder the question or have an opinion.

The last time I had psychic surgery, I floated away into nothingness.

And I liked it there.

I would have stayed in that floating warm bliss if I hadn't sensed Striker's voice calling me back to him. Yes, I'd leave bliss to find my way back into Striker's arms.

When I met Grandmother Sybil in the ether for the first time, when she used me as a conduit to save Striker's family, that whisper at the back of my head felt a little like that.

At least in the sense of being caught up in something bigger than I was.

It was hard to imagine any of that being at play here as we drove past the expansive Tanzanian vistas with flocks of birds and grazing wild herds.

This whole area seemed incredibly peaceful.

While Grandmother Sybil is one of the people I feel closest to in this world, I've never seen her in reality. Never spoken with her. I've sent letters. Doc has visited several times to learn from Grandmother Sybil's vast expertise in the ether.

Striker, of course, knew her and had visited over the years.

That last trip, Doc accompanied Striker as they took solar panels, lanterns, and electric camping stoves. He rented a digger and put in a well, saving the women long walks to the water and dangerous hikes into the surrounding forests to gather firewood. They were gratitude gifts.

But I was unable to go.

Honestly, I didn't strive to be on that plane with Doc and Striker.

I appreciated my relationship with Grandmother Sybil in the

ether. Corporeal would be different. Meeting her and her tribeswomen in the flesh would change everything.

Striker reached his hand across and covered my tightly laced hands. "Okay?"

He had come to a stop under a broad tree and moved the gear into Park without my even realizing it.

"Nerves," I said.

"Understandable." It was a single word, yet I knew it was rich in meaning for both of us. "Are you hungry? Let's take a break for lunch."

He reached around and pulled out the picnic basket the tourist agency had put together for us.

We sat in the rover—a generic name my friend Meg used for the kinds of open vehicles she took out into the Tanzanian bush. The warm breeze blowing over our skin. The animals startled into an abrupt silence at our arrival were tentatively squawking again.

Rustling returned to the tree limbs overhead. I looked up, and a red-tailed monkey stared down at me with curiosity. After a long moment of our doing nothing of interest, it swung on out of sight.

"What are you thinking?" Striker asked as my smile spread.

"Oh, about Kate and her baby. She's going to name her India Katherine and call her Indie Kate for every day."

"Cute." He sent me a wink. "What do you think that will indicate?"

"I said basically the same thing." I reached for the sandwich Striker had unwrapped and handed to me.

"And thinking of Kate's upcoming labor, I was remembering this beautiful birthing tradition I read about once, a tribe in South Africa. So, as I understand it, the child's birthday has nothing to do with the child leaving the mother's body. The birthday is when the baby comes to its mother's mind. When a woman thinks it's time to bring a baby into the world, she goes to a tree and listens to the wind and her heart beating. After a while, she hears a song and practices singing it over and over until she memorizes it." I took a bite and savored the spices that danced over my taste buds. "Mmm, this is so good." I reached into the basket for a napkin. "Once she knows the song, the woman goes back to the village, where she teaches it to the man who will father the child. As they make love, they sing the song together. And that's how the baby is conceived."

Striker pulled out a mango and pared a section with his knife, holding a piece out to me.

"Thank you. So, that's the beginning of the song. The midwife learns the song. The elders learn the song, and when the baby arrives, everyone sings that baby's song to them as a welcome." I ate the juicy piece of golden fruit then wiped the sticky moisture from my fingers. "So sweet!"

"The mango or this tradition?" Striker asked.

"Both. And it continues. So everyone has their own song. And everyone in the village knows everyone else's song, right? When the child gets hurt or sick, they soothe them by singing the song. They also use the song when the child is naughty. They bring the child to the middle of the village, and everyone stands in a circle around them and sings that child's song, not as a rebuke but to remind the child of his pure nature and the goodness he was born with. Can I have more of that mango?" I held out my hand as Striker prepared another slice for me. "When there are rites of passage, like our unity ceremony, they would sing your song and my song."

"Beautiful."

I slurped down the mango. "Isn't it? I love that tradition." Then I wrinkled my nose. "I don't love all the traditions, though."

"What's that one that you just remembered?"

"It's from Uganda, actually. The custom dates way back to before the Renaissance. It seems that it's the traditional role of the auntie to help with the wedding."

"Sounds normal." He put the mango seed into his garbage bag.

"The auntie is the one who introduces the groom to the family. And she's the one who attests to the bride's virginity."

"Usual stuff for back then, right?" Striker asked.

"The auntie also had to take the groom into her hut and have sex with him to make sure that he was virile. And after the couple was married, the auntie would hang out and watch the couple having sex."

"Because?" Striker pulled his brows in tight.

I shook my head. "I don't know, to offer pointers and suggestions, answer questions?"

"That would blow the concentration and enjoyment, don't you think?" He pitched his voice up higher. "No, boy, that's not the rhythm. Listen, I'll clap it out for you. Ready? Thrust. Thrust. Thrust. Thrust."

"Striker!"

"You get what I'm saying." He poured water on his fingers to wash them, then held the bottle out to me.

"Did you research the rituals here in southeastern Uganda? I didn't."

"Logistics did," Striker said. "I have a list. I read them over, and they didn't say I had to sleep with an auntie. I didn't tell logistics I was getting married. I told them we were attending a wedding ceremony. So, they might not have thought it necessary to add that bit of information."

I shot him a wide-eyed mock-fear face.

"I'm just saying, there are times an auntie is helpful. There are times when she is not. And I imagine if a guy's bride had an auntie that was off-putting for whatever reason, a display of virility might be hard to come by."

"Nice choice of words." I took another bite of my sandwich.

"Honestly, if the man loved the woman he was going to marry, yeah—I guess that's my culture speaking to me—I have no desire to share a bed with anyone but you."

"You know I'd know if you did," I said from behind my hand, my mouth full of food.

"No doubt. But that isn't working as some kind of restraint. I honestly can't imagine desiring someone other than you."

I leaned in to reward that sentiment with a kiss.

It was nice when he said things like that out loud.

AFTER PASSING over the border into Uganda and turning off the highway onto a cratered dirt road for about an hour, Striker came to a stop.

He parked the rover a good distance outside of the village. Grandmother Sybil and the women hated the sounds of motors; it sent horror and anxiety through their systems, and we didn't want to frighten them or cause any pain.

Striker had climbed out, saw me sitting still, and climbed back in to sit in silence beside me.

The minutes dragged.

Striker's eyes scanned the foliage by habit.

More minutes passed. And I was beginning to feel like a coward. My butt was beginning to fall asleep. My muscles became restless.

"Okay," I said.

Striker turned toward me and canted his head. A smile tickled the corner of his mouth. "Ready?"

"No. But let's do this thing." I shifted a leg out, and as my toes touched the ground, Striker held my arm. "Is your hesitancy about seeing Grandmother Sybil or about the wedding ceremony? Or is it something else?"

"No hesitation about our wedding."

"Good to hear." Striker sent me a grin.

"Yes, to Grandmother Sybil. A little bit, at least." I looked up and batted my eyes at the dust shimmering in the air, illuminated by a ray of golden sun. "There's something." I swept my hand through the air.

His gaze followed the movement, and he repeated, part curiosity, part trepidation. "Something."

I licked my lips.

"Any rhymes popping into your head?"

"There's one in front of me. It's not sizzling around the edges. It's just doing a loopy loop, like an earworm."

"Ah. Okay, let's hear it."

I shook my head. "Surely you don't want this humming through your head, too."

"We're getting married in the morning, Lexi. I'm willing to endure along with you." His laugh was bright merriment, and, once again, the forest fell into a shocked hush. I loved when he laughed—usually. I loved *this* kind of laugh, the way the golden flecks warmed his moss-green eyes. How his dimple winked, and his white teeth flashed.

"All right, Mr. Masochist, the song goes, *'If wishes were horses, then beggars would ride. If turnips were swords, I'd have one at my side. If "ifs" and "ands" were pots and pans, There'd be no work for tinkers' hands.'*" There was an odd unsettling as the wind swept those words, swirling into the tree branches…almost like an incantation.

I wanted to snatch them back and shove them into my pocket as they flew away.

I even called out, "Those aren't for you! I want them back." My words sounded miffed and scolding.

Striker's laughter came to an abrupt stop. He stopped unloading the bags onto the folding trolley he pulled from one of his duffels, his head on a swivel.

"No one's there," I said, sorry I'd brought any of it up.

He turned back to me. "Who were you talking to, Lexi?"

I shook my head. "I don't know. The wind? Nothing? I'm just a little spooked out here."

"Spooked by the forest? Spooked by something that I can't see?" There he went again, head on a swivel, using his SEAL skills to locate dangers in the shadows.

I shook my head again as I reached for my ruck.

"Do you know where that rhyme came from? What it means?"

"Traditional English rhyme from, I think, around Shakespearean times."

With one more scan of the environment, Striker lifted a basket we'd brought from Tanzania on top of the other bags and began tethering it all in place on the cart. "Didn't sound very much like something Shakespeare would write."

"No. Not great literature. But the first part cautions children that wanting something, wishing it into existence, isn't enough. Action is required. You have to make an effort for what you want."

"Keep going. What do you want?" He tested the security of his work. "What were you thinking about when this first started?"

"To be honest, I can't remember."

"Okay," he said, reaching for my hand and grabbing the cart handle. "Turn on your antennae."

"As if that were a thing."

We started off toward the village.

After that day of tumult when I first encountered Grandmother Sybil, I found great peace when I think of her.

When I meditate, to this day, I often feel her sitting peacefully nearby, as if saying, "You're safe to close your eyes, child. It's safe to go within and let go of the physical world. I will sit here and hold space, guarding you while you do your work."

That's what I felt as I walked along the path, surrounded by trees, like this was a sacred space, separate and apart from the tribulations of the outside world.

It is hard to believe that this beautiful place was filled with screams and gunfire.

As I walked along, the sun's rays reached through the leaves. Above me could very well be images in Indigo's task drawings from when Indigo asked about Striker's wedding. That he had come this close to my beloved grandmother ignited fury in my chest.

But I pushed it away.

I wasn't bringing that energy with me into their village.

Striker startled me from my thoughts when he said, "*'If wishes were horses, then beggars would ride,'* was the first verse. The next one is?"

"*'If turnips were swords, I'd have one at my side,'*" I chanted, reaching up to scratch my eyebrow. "Magical transformation of an object into a weapon? I don't know about that one."

He nodded. "Then what?"

"Ah, I see it didn't become an earworm for you. Good. Number three was, *'If 'ifs' and 'ands' were pots and pans, There'd be no work for tinkers' hands.'* And that line, I understand. My mother chanted that to me when it was time to do my chores when I was engrossed in anything else."

"Stories, wishes, hypotheticals—it would be nice if they worked," Striker mulled.

"Exactly, work is the emphasized word. A desire doesn't magically happen. It takes work and sustained effort. If we got everything we wanted when we wanted it, there would be no need for anyone to work."

"That would be a terrible state," Striker said. He had shortened his gait to match mine as we strolled side by side, the pull cart bouncing behind us. "By that, I mean I like my work. It's rewarding. I like how I use my time, my skills. I like my hobbies. What if I could just conjure my painting in my brain—think it into existence? What a loss." He reached for my hand.

I pulled a gift bag from my suitcase to get it out and ready. I balanced it on the basket to keep it from tipping and then secured it. "Each time we make a mistake, we have the opportunity to learn and grow. We build more synapses in our brains so they function better when faced with new tasks and obstacles. But would that be necessary in a world where all could be conjured as a whim?"

"We would only need the wishing part of our brain to work."

"The rest of our gray matter would be mush. Maybe the desiring part of our brain would need to be functioning, too. One would have to be able to reason things out. There's that idiom 'Be careful what you wish for.'" I took his hand, and we started off again.

"This is a weird conversation."

"There's a monkey following us."

"Curiosity."

"Hopefully. Is it about a quarter mile from here?"

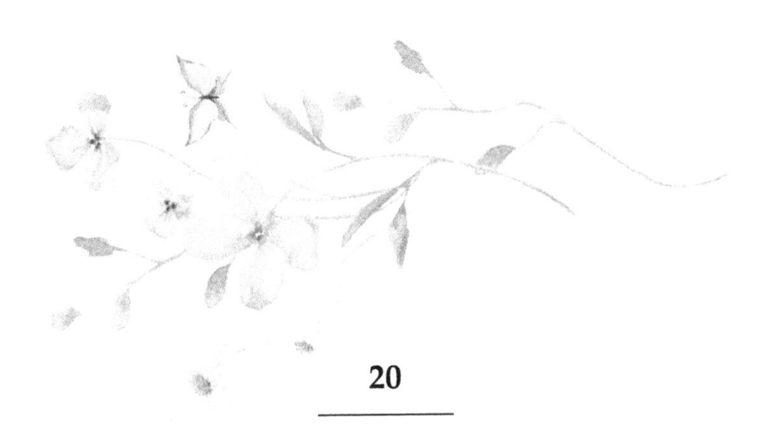

20

Nothing was a surprise to me. As Striker and I made our way into the clearing, it was like coming home. I closed my eyes and took a deep breath in, sighing it out again.

Striker squeezed my hand, then let me go so he could return the wave coming from a figure in the distance, calling out, "That's Denbe."

"Oh?" I stopped and smiled her way.

She rode a tide of sound as about a dozen goats quick-stepped our way with their musky scents and clanging bells. The herd had trampled or eaten the grasses in the broad meadow. The surface glowed golden in the late afternoon sun.

Women swarmed from the other side of the hill, calling out their welcomes. They were focused on Striker, as well they should. They knew him as he rid them of the scourge that had tormented the village. And these many years later, as the man bearing gifts of gratitude for their work in saving us—electricity and water. A perfect circle.

A few more paces in, I could see how the huts spiraled inward like a labyrinth that hadn't finished its coil. The thick straw roofs and baked mud walls looked like they would keep the families cool and comfortable when the noonday sun beat down.

Home.

I had only been here in my mind's eye. And it was perfect.

"Grandmother waits for you," Denbe told me, pointing off into the distance.

As I walked where she directed, Striker trailed behind as he greeted his friends. My gaze swept over the village. I knew the basics of what had unfolded here, and I could feel pain from the earth coming up through the souls of my feet—the soil wetted by the women's tears and their loved one's blood.

Any pain I have had in my life was so small in comparison.

I walked toward the flat rock where, in my dreams, Grandmother Sybil stroked my hair and reminded me of my strength when I had never in my life been so weak. Grandmother reminded me of my power when everything around me said I was powerless. And there in the jail, when a metaphorical wild cat was at the door, hungry to rip me to pieces, Grandmother Sybil screamed for me to run. Run!

Grandmother Sybil was strong enough to be here in the natural world with the ancient rhythms to her day, and she was powerful enough to let her mind travel halfway around the world to protect insignificant me.

She sat peacefully on the flat rock surrounded by grasses. Elegant and royal. The sparse tendrils of her long hair followed the curves of her scalp in intricate braids to the top of her head, where the bun was shell-studded. She was tiny in her old age. She looked as if her bones had lost the weight of the inner marrow, that she had become bird-like with age and wisdom. The breeze might swell at any moment, and she would be aloft and gone.

As I came closer, I could see the deep wrinkles of her papery skin.

In her eyes, black and shiny like the obsidian I'd brought in my gift bag, there was intelligence earned through a lifetime of experiences.

"Grandmother." I bowed.

She smiled and patted the rock.

As I leaned down to take a place near her, I realized that many of her wrinkles were, in fact, scars. And not the beautiful tribal skin art that I have seen in pictures.

No, this scarification came from an evil hand.

How anyone could raise violence toward this woman mystified me.

She shifted and then opened her arms. "My child, lay your head in my lap as before. You've had a long journey, and it's time to rest."

In my dreams, this had been the natural thing to do. But it felt selfish and irreverent here on the rock. I crouched and reached for my bag. "Grandmother, I've brought a gift."

Striker leaned over, unbuckled, and untied the strings, then lifted the bag closer to me.

From inside, I drew a copper bowl, broad and shallow, with intricate etching. Next, I pulled out a bag of polished gemstones. Into the center of the bowl, I scooped the rocks, mounding them into a hill of color, making the platter too heavy and tippy on that part of the rock.

Striker came up beside me and held it in place.

"Miriam?" Grandmother asked.

"Yes, she washed the stones under a full moon and blessed them for your family. And the bowl, this comes from where Doc lives. The etchings on it were made by an artist who loves the wild open spaces."

"This is very good. I like this very much. A marriage," she said with a smile. "It's a beautiful thing to love and be loved. I am very happy you decided to marry here with your faraway family." Grandmother turned to Striker. "Would you take this to Denbe?"

Striker stood and did as he was asked, walking toward the community area, a roof with open walls where the children went to school and would gather away from the battering sun.

Before she turned back to me, Grandmother reached out a hand, and I cupped it gently in my own, bending to kiss the dry, papery skin, feeling blessed to meet her here in person instead of in the ether.

I have no idea why I had feared this.

Everything was as it should be. Grandmother Sybil felt exactly the same to me in both realms—the physical end, the etheric.

Grandmother turned my way. "You have journeyed a long distance. There is joy in that you and Striker will be united."

"We're so honored that you will be the officiant, Grandmother." I smiled as I crouched by the flat rock where she liked to sit. When I was in the Honduran prison, I would travel in my meditations to be here and have some freedom from the dank walls of my solitary confinement.

"Yes, I remember your days of imprisonment," she said.

I wasn't surprised at all that she heard my inner voice as easily as the voice I used to say words aloud.

"A very difficult task was before you to reach safety." She caught my gaze. "And an important one. As you must know, if there is an agreement in this lifetime between two people, it is a rift in the universe when wrenched from the task of fulfilling their life's purpose. But, too, it sends waves through the continuum that others cannot fulfill theirs. Imagine the devastation if you and Striker were not wed. It took courage and tenacity for you to reach this point of your journey."

"Thank you, always, for your support and kindness. That was a difficult time."

"You know that many of our traits are passed down through our life's energy. My great-granddaughter tells me that the proper word for this is DNA. DNA holds the stories of our ancestors. My family's DNA says that we are a village. We are meant to stay in this place." She laid her hand on the rock. "To work and play and support each other. This is the way my ancestors survived. And their tale of survival and our desire to be here as a village flows through our veins."

"Yes, ma'am."

"You wonder why we stay when there is pain in this ground."

"Oh…I…"

"This pain is not new. This pain has been layered generation after generation for over a thousand years. It is our birthright. And we use this knowledge to continue. To leave would abrade our souls. We stay, and our ancestors are here with us."

"Yes, ma'am."

She smiled toothlessly. "You cannot understand such a pull. The earth here, we are tethered to it like an umbilicus. Here in Uganda, the temperatures are always temperate. There are times that are dry, and there are times of rain, but always comfortable. The lands allow for crops and grazing herds. You and Striker come from a different line of stories. Your family comes from a place far to the north, as far north as there is land. There, in the north country, it was very different. The weather was harsh, the land rocky. In order for your people to survive and prosper, they had to take to the seas, to explore, to fight. For some women, they went, too, on the boats. Other women stayed in their homes and raised the children. They were the heads of households. Should a woman wish a man to leave, she merely set his boots outside her door and locked the door behind her. She was not faint of heart. She was the healer. The thinker. The plotter and planner. And, like our village, your foremothers made sure that the clan was cohesive. Does this sound familiar to you in your life with Striker? That you are living the story of your DNA?"

"I hear in your words how I feel about making sure that I have an extended family of people I love and that we can all help each other. I hear my job at Iniquus is to think and plot to keep my brothers on Strike Force safe. And I hear Striker's story, too. That he travels out, and thinks of his task, and does his work. And then, he turns his boat homeward where he trusts that all is safe and sound."

"Yes, this." Grandmother reached out her index finger and tapped my wrist. "My great-granddaughter tells me that there is a kind of DNA that is handed down from the mother's side alone. A mother's story passed without changing down through the generations. She says that her Mother-DNA is the same as mine, and mine is the same as my ancient ancestors, two hundred thousand years ago. The scientists say that we all have the same mother. I could have told them that, but they would not have believed me." She tapped my wrist again to focus me on her words. "I tell you this because at some place in time, our ancestors diverged, but the great mother allows you and I to reach out to each other in spirit."

"I'm so glad that we can." I leaned forward so my knees reached the ground, then sat back on my heels. The grasses tickled me through the thin fabric of my tactical pants. "Though I'm sorry it's often under unhappy circumstances."

"My daughter, I have dreamed about you of late. These last days have been frightening ones for you because you are afraid of the young one and her abilities in the ether, and you have questions about that and about your own situation. I have discussed this with Doc yesterday evening. I am not of the mind that Cammy burrowed within you at the time of great fear, and you carry a portion of her with you still today. Though it's possible, Doc was offering a suggestion as an explanation. That is not what I saw. That is not the situation you find yourself in."

Thank heavens! I nodded.

"The child, Cammy, was a tender age when my family worked with you to save her and her mother. She was still at a time in her life when physical reality was only a portion of her awareness. Her imagination was still vivid, and her ability to believe was strong. She was given a shot of medicine, but she fought hard against this."

"Yes, ma'am." I clasped my hands so tightly in my lap that the skin around my knuckles pulled and ached.

"In her fright, she conjured a magical helper as in one of the bedtime stories that parents tell to their children. And as she slipped behind the thick cloud of medication, she saw you. This is where she was both a physical child and a spirit child. You will understand what I am saying because you have had this ability. When you were saving her life, you were both having a physical experience in one location and a spiritual experience in another. She is whole now. And she does not leave her body to explore at night."

"I'm so glad. I—" Turning, I saw that two women had come up.

"Grandmother." Denbe grinned. "Lexi's spiritual aunties are calling you to the circle. There is somone who wishes to speak with you about a very important matter."

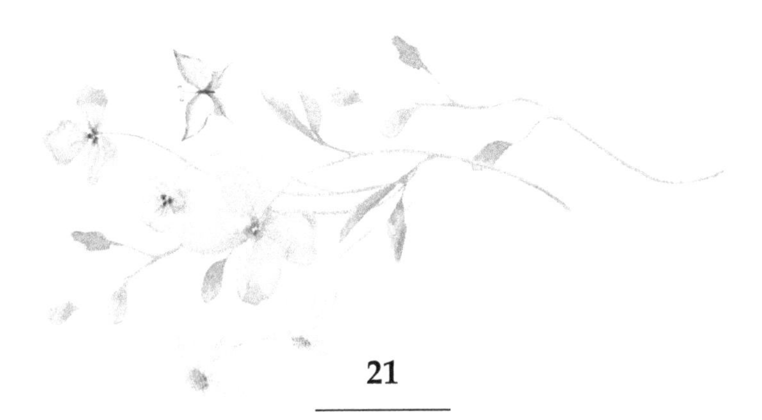

21

WHEN I WALKED TOWARD THE CENTRAL FIRE CIRCLE, STRIKER STOOD in a hut's entrance, signaling me over. He had changed out of his hiking clothes and was wearing a pristine pair of white pants with a long white robe over it and a white kufi cap on his head.

"What are you doing?" I asked.

"So logistics gave me a rundown on how things might unfold. And I prepared for that. I have had a discussion with your spiritual aunties."

"A discussion."

"We sat and talked, a discussion. And they have agreed to introduce me to the elders as a man who wishes to marry you."

"Interesting." Striker was taking this very seriously, and it tickled me for some reason.

"Usually when a groom meets the bride's family, they show up with gifts, livestock."

"Did you pack a goat in your ruck?"

"Stop. This is serious. What would we do if this doesn't go well, and the elders don't want us to marry?"

"Sorry. So, no goat, what's Plan B?"

"I'm prepared. Normally, there's a spokesman for the groom who gives a formal speech, and that's when they ask for permission to seek out the bride."

"The bride doesn't have a say in it?"

"She does, Lexi. There's a courtship. We're speeding past all that. And I don't have anyone to stand up and present me, so Denbe said she would do it."

"All right, what do I do?"

"I don't know. Maybe stand beside me until someone signals that you should go somewhere else?"

I looked over my shoulder, "Well, it looks like they've assembled. Should I change my clothes?" I had no clue what logistics had packed for me or what the proper thing would be to wear to a council meeting.

"I think that I'm the one that's accepted or rejected. You're probably fine. Denbe told me to change into this. She didn't say anything about your clothes."

"You're nervous," I whispered.

"It's been a weird week." He lifted a small backpack and traced the strap over his shoulder.

Denbe arrived at the door, her smile wide and bright. "We go. Everyone is assembled."

As he moved forward, all of the villagers swayed and hummed. I wished I knew this song; I wanted to join them. Denbe ushered us forward, and there we stood in front of Grandmother Sybil. They told me that the women standing on either side of her would be filling the role of my spiritual aunties.

"Grandmother." Striker put his hand over his heart and bowed. "I have come to ask to be born into Lexi's family."

Well, that was an interesting choice of words.

He looked over at Denbe. "Now?"

She lifted her hands as a signal to move ahead.

Striker put his pack on the ground at his feet and untied the cord to pull out a jewelry box.

My aunties—whom I found out later were Grandmother's

youngest sisters—approached. One accepted the box with two hands. They both bowed.

They returned to Grandmother Sybil and opened it. From where I stood, I could easily see that it was filled with rectangular bars of gold. I willed my brain not to calculate, not to play the "how many gumballs in the vase for a prize" game.

There had to be at least fifty in there.

That would be over a hundred thousand dollars.

It was a lovely gift. And absolutely, I wanted Grandmother and her people to have this money after all they had done for Striker and me. No amount of money could come close to paying that back. It was just that this was such an unexpected exchange.

This must be why Striker left me alone for over an hour at the Dar es la Salaam airport to "run a quick errand." It just kind of freaked me out that we had traveled with that amount of money all the way out into the African bush and all the way over the Tanzania-Uganda border to bring it here, and I never knew.

And here I thought my bowl of tumbled rocks was a lovely housewarming gift.

I honestly regretted that I hadn't read up on Ugandan marital rituals.

Maybe they *would* assign a ceremonial aunty to test Striker's virility.

For some reason, I had assumed our unity ceremony would entail some words and some dancing.

As my mind scrolled through these ideas, I landed on the reason that box of gold was so off-putting.

That was a dowry.

I wasn't sure how exactly I felt about that. Not good.

Grandmother Sybil nodded, and her daughter closed the lid and left the circle.

Now, I wondered if she and Striker had spoken and had arrived at a price for me. If Doc had haggled my price over the phone.

Dowry.

It was more unsettling than I would have thought—like a family's chattel they were selling.

Obviously, that wasn't true. *Still,* this felt bad.

Striker must have sensed my discomfort because he reached out his hand to take mine and squeezed it gently.

I sniffed and adjusted my shoulders back to stand a little taller, not daring to snatch my hand away lest an elder see and not give her consent.

"Grandmother, I respectfully ask for your wisdom," Striker said. "I seek to marry the granddaughter of your heart, Lexi Sobado. I wish your blessing and permission to do so."

After he said that, the woman who had taken the box returned to the circle. She and two other women stepped forward and took Striker by the arms. Smiling, they gestured toward one of their huts.

He looked around at me. I have never seen such a startled, confused, apprehensive look on Striker's face before.

It would be laughable if I had any clue what would happen next.

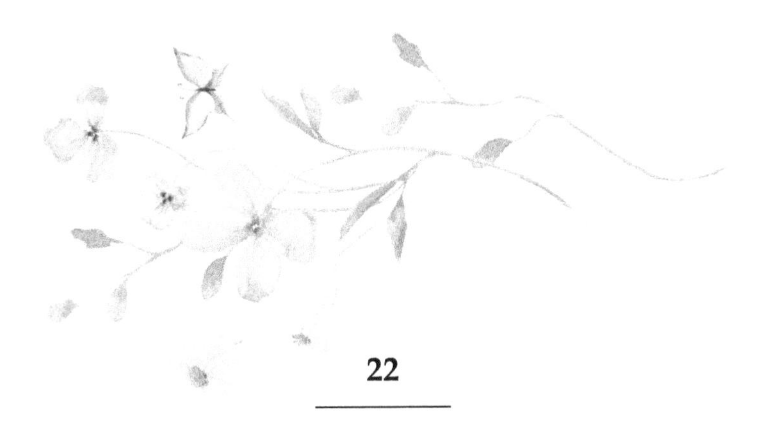

22

"My child," Grandmother Sybil said. "They must perform the steps of *Kwanjula.* Striker must be investigated by your aunties."

"Yes, ma'am." Oh, dear.

"This is tradition."

"Thank you, ma'am." Well, that's what we signed up for—a traditional unity ceremony to allow us to be married. I cleared my throat. "We have brought coffee beans with us." I gestured toward the cart we'd dragged in. "Where can I place the sack?" I needed something to distract myself.

Three ceremonial aunties? That was a lot.

Denbe arrived at my side, her hand rested gently on my arm. I think she was our designated "known face," the person who would keep us heading in the right direction during our visit. And I was so appreciative. "We are doing things quickly as we know your time with us is short."

"That's very kind."

Iniquus logistics had a feast sent from the nearest town as that would be ours to provide. I knew that traditional clothes were in the bags. I hadn't imagined the outfit that Striker had on for the presentation of my dowry. *Dowry, it might take me a while to get past that.*

Logistics knew we would be attending a ceremony; they didn't know we'd be the central figures in that ceremony. Hopefully, it would be right, and we conducted ourselves appropriately.

I had been incurious.

I had so much circulating through my mind about Spyder and Sylanos and Cammy.

Well, it was time to focus on the present.

I was here to, at long last, get married to Striker.

"Denbe, can I help with dinner?"

"We can prepare your plates. You will eat tonight with Grandmother."

I was willing to do anything that would distract me, and I didn't want to think about what was happening behind the blanket.

She led me over to a woven mat with an array of steaming baskets filled with fragrant foods.

I held the plates, and Denbe filled them, naming each dish and telling me some of the ingredients, some of the names I recognized.

When Denbe looked up, I followed her gaze.

Striker emerged from the hut, looking relaxed.

Too relaxed?

I caught his eye, and he winked. He did that on purpose to tease me. Nothing had happened in there, I was sure.

Pretty sure.

With the plates of food in hand, we followed Denbe to Grandmother Sybil's hut. After Denbe handed Grandmother a plate, she left, lowering the blanket over the opening.

"Come, children." She scooped her hand to welcome us, then gestured to the grass mat.

We lowered ourselves to sit cross-legged, hiding the soles of our feet.

I set my plate down in front of me. My stomach was churning, and I wasn't hungry.

"Lexi's spiritual aunties have agreed to this marriage," Grandmother told Striker. "They will speak for you at the tribal council tonight. Before I can agree to this union, we must speak. Decisions must be made." She turned shining obsidian eyes to Striker. "We have two things to discuss before I allow the ceremony. There are two bright questions in your heads. It is right that a couple shares the same concerns. One concern is whether Lexi should have psychic surgery, and the other is about the safety of Cammy in the ether."

She turned her gaze toward me. I felt a warm glow on my face.

"Now, Lexi, Doc says that the two of you discussed your soul's injury when you were there three days ago. The tear. And that she has advised that I repair this."

"Yes, Grandmother."

Striker shifted into stoic mode. Solid as a boulder. Something I loved about him and something that I didn't like very much.

"That leads you to worry." Grandmother's focus was only on me. "Will you be able to sense a need in your loved ones, and will you be able to go to their aid if you are healed." She placed her hands on her knees and lifted her chin, looking above my head and breathing deeply. She lowered her gaze to mine. "I don't know the answer. Perhaps it is that you have traveled through the ether so frequently that it is as easy for you as standing up and walking across our field. I can imagine that you would still be able to do this, see the shimmer, and decide if you wished to go and see what the universe had to share with you." She paused to breathe. "I have contemplated this since I performed psychic surgery the last time to remove the soul attachment that Indigo forced between you and Angel. Perhaps it will be that you will find information, as I do when I travel to see. I do not suffer as you do. With your skills and the healing, perhaps you will be this way as well. Will this limit you? Of course, in some ways. But if you can see with their eyes and hear with their ears, do you need to share their body experiences? Do you need to take their blows?"

"So I can do what I do now, only in a safer way?" I asked. I promised my team not to use my skill except to save my own life or theirs. They were adamant that I not go behind the Veil and risk all.

But if I was just eyes and ears, I could use my skill to help when I saw the shimmer.

"I can imagine that that is a possibility. But I believe that, after hearing what you have been able to do all your life, that walking behind the Veil is a gift from your ancestors. Without a wise woman of your own background to guide you—though I know that Miriam tried—I believe you learned about this skill because the slice made your birthright abilities something you could not overlook."

This, again, was speculation when I would love a concrete understanding.

"Since both you and Striker come from the northlands, and so too does the DNA that flows through Cammy, handed down through her mother-line—Striker, what was your mother's family name?"

"My mother, Jones? Her mother came to America from Norway." Striker looked over at me, not following this conversation. I made a mental note to fill him in later. "That family was Karsten."

Grandmother gave me a knowing nod. See?

"I believe that Cammy's experience behind the Veil seeing Lexi work," Grandmother told Striker, "and having my village support her, opened her up early to skills that might otherwise have laid dormant."

"Can you close her eyes to this again?" Striker asked.

"Perhaps Lexi's cut allows Cammy to share visions in the dream state, as Doc suggested. I think it is wise to close the incision and answer that question. I have long been worried about this wound. An open cut will fester."

Didn't that sound horrible? A festering soul. "Yes, ma'am, I ask that you heal me."

"Good. We will do that tonight." She turned to Striker. "And now, I would like you to present your fear concerning Cammy."

"Yes, ma'am, I'm not sure what to say. Let me begin with the fact that your skills, Doc's, and Lexi's are very hard for me to understand. They are skills that are lifesaving and skills that, if poorly used, like Indigo's were, can torment and endanger."

"These two things, yes." Grandmother nodded. "Both are very true."

"I have been very close to my niece from the time she was born. And up until the time when you and Lexi saved her through the ether, she never showed any signs of being psychic or having any kind of skill with the sixth sense." He turned to me and held out his hand, which I grasped. "Lexi has people in her life who have known her from the time she was in diapers. In their stories, Lexi has always had the ability to *know*." He shifted from hip bone to hip bone. "The first time that I realized that something had changed for Cammy, Lexi and I had gone on a trip to a place called Miami, where my family lives, where Cammy's mom, my sister Lynda, was being treated for her injuries. Cammy kept talking about her 'fairy godmother,' and Lynda thought it would be a good idea if Cammy, who was turning four at the time, could see that Lexi was a person and not a magical being."

"Ah, but Lexi is a magical being," Grandmother countered.

Striker released my hand and pulled one leg underneath him. It seemed as if he was kneeling in reverence, like a knight before his queen.

Queen? Was this the queen?

If so, the vibrator-thing made no sense. But those were Western eyes viewing the object. It might be a ceremonial something she had from her own cultural traditions.

"Lexi is magical, yes. But not in the way that my niece was imagining. Lexi doesn't have a magic wand with which she can make wishes come—" Striker stopped and lifted his chin, looking at me as he quoted, "*If wishes were horses, then paupers would ride*." He sent a hard, worried stare my way.

A connection? I let that tumble through my brain, and it didn't land anywhere.

Grandmother waited.

"Lexi can't wishfully manifest things like a pretty party dress," Striker clarified.

"I see." Grandmother nodded, encouraging him to continue.

"Lexi and I went down to Miami, and when Cammy saw Lexi for the very first time, Cammy knew who Lexi was without an introduction. Cammy crawled onto Lexi's lap and talked about how Lexi's hair was curled." Striker looked over at me. "Lexi and I realized that when Cammy was in an altered state with the medication, unconscious, she was not only aware of what was going on but recognized Lexi in physical form." He turned back to Grandmother.

"This is quite interesting. And not the first time I have heard of this. Doc and I have discussed it. And Miriam."

"Recently, Cammy came to live with us. Just before her move, a children's poem kept circulating through Lexi's mind. '*Three blind mice, see how they run.*' Every child that grew up in the United States has heard this rhyme. And you know that Lexi often gets messages through children's stories, rhymes, or songs."

"Yes." Grandmother turned to me. "The words Striker said earlier, the ones that send ice down his spine about '*if wishes were horses.*'"

"It is a children's song. It is in my mind. It doesn't show up as a *knowing.*"

Grandmother nodded and turned back to Striker. "But it frightened you."

"Yes, ma'am. You see, the three blind mice weren't a *knowing* either. Lexi was traveling in a different country, and she was getting on the plane. She felt great pressure to reach out and check on Cammy. She called, and no one answered the cell phone. Lexi called again and again until finally Cammy came on the line and said, 'Thank you, fairy godmother,' then hung up."

"The situation was that they were in the dark and needed to find their phone," I explained. "My calling helped Striker's parents find it in time to call medical help for Cammy's mother."

"Yes. Very good."

"Striker's upset because when Cammy came to our house, she

was singing that song. And when we asked what she had been thinking about, she said she was thinking about my calling her."

"Ah, an ethereal connection." Grandmother Sybile nodded. "She will need training if this continues past her first moon cycle. But that is many years from now." She turned to Striker. "It is important that Cammy not share with anyone that she has etheric skills."

"She doesn't seem to know she has them," Striker told her. "We don't point it out to her. We give her no affirmations."

"Right now, Striker," Grandmother said. "You are afraid that Lexi's fate in the ether will become Cammy's."

"Grandmother, I have to protect my niece." He put his hand over his heart. "I have no skills to safeguard her in the ether." Striker sent a glance my way and reached for my hand. "Or Lexi, for that matter. Watching Lexi being tortured when she's behind the Veil is hell on Earth. I *can't* let that happen to my niece."

23

"WHILE THE '*THREE BLIND MICE*' SONG HAPPENED BEFORE CAMMY moved in with us, there was another thing that happened." I tugged my bag from behind my back, pulled out my tablet, tapped the On button, and scrolled to the picture of the purple rat. I held it out to Grandmother Sybil.

She took it into her hands and examined the picture of the web and dangling spider, the rat with its open mouth.

After a moment, I reached for it back. "Cammy drew that in class." I scrolled to the same picture done as a task rendering. "Galaxy's Herman Trudy did this drawing. He was working on a task commissioned by Spyder. The task read: What dangers surround Lexi? And the conclusion had two elements. Trudy wrote, 'This was planned.' And then he asked, "How did Cammy find out about it?" I held out the picture, and she looked at it and returned it to me.

"Then there was another picture Trudy drew on a clarification task." I scrolled and handed the new image of the seeds and stump back to her. "It seemed to indicate that the seeds for this picture," I reached out and tapped my tablet, "were planted five years ago. The task was: More? Referring to the spider and rat drawing. And the conclusion was 'It's time'."

"What more do you know of the spider and rat images?" Grandmother asked.

"I believe I understand who these people are in the picture." I pointed toward the tablet. "Cammy would not."

"And yet you dream of this." Grandmother was making a statement, not asking a question.

"The rat, at least. Yes, ma'am, I do."

"And Cammy is in the house with you." She placed the tablet in front of her. "Our dreams reach out and dance in our space. If Cammy found them interesting, perhaps she took them into her own world."

"That would be a happy understanding. And that is what I thought at first, too, the idea of the collective unconscious."

"Collective unconscious." Grandmother pronounced slowly. "I like these words. They describe much. "You have been dreaming these images. It is possible that she learned these symbols from you."

"That's what Doc suggested to me." I leaned forward. "For me, this spider is Spyder McGraw, whom you know." I pointed. "And this rat is a man named Sylanos. The timeline went like this: Spyder brought me a crime puzzle to solve. It was very intricate. The crime puzzle had to do with a man named Sylanos. After I figured it out and handed the answer to Spyder, he left on a year-long mission. My mother died. Indigo slit my soul. I had my first walk behind the Veil, in which I wasn't an observer but actually integrated with someone else, and what happened to their body happened to mine. Indigo performed psychic surgery to sew Angel and me together. Then, a fire burned down the building where I lived my whole life. That night, I met Angel. Three weeks later, we were married. And so it was until the pieces of this slowly unfurled."

"Sylanos is a rat?" Grandmother asked.

"He is a very bad man. We don't know whether he is dead or if he faked his death. The crimes may be committed by his crime family, the Sylanos Cartel."

"What happened with the crime that you puzzled? You brought that up for a reason," Grandmother said.

"My life, my thoughts, were very full at the time."

"How long ago?" She looked down at the image again.

"I was nineteen. So—" I turned to Striker.

"About five years ago. But that could be happenstance," he said.

"It could be, but I doubt it," I said. "The picture Trudy drew answered, 'What dangers surround Lexi.' Trudy came up with a picture of a rat with a freaking tracking collar."

"What came of you solving that case?" Grandmother asked.

"I put the case to the side. I thought I was done with it. After a stalker attacked me, Striker and his team took me into the safe house —the house where you found me to help him save his sister and Cammy. There, I told Striker that Spyder was my mentor. And I mentioned the case I had just finished solving, the one about Sylanos. Striker said they weren't given the answer to the puzzle, so I went through the files to figure it out again. And that's when the dreams started."

Grandmother had closed her eyes as she listened. And with her eyes still shut, she asked, "This man, Sylanos, is on the same team as Indigo was?"

"Yes, ma'am. They were partners. When the people in charge of the case were given Sylanos's name, they decided to follow Sylanos to see what he did in the hopes that they could take down the entirety of the criminal enterprise. But Sylanos might have died. Everyone thought that he was dead."

"And you did not think this." Her body swayed gently like a ribbon in a breeze.

"I don't think I'd be dreaming about him as a rat with a tracker on his neck if he were dead," I said softly. "He feels alive to me."

Grandmother opened her eyes and tapped the picture. "What do you see in this image?"

"That the rat is opening its mouth to eat the spider."

Grandmother leaned forward to look at the picture for a long moment. "Interesting. When I saw it, I thought the rat was laughing at the spider web and didn't see the spider descending upon it."

"Those are two very different ways to interpret this image," Striker said.

"And both, in this moment, could be correct. Perhaps either is available, and a decision has not yet been made in the outcome of this picture," she told Striker. "But I feel that both your energy and Lexi's are tied to this picture. You will soon see for yourselves how this tale will unfold."

Striker shifted beside me, but Grandmother Sybil lifted the tablet and said, "Show me the other picture that concerns you."

I pulled up the picture of the alien and the queen and laid it in front of her. "Indigo went on a series of tasks, questions to which he was searching out answers. In one of these questions, he was asking about Striker's wedding. He was shown sunbeams and leaves. He tried a different way to determine whether his daughter Scarlet married Striker. The question he asked was: 'What happened right after the wedding?' He asked it three times. The first picture he drew made little sense to Indigo or me. It looked like a blob with a smile. But this is the picture from the third time he went into the ether looking for the answer to his question." Grandmother lifted the tablet and looked at it for a long time—what felt like a long time.

"Indigo's picture is dated to a time before he experimented on me with psychic surgery," I said. I reached out and scrolled to the next page with the scientific documentation.

After she read, she said, "My child, you know that time only happens on a physical plane. In the ether, there is neither time nor place. You can go anywhere. He is dead, yet he has seen what happens after Striker's wedding. The task says this is where Striker goes after he is married."

"Which leaves me with so many questions. If he was asking what came next for Striker as associated with his wedding, why this picture?"

She set the tablet down and took a sip from her cup. "I have talked at length with Doc about Indigo. Doc told me the story of when you felt called from behind the Veil to help Lynda a second time. You felt a great deal of guilt because you had told Spyder about a necklace that would lead to information about this rat-man Sylanos. His name is not new to me for this reason. When Indigo was asking Lynda questions, he asked about a man with blackberry skin who has the necklace, and he had no other information."

"Correct."

"He was able to see the slightest blur of his skin, and that is all. It infuriated Indigo. He knew that this was a great enemy who would be able to hide from him. Spyder is energetically impenetrable. He is safe from being spied on in the ether."

"That can be both good and bad, I guess."

"All things are," she agreed. "When Lynda was captured this second time, Indigo asked her about your skills. Doc says that you are frightened that others will know of your talents and that this will put you and your loved ones in harm's way. I have thought about this at great length."

I stopped breathing.

"Before Indigo spoke with Lynda, Doc said that these things had already happened: Indigo had performed psychic surgery on you. You were kidnapped, and General Elliot hired Trudy to find you. Trudy reached out to Indigo to be his assistant. Trudy saw you in the cell and that you were gone from your body. He didn't know what to make of this. He thought perhaps you were, like he was, a viewer. But that felt wrong to him. Trudy went to see where you were and what you were doing, and it took him to a meeting of The Assembly. There, they were talking about things that were psychic in nature. And you."

"Yes, ma'am. Trudy thought that perhaps my soul went to where my name was being used because I was very close to death."

"And you were," Grandmother said gently. "My tribe worked very hard for many days to heal you. You were very ill, and your body wanted to give up. Your soul was weakened, as well."

"I am so grateful for all of your help while I was imprisoned. Your counsel, your healing, the respite of coming here in spirit to rest from the prison walls. So grateful."

"And we are grateful to Striker for our survival and release from slavery, and we are grateful to you for allowing us to help our dear Striker in his time of need. This is how families support each other."

I remembered lying on that shelf in the Honduran prison. I was boiling hot and freezing cold. I couldn't make my way to the toilet, or the water faucet, or the food. My soul didn't want to stay in my body. My body hurt so badly, and my soul was free of pain as it floated away. I didn't want to go back. And I really don't remember what happened next to change that. But what Grandmother was saying made perfect sense to me.

"I speak of this," Grandmother continued, "because Trudy tells me that he was confused by what he saw on that task. He discussed it with Indigo. I feel sure of this. As he wrote the report, Indigo would have pressed for more answers. Indigo didn't know what your skills might be, and he certainly didn't know if he had caused them through the psychic surgery."

"Indigo asked Lynda how Lexi saved her from the cabin where she was beaten," Striker said.

"Indeed."

"How would he… he had to task himself to go to a time and place where he could understand what I could do, right?" I asked.

"What we know from our visions," Grandmother said, reaching for my hand, "is that Indigo was furious that Striker had found his way to you when you were recovering from the stalker's attack in the hospital. Indigo tasked many questions, trying to discover what was happening. We feel that one of the times he sent himself out to gather information, he found his way to the cabin where she was being beaten. The night that we worked to protect Lynda and Cammy, you were with Lynda for a very long time. You were receiving each blow that she took like a warrior. In that otherworldly state, he saw you briefly as you left Lynda's body and flew out of the cabin and back to the safe house, much like he was fleetingly able to see a glint of Spyder's blackberry skin. And next, the helpers arrived with medical assistance. When we were in the cabin with you, we saw a flash of blue energy shaped like a man."

"That's how I've seen Indigo, too," I whispered. "Yes, ma'am, that would line up. That would make sense. And that would explain why he knew that I saved Lynda but didn't know how. Though, he seemed to put it together on the day that he was questioning her because he was ordering his bad guys to gather everything, collect Lynda, and leave immediately. But our police officers were already there. It was too late, and the SWAT team was able to rescue Lynda."

"The night of the cabin, you returned to your body at the safe house. And Indigo knew the location. Already, he had gone there to observe you. This was possible because of your physical and mental state. We saw this blue energy and stayed to protect you."

A sob escaped my mouth that I didn't know was accumulating there. "Thank you."

Striker smoothed a hand over my head and left it resting, warm and supportive, on my back. I could feel guilt radiating from his palm.

"We deepened your recuperative trance," Grandmother said. "We wanted you strong when you woke. You would need to act straight away."

"Yes, I was unconscious for much longer than I had been before." Well, when you know, you know. This was going to take some time to integrate. "Now that I'm looking back at my time in the safe house, I felt Indigo there as what I call heebie-jeebies. I think it was two things. I felt him on my skin, and my psychic early warning system was alarming."

"This is so." Grandmother nodded.

"But I *didn't* know about Indigo at the time. I've always interpreted that feeling with my *knowing* that Wilson knew about the safe house. When I awoke from my recuperation, I remembered that I had been told to go live at Iniquus in the Barracks. I didn't know the name, only the description."

"Wilson is the name of your attacker?" Grandmother asked.

"Yes, ma'am."

"No, he did not know where you were until you returned home. No matter what you might have understood in the past. As far as I can see, the safe house was safe from Wilson. Indigo was the danger. It was my acolytes and I who sent you to Iniquus. That land, like ours, has a protection over it and cannot be penetrated by viewers like Indigo."

I swallowed. Well, this was a paradigm shift.

"Indigo watched you while you were at the safe house. Why?" Grandmother asked Striker rhetorically. "For two very important reasons. One, his daughter wished to marry you. And in that safe house, Lexi slept in the same bed as you."

"Yes, ma'am," he said, his voice gruff.

"Also, he had performed psychic surgery on you, Lexi, to tie you to Angel. He wished to know the effects of this surgery."

"I stayed loyal to Angel. I felt the pull as I always had with Striker. I had fallen in love with Striker before he knew me. While I worked for Spyder, I was forbidden from telling Striker who I really was." I turned and smiled at Striker. "And I remember that I loved and longed for him to be mine up until the moment when I saw Angel." I turned back to Grandmother. "And that changed everything for me. I felt like I had found what some people call my twin-soul."

"Which is what Indigo tried to create."

"Yeah, yay him." I held up jazz hands. "It was a success in many ways."

"Have you read any of Indigo's tasking from this time?" Striker asked.

"I haven't. I searched for where he mentioned Lynda or Cammy, and I couldn't find either name." I shifted and sucked in a be-brave breath as I crossed my fingers. "Grandmother, do you know if Indigo ever understood my skills? Did he tell anyone else?"

"These are questions, my child, that I cannot readily answer. I don't know what other tasks he witnessed and what he put together. I don't even know at what point in his timeline he would have traveled to the safe house. It could have been moments after the surgery. It could have happened days before his death. All we saw was his energy, and we acted accordingly."

"There is no time in the ether," I murmured.

"As always, my child, this lesson is a very difficult one to teach the brain."

"All right, well, we know Indigo influenced what happened in the safe house. And I'm afraid he is influencing now. I have felt him in the ether at my divorce from Angel. More concerning is this picture that explains where Striker goes after we are married tomorrow." I reached out to tap the picture of a spider dangling over the alien and the queen.

Grandmother said, "There was a man who harmed you. He was the reason that you went to the safe house. Not the man Wilson who used the razor on you. Wilson heard evil voices in his head that asked him to do terrible things. There was another man who knew this and decided to use Wilson as a tool, as a weapon. Do you know this man?"

"Yes, ma'am. His name was Frith."

"Frith worked with Indigo or Indigo's people?"

"Yes, ma'am."

"I see this, that Frith knew of your association with Spyder. He kept much information from Indigo. Indigo never had the name Spyder whispered into his ear in connection with Striker at the time he did the searches that you have in those pictures. Indigo did not know about you or your connection to Spyder and would not understand the picture at that time. Indigo found you because of your connection to Striker. He sent Frith into your life, and Frith discovered Spyder there."

I thought about that for a minute. Didn't General Elliot mention Spyder on the tasking sheets that Trudy drew along with Indigo when I was in the prison? Yes. Yes, I remember that he did. But General Elliot would have received the reports and made his notes. Indigo wouldn't be privy to them, especially if General Elliot looked at the tasking sheets at Iniquus, protected by the Tsukamoto art.

And I remembered reading how Indigo was mad that while helping Spyder, Spyder had not testified for Galaxy. But Spyder would have been a name. Indigo didn't know what he looked like. Trudy had said a "man named Spyder" in one of his tasks, but Indigo probably paid no attention. The tasks had a forty percent chance of being wrong. And Indigo probably thought Trudy misunderstood the monsters in my fever dreams or maybe thought of it as a metaphor. And too, Spyder said that he had been saved many times by Galaxy's information. If Spyder had offered a task and Indigo went off to find the answers in the ether, all Indigo would have would be a string of tasking numbers, possibly even Spyder's name.

As a matter of fact, I found out that Trudy didn't learn about Spyder McGraw's connection with Galaxy until after Strike Force rescued me from my plane crash. At the time when Trudy was doing the remote viewing of me in the prison, Spyder's name meant nothing to him, thank god. They didn't meet until Trudy moved to Wyoming near the other Galaxy viewers. The universe, I thought, was a tangled web. One just hopes it's a compassionate and clever spider that traces the silk of one's timeline.

I held out the picture of the alien and the queen to Grandmother Sybil.

"So, whatever this is?" I asked her. "We don't understand it, but neither did Indigo, right? When the task mentions danger surrounding me—whatever was seeded five years ago—but now it's germinating, Indigo wouldn't have done something to influence it, right?"

24

My arms wrapped Striker's waist, and I leaned back so I could read his eyes. "You look like you've psyched yourself up to go to war."

"I'm not loving this. And I feel that you are going into harm's way, once again, for me and my family."

"I am going to go have a cut repaired," I said pragmatically. "I was attacked by an evil crazy man, who is now dead."

"He was dead the last time you had psychic surgery performed. They called me into the tent, and you had floated off into the ether. They were afraid they'd lost you. As in, you were never coming back."

"But you called me. I heard you, and I came. Look, we aren't married yet. That is one of my soul's assignments in this lifetime, or so it seems. Your voice will be my beacon if I'm lost in the ether. I'll always come home to you." Wow, the conviction in my words was powerful, yet there was a piece of me that said I was playacting to placate Striker, and it wasn't the truth at all. "The last time I had undergone soul surgery, I was like a conjoined twin. It seems like a much bigger deal compared to what's happening now. Grandmother would find the cut, heal anything surrounding it, seal me back together."

"Simple. Right?" He was sweating. "I liked it better when the team was here. Gator. Doc."

"I mean, we could call them and see if they could participate, but if my knife slipped while I was cooking and I went to the emergency department for stitches, I wouldn't be calling in the cavalry."

"Gator has that trick he can do in the ether to pull you back into your body."

"If you'll remember, he sat next to me last time and said I slipped right by him. He couldn't grab hold. *You* called me back. I came to *your* voice. And you will be with me."

Striker's grip around my waist tightened. "I am all kinds of outside of my skillset here."

"You love me. That's the skillset required."

He gathered me tighter in his arms, pressing my head to his chest. His heart pounded. Energy buzzed along his length. He was scared. And masking it well. "I've been with you too many times and seen too many things for me to think this is going to be a walk in the park."

"Please don't think those thoughts. Thoughts have energy, and I want this to be easy. Besides, I will remind you that this journey will be supported by Grandmother's acolytes. I didn't save Lynda and Cammy by myself—much of the time, I was simply an instrument that these women were able to use. They were the ones who saw the danger and intervened. It was their drumbeats that allowed me to channel Grandmother Sybil. Their chants allowed me to see and act in ways I didn't know were available to me. Knowing their strength, I'm putting my trust in them."

"Okay." He kissed my hair. "I'm trying. I really am."

"Tonight, surgery. And if I am rested and comfortable, tomorrow we will get married. We file the papers, get our marriage license, and go home a happy couple."

"Let's work that plan."

What was that military truism? Plans only last until first contact with the enemy.

Did that phrase have any meaning here?

"WE WILL TALK as we wait for your tea to take hold." Grandmother Sybil nodded toward the door. "The air feels good on my skin now. When you drift off, I will pull the blanket over the door. Striker has the fierce eyes of a warrior. And that energy should stay on the other side of the fire circle."

"He loves me." I smiled.

"You should know that we are safe from observation in here. Above us in the ether is the man that you call Indigo. He cannot see us or hear us in our village. Though, he knows that you and Striker are below the distraction."

Indigo.

Was it the tea, or was it that name creating this strange sensation? As adrenaline flooded my system, it seemed to cleave my body from my awareness. Looking over at myself, I saw sweat on my brow. I could smell the fear emitting from my pores. I could see Striker looking up at the woman who was there to communicate with him. He pointed toward the door.

Striker knew something was wrong.

She pressed his shoulder to keep him seated.

Behind the hut, I heard a drumbeat begin. Chants rode the air current.

And just like that, I settled back into my body. "Indigo is dead, Grandmother."

"He is here as an observer. In the ether, there is no such thing as time."

"Yes, ma'am. I don't fully grasp that concept. Though, I understand that in the past, Indigo could task himself to go to a time and place in which he might grasp the answers to a question that he posed."

"Yes, I believe that after he performed the slice as an experiment, he moved forward in time to see if it healed and arrived here, where he will learn nothing. He is outside of our protection, and we are showing him moonbeams and dancing leaves."

"You recognize him, though, right?" I asked. "Was he there when you separated Angel and me?" I wondered if that was why I had trouble finding my way back into my body, and Striker needed to reel me in.

"He has, from time to time, shown himself to me. When he comes into my awareness, I forbid his contact as I am doing now. I know who he is through discussions with Doc."

"How does this no-time or space thing affect me now, Grandmother? I mean, could he come in behind you, and undo your healing at some future time?"

"This is not allowed, or our future generations' paths would be landmines of ancient manipulations. There are universal laws. No, what we do is in present time, and I will clear your timeline from the beginning into the future. Doc has described ancestral memory to you?"

"Yes, ma'am."

"I will clean along your timeline in such a way that your children and your children's children will not suffer the effects of this man's interventions. You were an innocent, and you have suffered much."

"Grandmother, I am wondering…" I let the thought trail away.

"Ask your question."

"My beloved Spyder, you know him."

"I do. A formidable warrior, we have walked through lifetimes together. We—you, Striker, Spyder, and I—are of the same soul group, and each lifetime, we find each other and recognize each other. We show up in different configurations in each other's lives. In this lifetime, Striker is my savior. I am the healer. You are my granddaughter. And Spyder is a warrior for the light."

"I have seen two pictures of spiders, and both, in my mind, have to do with psychic manipulation and danger."

"Yes, with one of the pictures, the one that Indigo drew. It was created at about the same time as your soul was attacked and sliced."

I thought about that for a moment. And Grandmother was right; when I looked it up, the tasking for this was about Striker's wedding and what happened next. It was the same time frame that he'd noted that he'd taken his dog to be spade, and the surgery to prevent bloat had inspired him to sew me to someone else to open a possible surgical path for him to realign his daughter Scarlet with Striker.

Sew me to Angel, then sew Striker to Scarlet, do-si-do around we go.

Indigo made the first slice to see how things would go. I missed reading a task where he went forward in time to check on his handiwork. But yes, the slice, the wedding, the rat with the spider web were all right there next to each other in the notebooks. "Yes, ma'am, that's correct."

"This man, Indigo, didn't work alone. He was like an octopus in the ocean. I am told by one of my great-grandchildren, who loves all things that live in the waters, that an octopus is one being, but each of its arms acts independently. That each arm has its own brain. The goal of each arm is to help the octopus as a whole."

"Yes, ma'am, this is the description."

"Indigo is no longer here. That octopus's arm was severed. I caution you that the destructive energy of this octopus is profound for an entire people."

She poured me another cup of the bitter tea, and I continued to sip.

"Indigo is a man of great vanity. As I sense him, he has a god complex. He laughed when he drew the picture you showed me of the queen in the water. I feel his delight. He believed this was when a great adversary would meet her demise."

Her? Could the 'her' mean me?

Cold washed over me like an arctic blast.

"Indigo is still here. I wish he'd go," I whispered, pulling my shoulders up to my ears.

"He is perplexed and curious by what means my acolytes shield us. He has been looking for a way to hide information as another tool. He is testing my perimeters to see if he can't find a way to penetrate them."

"If he can't find it now, he'll just keep coming back, won't he?"

"This is already his fifth time coming back. This last time, he is here because he is worried. At this point on a physical-world timeline, his daughter has offered a contract to Striker's company. That contract included vibrational writing that no one else could see. Had it been Striker himself who signed that contract, things would have become a lot more complicated for his soul and for your marrying."

"I have so much to learn." I blinked heavy lids. "That all makes very little sense to me."

"Indigo's attempts to manipulate soul trajectories have largely been thwarted." She patted my knee. "With this healing, we will do much to reset many lives."

"Yes, ma'am."

"Very quickly, my child, this will begin to unravel. Focus on the webbing. It holds the answer." Her voice was musical notes that played in my ear.

The webbing… holds the answer.

The webbing…

The…

25

THE SMELL OF INCENSE TICKLED MY NOSE.

I rolled over and blinked away my disorientation.

Denbe sat on the sleeping mat beside me in the glow of a solar lamp with a smile. "Good morning to the bride. The sun will soon smile on you." I pushed up onto my elbow and took in the room. My three aunties sat to one side, and other elders sat on the other.

How had I slept through their arrival?

When I pushed myself to sitting, I grabbed my head as it clanged.

"This is expected," Denbe soothed. "Drink this, and your head will quiet."

It was a strange compost kind of taste that pulled my face into a full pucker. I absolutely did not want to drink this brew.

"Yes, you do want to drink it. It is difficult, I know. But it will be the antidote to last night's tea." She turned an *I've got a secret* eye to the women and cryptically said, "This tea turns back last night's tea for you. And later today, Striker, too, will have a turn-around tea."

The women laughed. And my head hurt too much to care what they were talking about.

I didn't want to get married feeling like this.

A large tub was brought into the hut. As younger women filed in, they filled it with steaming water.

Denbe pressed her finger under my cup, tipping it toward my mouth. It was drink or spill.

I reluctantly drank, feeling the bitterness travel down my throat.

She pulled it away, looked inside to ensure I had the last dregs, and said, "There now, we have breakfast ready for you." Her graceful hand gestured to a platter beside me. "Striker is now having the same foods. And receiving the same counsel. There is but one other man in the village, so he has taken it upon himself to serve as Striker's uncle."

"Oh?" I had only seen boys in the village, no men.

"On this platter, we display the foods that speak of the marital journey. There is honey spread on your morning bread." She pointed. "This bread is sustaining you. And the honey shows the sweetness that the heart feels when it is loving someone and that love is warmly returned. But not all will be sweet. This salad is cucumber in vinegar. Life will sometimes be bitter with bickering and fights, and you must swallow it down. This chicken has a cayenne paste, which is the spice of passion. A marriage is a meal of tastes, yes? And here we have the mango fruit, our wish that your life is juicy and full of flavor."

"Thank you, you are very kind." As the compost flavored medicinal tea worked its way into my blood, I did feel better. And hungry. I looked at Denbe for instruction.

"Yes, you must eat and bathe, and then we will dress you. It is good to be married as the dawn breaks, and you start your new life at the start of a new day."

After eating the food, unabashed, I took off my clothes and climbed into the tub the girls had filled. The hot water felt so good on my muscles, stiff from slumbering on a sleeping roll, which my body was unaccustomed to doing. The aunties came over with baskets of leaves. They spoke to their leaves in a language that I couldn't understand. But I heard the poetry of their cadence.

Oh, they smelled so good.

"Denbe, where is Grandmother?" I asked as I soaked.

"She sits in meditation, speaking with the ancestors, preparing herself for your ritual."

"Thank you."

As the women sat again on the floor, the hut filled with a soft hum of a song. A song that I could peacefully ride as I closed my eyes and absorbed the sensations of the ritual bath.

With each new song, the beat lifted a little and became more energetic.

With this last song, clapping was added to the lyrics, and outside my hut, I could hear the other villagers pick up the music and sing it, too.

This was an amazing experience.

I hoped Striker was enjoying his preparation as much as I was.

When Denbe brought me a cloth, I rose from the tub. The aunties dried me and rubbed me with perfumed oil until it was absorbed into my skin, and I glowed.

Next, I saw that my pack was opened, and a colorful dress was laid out with bejeweled sandals.

The aunties pulled this over my head.

Denbe said, "Your wedding dress is beautiful," as I stepped into the sandals. I sat on a stool as Denbe picked up the length of fabric that was under my dress. It was peacock blue. Denbe began working to fold and pleat the fabric into a hat for me. It felt like a crown. I felt like a princess.

Again, there was a change of drumming and singing.

"Grandmother has entered the circle. Elders." Denbe bowed. The women left except for my three aunties and Denbe.

"We shall escort you. We wait for our song."

There was silence in the hut. Then, there it was, a different beat.

My escorts walked me out of the hut. Denbe took my arm on one side, and Auntie took my arm on the other. One auntie walked ahead and one behind. They protected me and supported me from all sides.

The villagers were shoulder to shoulder as they curved around in what I thought was the shape of a nautilus, the curve of a labyrinth.

We walked slowly with the beat. And I swear that my heart rate changed to match the drums. As we reached the part of the swirl that included the elders, the front auntie stepped aside.

There stood Striker.

Painfully handsome.

Spyder to his left, Grandmother to his right.

Oh, my head spun.

My breath caught.

I could not believe that the moment had arrived.

I had waited; it felt like a thousand years.

It felt like evil had conspired against us. Pain. And… Fear. We had overcome so much.

Striker held out his hand to me as he stepped forward.

I had held myself together until I saw the tears on Striker's lashes.

My dam broke, and my own tears flowed in silent streams.

We made it.

We were here.

This was it.

We were soon to be one.

I reached for his hands.

"I, the father of the bride, come forward with confidence," Spyder said as he took a step closer to us, "that this man and this woman will love and support each other for all their days."

I looked over to catch Spyder's gaze and mouthed, "Thank you." Thank you for being here. Thank you for that confidence. Thank you for being my second father. Thank you. Surely, he got all of that.

"I," Grandmother Sybil said as she took a step forward, "the ancient mother of the bride, feel confident that she is well prepared for her journey as a wife. And I welcome Striker as he is born into Lexi's family."

Denbe arrived with a piece of cloth that she handed to Spyder.

Denbe lifted our hands, layering my hand on top of Strikers. When she stepped back, Spyder knotted the cloth around our wrists.

An elder stepped forward and laid a broom at our feet.

"With my blessing, your paths are joined," Grandmother announced. "The first steps you will take as man and wife will be to jump the broom. This will sweep away the past and bless you with a fresh future."

We looked to Denbe, and she gave us a nod.

Striker laughed as he said, "Three, two, one." And we jumped together.

In the air, it was as if I had wings, as if I was flying with him into that bright future.

Oh, I loved him. I *loved* him. It was here. Our time had come.

The village erupted in cheers as we landed on our feet.

We had done it!

"You are now Mr. and Mrs. Rheas. May you always be blessed," the aunties chanted.

I had no idea what to do next other than to stare wide-eyed into my husband's eyes.

Denbe leaned in. "The knots that Spyder tied will not be untied until the marriage is consummated."

"Oh, okay," I said, smiling at Striker.

"So now you will start your married life, learning how to eat and dance as one." She smiled.

And it was incredibly fun. The whole of it. The speeches and good wishes. The toasts and the storytelling. The dancing and the incredible festive breakfast that covered the tables. We watched the children play games, sang, hopped, and tried to keep up.

The joy! I have never been surrounded by people who understood how to vibrate with joy like this.

Finally, a horn blared.

The aunties brought a tray decorated with flowers and two steaming cups of tea.

Smiles slipped behind hands, and everyone stilled.

Grandmother made a symbol over the tray. Her black eyes glittered with amusement.

Denbe leaned in and said, "Drink your cups."

Lifting them with our free hands, we held them aloft like one does in America when accepting someone's toast. Neither of us knew the significance, so neither of us offered any words.

Mine was cinnamon and other spices like a chai.

Striker's seemed to be a different color, but he seemed to enjoy his, too.

We replaced the cups on the tray. The tray was removed. And everyone waited in giggly, silent expectation.

Striker's face pinked.

He turned to me and stepped closer.

The giggling turned to laughter as everyone watched us closely.

Denbe leaned in. "When a woman is married, she is offered a tea of warm spices to warm her womb, preparing her for the marital bed and the blessing of children."

"Oh," I said, silently moving through my memory to ensure I hadn't missed any of my birth control pills.

Striker's face was growing redder, and he looked…uncomfortable.

And like he wasn't sure what he should do.

He turned his hand where we were bound and gripped at my fingers.

Denbe leaned in again. "When baby boys are born, they have baby erections. The elders give them tea to settle that energy so the boy can grow in peace. The men are offered a tea that will undo the baby tea at the marriage ceremony. And a man will bloom."

"Bloom?" I mouthed at him.

His brow drew in tight. There was a whole conversation raging in his eyes. This was definitely *not* stoic Striker.

"The tea will fill him with much virility and stamina," Denbe said. "But his bloom will increase." Denbe was pushing on our backs as if to move us forward, and Striker was adamantly holding me so that we stayed facing each other.

The villagers were having a ball with the situation.

"Striker will be in much pain if you do not hurry to your marital bed. As you see, the tea has a very strong effect on him. Your hut is prepared for you, there." Denbe pointed at a hut set at a distance from the others. "But remember, your wrists must remain tied until the consummation is complete and untied by the grandmother."

I turned to Striker. "Can you make it that far?"

"That far and no further," he said as he started forward very fast, and I had to jog to keep up with the length of his stride.

The cheers followed us as we plunged through the blanket covering the door.

"Virility tea." I laughed as I tugged at Striker's string to loosen his pants to find his raging boner. "Oh," I said as if taken aback. I held my eyes wide as if startled. "I could make a balloon animal with that."

"I see what you did there," Striker said as he lifted me into his arms. "Come, Mrs. Rheas," he said as he took a step, then gently laid me down on the sleeping mat.

"Oh, I'm very sure I will."

26

Striker and I sprawled naked on the mat, catching our breaths as the predawn animals woke and called to the new day. "I think that last one finally did it," Striker whispered. "Whatever was in that tea should be illegal. Are you all right? That was—"

"Magnificent." I stretched my free hand over my head, luxuriating in a state of utter contentment. "Aerobic, for sure. And full of vigor." I laughed. "For a wedding night, it was fun. But not a tea for every day."

Striker laid his free hand on his chest. "No, I think it would kill me if I had to have that many orgasms in a single night on a constant basis."

"Same. That was quite the adventure. Normally, you send me into a coma by my second orgasm. But strangely, I kept up. Yeah, that I'm talking right now is a miracle. Must have had something to do with the concoction they handed me as well."

"Striker, I hear your voice." Spyder was outside the hut. "Cover yourselves. I must come in."

In the dark, still tied together, we groped for anything to pull over our naked bodies.

"Okay," I called out.

Spyder had a solar lantern with him. “There is an emergency. I have received a call from JSOC. Our country asks for our help, and I am going now,” Spyder said. “Learning that you were here in the village, JSOC asked that you accompany me. It is of dire consequence.”

I blinked at him. This was quite the one-eighty from where my thoughts were a moment before.

I held up my hand, tied to Striker’s.

Spyder lifted the cloth door covering.

Grandmother came through. She walked to the bed and spoke words in her own language over the binding and continued the chant as she untied us. “And so you are bound,” she said in English. “Your new life has begun.”

“Thank you, Grandmother,” we both said.

Grandmother Sybil pointed upward. “The picture of the purple rat,” she said. "It is time. Go, my children. May you be blessed as you face your futures and fortunes together.”

Both Spyder and Grandmother left.

Denbe replaced them at the hut’s door.

She had a basket with a fresh set of the same kind of tactical clothing we’d worn into the village on the first day. She set our hiking boots on the ground. “Your bags are packed and outside the door. May you be blessed as you go to their aid.”

Go to their aid?

Striker and I each grabbed at the clothes in the basket, jumping into our underclothing, dragging our T-shirts over our heads, pulling our pants over our hips, tugging at the zippers, whipping the belts through the closures, and securing them.

I dropped to my butt to tug on my boots and tie my laces, triple knotting for security.

Gathering a quick ponytail, I thrust the length of my hair through the back loop on my ballcap.

With a flick of the button, my headlamp glowed red. I tugged the elastic into place so the light rested on the cap’s visor.

Striker reached his hand to me and gave me a tug that sprang me onto my feet. He didn't let go of my hand as he dashed through the doorway.

There, for the first time in almost twenty-four hours, we let go of each other.

And that felt wrong.

It was for just a moment as we threw our rucks onto our backs and clasped the hip and sternal webbing around us, but I was happier when my hand was back in his.

Spyder nodded, turned, and bolted forward in the direction we had traced from our vehicle into the village.

Spyder was tall and thin. He was the strongest, fastest man I had ever known. I ran a 10k most days. I worked to keep my speed up. But as Spyder gracefully and effortlessly loped forward, I sprinted to keep him in sight.

Striker was six foot three to my five foot six. His stride was much longer than mine. He adjusted to accommodate me. I hoped that I wasn't a liability on this apparent rescue mission. Striker had trained his speed in his SEAL days and maintained it through daily workouts. His holding my hand helped spur me forward and kept me from splatting out over the roots that intersected the path.

My headlamp illuminated little in the stygian night.

No moonlight filtered through the branches to help us along the way.

Striker's years in the jungle gave him the ability to navigate.

As we burst from the path, I bent, gulping at the air after my effort. Here, I could make out the shadowy hulk of two rovers.

"We take my vehicle. I have equipment with me," Spyder called as he rounded to the back. He tossed a helmet to Striker, then one to me. I jerked my ball cap with the headlamp from my head and tossed it onto the seat. Pressing my helmet into place, I watched Spyder attach his chin strap, then pull the affixed night vision goggles over his eyes.

Neither Striker nor I had NVGs.

"Get in," Spyder said.

I climbed into the back, leaving the front to Striker and his long legs. Pulling my safety belt into place, I cinched it down tightly.

The motor revved. Spyder threw the vehicle into Reverse just long enough to clear the tree line, then put us into Drive as he steered a tight circle.

We bounced at breakneck speed over the dirt road toward the highway.

I wanted answers, but Spyder was absorbed in concentration as he flung the rover through the night, focusing through night vision goggles.

I didn't dare interrupt. The pocked backroads put us at risk of missing one, tipping us. Then we'd be out in the bush with no vehicle, not powering toward anyone's aid.

What did I know already?

Spyder got a mayday from JSOC. He had a satellite phone, of course. Obviously, Spyder had communicated where he would be and possibly, probably, why he was in Uganda. JSOC had directed Striker and me to go to Uganda for our wedding. But they probably didn't know that we had acted on their directives with such alacrity. Yes, Spyder must have told them either on the way in or after receiving the emergency call.

I'm not on par with Striker or Spyder in this scenario.

I have limited tactical experience under my belt.

Yet, no one had suggested I stay behind safe in the village.

Grandmother mentioned the purple rat from Cammy's picture, the same picture that Trudy had drawn on his task. The same rat with the message, "It's time." The same message that said that this event, whatever it was, had been seeded five years ago.

Where could we possibly be going and why?

It felt like the sky should brighten. It felt like the sun was out there peeking over the horizon, stretching beams to light the sky, but it remained hazy. Uganda was a temperate country. The coolest months were in North America's summer. Why did the air feel hotter to me here than in the village?

"Do you smell that?" Striker's voice broke the quiet inside the bubble of my helmet, equipped for communications.

I sniffed and coughed. Smoke.

Spyder pressed the comms button that would link him to a TOC —Tactical Operations Command Unit—he spoke in a foreign language I didn't recognize.

Through my helmet, I couldn't hear anything going into Spyder's ear. If they were speaking the same language as Spyder, it wouldn't edify me except that I'd be able to hear the tone. Not from Spyder, his tone was always relaxed, but from whoever was on the other end of the communication.

Spyder jerked the wheel and abruptly stopped at the side of the road. He pressed the NVGs onto his helmet and reached past my knees to the tactical computer on the backseat floorboard. With a glance at the sky, Spyder extended a satellite antenna. "Bush fire," he told us, tapping the computer awake, entering his biometrics, and opening a file. He turned the screen so we could all see that satellite image of a stretch of bright orange against an almost black backdrop.

"Grandmother Sybil!" I shrieked. "The village!"

Spyder caught my gaze and held. I felt the calm and steady of his being seep into my bones and relax me like the warm, leaf-strewn waters of my bridal bath. "The winds are northeast. They blow away from the village."

I was able to breathe again. I offered a nod.

"This fire was not raging when I received the distress call. This is new and sudden. It is without explanation from those who are watching this area. There is no lightning. There is no sun burning the dried grasses. Fires do not start on a whim in the night. And they do not start at an abrupt length."

Spyder pressed a button, and we were looking at a black screen. A moment later, a ribbon unfurled—a length of orange and red.

"Someone poured an accelerant and lit a match," Striker said.

Spyder rapidly typed, and the page was back to the devastation of the fire. “That is the conclusion of our overwatch,” Spyder said. “Rain has begun to fall south of us. The storm should move into the area soon with enough vigor to put these flames out. Here, we are less than a mile from the fire that crept along the dried grasses.” Spyder pointed out the small green box very close to the edge of light.

Spyder turned my way. “I understand that you went into the Indigo files to perform a search.”

“Yes, sir.” My brows drew in tightly.

“Galaxy indicates that one of the tasks you found answered the question of where Striker goes after his wedding.”

This was after his wedding.

Shit!

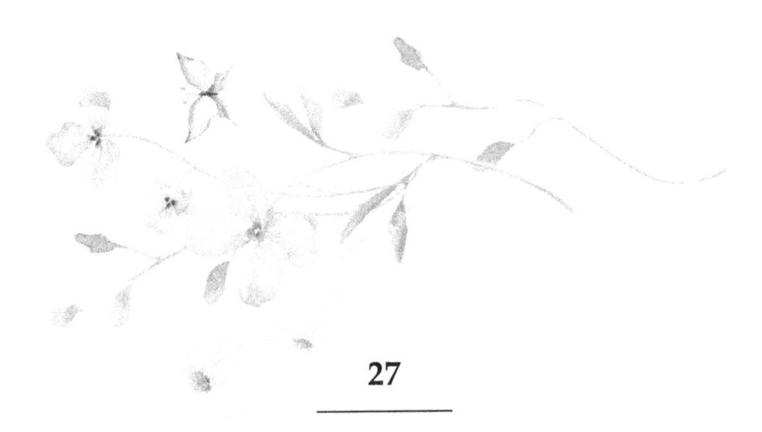

27

"May I see Indigo's rendering of the alien?" Spyder asked.

I patted my leg to find my phone, and of course, it wasn't there.

Pressing the latch on my safety belt, I freed myself to turn. Up on my knees, I reached into the cargo area, dragging my ruck to me. I hadn't packed it and held my breath, hoping my tablet hadn't been accidentally left out. But there it was, safely stashed near the top.

I flung myself back around, pressing the silver ON button and waiting impatiently for it to boot up.

"There are three iterations from Indigo," I explained. "This is the first I came across. The blob with the smile." I swiped. "Here is the alien and the queen." I swiped again. "And this one." I showed him the task that had a spider dangling from a helicopter in the third attempt. "He did the search using the tasking code of the last and asking for more information."

Spyder took the screen from me, scrutinizing each image, opening this section wider, then another. He scrolled to the bottom right of the iteration that included the spider and the helicopter. "What is this here, G. 15:17?"

"Indigo didn't mention the numbers in the session notes," I told him. "I speculated that perhaps it was a time stamp. It had nothing to do with the date or time when Indigo undertook the task."

Spyder rubbed his chin. His eyes had a faraway look as if he were searching through his vast files of information. "Hold this, please." He handed the tablet to Striker as he positioned his computer back on his lap. "I'm accessing the Iniquus AI system." The system could cull through an enormous trove of data in mere seconds.

With a tap of the button, the screen began to populate.

Spyder swiped his finger over the screen, the data flying by as his eyes scanned.

Suddenly, he stopped and read, "'Genesis 15:17 It came to pass that, when the sun went down, and it was dark, behold, a smoking furnace and a flaming torch passed between these pieces'." He gave me a raised brow look of significance. "Perhaps the object in the woman's hand is a torch and not, in fact, a vibrator."

"Hey, I wasn't the only one to think that. Striker thought it was a dildo."

"I said a magic wand," Striker said with a laugh that ended in a cough. The smoke was getting thicker.

"Okay, you two," I scolded. "What are we doing here? The line of fire, at least the smoke, is getting thicker. Spyder, will you check again on the weather systems and Grandmother Sybil."

Spyder did as I asked. "The rain is approaching in about a half hour. It is perhaps lighter than we wish for the fire and harder than we would wish for the rescue. The fire is not moving toward the village. It is, in fact, tracing along the edge of the road and heading in our direction, though the breeze blows very gently away from us. Since there are no trees in this area, all is well unless the sparks fly and ignite the dry grasses across the barrier."

"Can we please drive away from the fire?" I asked.

A tickle of fear raced up my spine. I lifted my head, holding my breath, trying to see if there was a sense of heebie-jeebies or a *knowing* to edify this moment. I had nothing other than the icy finger painting along my spine. Had I lost my psychic skills in the surgery?

That thought left me awash in terror. Would I wish a sixth sense on anyone? No. But it was a sense I had used all my life. And I'd imagine that losing it would affect everything about how I moved through life, just as anyone else who lost the sense of taste or smell during the pandemic.

Spyder reached out and covered my hand. He must have seen something in my face that made him want to offer comfort. Spyder's touch was always a balm.

But frankly, this wasn't the time to assuage my fears with a kind pat. Not with a fire roaring toward us.

He put the rover into gear, and once again, we were heading up the road.

"What did you see in the picture," I asked, knowing Spyder and Striker could hear me over the helmet communication system.

"The trick is to find what changed from one iteration to the next," Spyder said. "What was the constant?"

"The shape of the blob," I said.

"What changed?" Spyder asked.

"In the first, the blob smiled. The smile was a sliver in the next, and it had opened its eyes."

"And you say this because?" Spyder asked.

"That's what Indigo said," I replied. "He was there in the ether, not me. I haven't reached any conclusion."

"The alien blob happens to be the same shape as Lake Victoria," Spyder said. "Almost exactly."

I moved my shoulder belt out of the way and leaned onto the back of Striker's seat to look at the blob in that context. "If this is Lake Victoria, the smile resembles a boat in the first iteration. Given the size of the blob and the size of the smile, it's a large boat." I swiped to the next iteration. "If we assume it's a boat, then there's a queen in the water. And the boat is a sliver. It could mean that the boat sank. And, of course, the queen could refer to the name of the lake. Indigo drew the queen wearing a hoop skirt, the style that Queen Victoria would have—"

Spyder let me have a moment while my brain churned, then quietly asked, "What was that thought, Lexicon."

"I was remembering something historical."

"Yes?" he asked.

"Are we getting closer to where we need to go?" I turned to look over my shoulder as the fire closed the distance. We could only go so fast until we reached the highway. A fire can travel almost fifteen miles per hour. A human can't outrun it.

"We have time to hear your history lesson." As I turned forward again, I caught a flash of Spyder's smile.

"Okay." I pulled my T-shirt over my mouth and nose. "Striker, just so you know, I'm going to ramble about Queen Victoria because I'm anxious, and it makes me feel better. And, of course, if I don't start rambling before Spyder senses my unease, he'll assign me some quote to interpret in light of the present circumstances. Won't you Spyder?"

"This is the correct course of action, Lexicon. It allows the brain to be at ease. When it is held taut, a muscle becomes stiff and inflexible, and any useful technique that can allow you to remain in the flow of the event is welcome."

"Fine. When Queen Victoria reigned, there was a theory that it was bad for men to ejaculate. They were cautioned against having sex except for procreation and warned that masturbation drained the body of energy." I thought of the vigor tea that Striker had drunk down at our morning wedding and that it had given him the stamina to continue for almost twenty-four hours. Granted, I was a little sore from our playtime, but it didn't look to me like it had diminished Striker's energy. "Yeah, the men were made to think that sex, even in their marriages, needed to be rationed, or they would lose their faculties."

"Just so you know, Lexi," Striker said with that drop-my-panties smile of his, "that wouldn't have any effect on us. I'd happily render myself catatonic to be with you."

"Aaaaaand, Spyder is listening."

"I'm sure Spyder wants you to be happy."

"I am," I said. "Blissful. Which leads me to the next part of that history lesson. "There was an inventor at the time. His name was Dr. Joseph Mortimer Grandville. He invented something he called Granville's Hammer. The goal of the hammer was to treat muscle spasms. Okay, now back to the men that were afraid to orgasm. If the men weren't putting out, the women weren't getting any. The ladies at that time were extra grumpy. And angry. The male medical establishment called this 'female hysteria.' And I don't know who or how the women discovered they could use 'Grandville's Hammer' to get some relief, but they did. And Grandville was pretty ticked that that's what his machine was used for, getting women off."

"Where did you get that factoid?" Striker asked.

"My mentor, Chablis. She did a lot of research to make sure her clients were satisfied with her work."

"Lexicon, go back to the vibrator. I wish to know beyond you believing that it is a vibrator, and that is a story you know, did Queen Victoria use one? Could it help to establish the image of the queen as a symbol for the name?"

Could Spyder think it was a person? Maybe in a ball gown on a party ship?

"That," I said, "I don't know. But I do know a bit about Queen Victoria's history that would lead me to believe that she very well might have. After her 9th child, the doctors advised her not to have any more. And she was upset that she wouldn't be able to have sex anymore. Did she turn to a vibrator and non-penetrative sex? Maybe."

"The Hammer sounds aggressive," Striker said.

"I'm stuck on the eyes in the water." I leaned in to look at the tablet. "They have eyelashes and eyelids. Suppose that was a boat on Lake

Victoria. Then that's what we're doing right now? Pulling people out of the lake? And if JSOC needs American operators in the water pulling them out, they aren't just anybody's eyes. They are eyes that are significant to the United States government. And so the phrase comes to me, '*I spy with my little eye.*' And I will guess that there are intelligence sources that were attacked and are in the water, and we have to get there and get them out before anyone else does. And now that I say that and think about this terrible smoke and fire, it can serve two purposes."

"Exactly, Lexicon, continue with that thought."

"They wanted to make sure that if the spies were swimming to shore, they couldn't get out of the lake. And if the boat radioed for assistance, that rescuers could not get into the lake to save them."

"From the time the fire sparked on the satellite image," Spyder said, "I calculate the fire was set just before a good swimmer could reach shore. By not setting it when the ship was hit, it assured that the flames had not consumed the vegetation."

"Hit?" Striker asked.

"Our target seems to think that it was a water drone."

I coughed to rid my lungs of the smoke. "If that's true, Spyder, we're going in the wrong direction. What's your plan? How are we going to get there in time?"

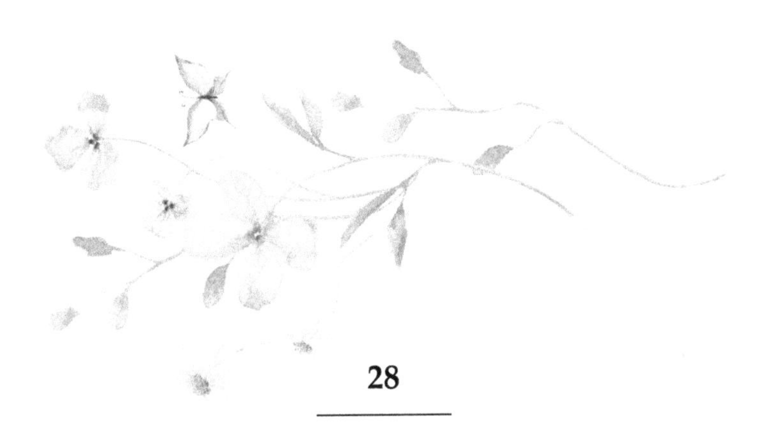

28

Beside the road, the margin of land was now slender enough that I could see the lake to our left.

Spyder was scanning along the shore.

"That would mean they wanted the spies to drown. They weren't interested in capturing them. Right?" I asked.

"Not—" Without finishing that thought, Spyder stopped the car, using the steering wheel to pull himself up a bit higher, snapping his night vision goggles down over his eyes. He blinked the headlights twice, signaling someone.

A congress of baboons ran out of a billow of smoke. The babies clung to their mothers' backs.

I pulled my helmet from my head, and now, I could hear the roar of the fire and the terrified screams of the wildlife.

"Sit down!" I yelled. "Sit down! We need to get further down the road."

A spark riding the wind landed on Spyder's shirt collar. I beat it out, and it left a hole.

I swung my head to the back of our rover, where a twenty-gallon plastic gas tanks were strapped to the tailgate, and grimaced.

"Striker, the gas?"

Striker leaned in and checked the gauge. His mouth moved, but the wind whipped his voice away. The best I could make out, Striker was suggesting we put what gas we could into the tank and drop the rest. But I could be making that up.

I reached for my helmet to pull it back in place to use the comms, when Spyder jumped from the car. In one fluid motion, he was racing down to the lake.

I pulled my field glasses from the front of my pack to watch. There, he spoke with a man. Spyder's gestures were broad, but I couldn't tell what was happening. Cupping my hands over my mouth, I shouted toward Striker, "Do you think he's asking if he's seen any bodies washing up?"

Striker put his lips near my ear, his words tickling along his exhale. "The lake is full of crocodiles, Chica."

"You don't think the bodies will be recovered?" I pulled my clothing cube from my bag and tugged out three T-shirts. I handed one to Striker and tied the other one around my mouth and nose. The third, I reserved for Spyder when he returned.

"Chica, there are hippos and crocodiles. Both threats lead to horrific ends."

"Why would the people on shore set the fire if there are crocodiles?

"Someone could get lucky," Striker said.

Spyder arrived at the vehicle. Wordlessly, he climbed back in and rolled the car slowly along the roadway. He jerked to a stop, put us in reverse, and made a sharp turn toward the water.

There stood a man waving us forward.

I squinted against the burning acidity of the smoke.

I wasn't worried about Spyder being able to follow the man's gestures. He was wearing fusion vision goggles. I was worried that we were in the grasses now, and the tires rolled over burning patches.

The rover climbed the rocks. The wheel skated to the left, and we shifted to a crazy angle. Striker gripped the roll bars to hold his weight away from the door as the vehicle came up on a shimmying, wiggling, two-wheeled balance.

I cinched my seatbelt that much tighter. Did I know if that was the right move or not? No. No, I had never trained to roll in a car, let alone one without sides or a top. I flung my body to the left as far as possible, trying to add my weight to Spyder's to counter Striker's size.

Finally, we flopped back on four tires.

With deft movements of feet and hands, Spyder maneuvered the vehicle into a recess surrounded on three sides by rock and ahead of us water and a boat.

"Grab everything of technical value. Water. Food. Leave everything else."

Spyder had always taught me to pack in labeled cubes, clothing, climbing gear, wash gear, and so on.

Spyder said technical gear comes with us. Okay, computer and tablet, I wrapped those into a dry bag along with a charging brick and quickly rolled and fastened the top. I slid my phone into the SCUBA lanyard that Iniquus used. The rule was that if you were an Iniquus operator, you could never be more than an arm's length from your phone. And that meant when you were swimming as well. Of course, out here, it wasn't much help with zero bars.

I grabbed the extra battery. We were obviously going onto the lake, and I had no idea how long we would be there.

First aid kit. Two MREs. My camelback filled with water.

I also grabbed my water straw with the UV super-duper germ-killer light. I slid it into my phone lanyard to keep it close. Air was most important to survival. Shelter and drinkable water stood side by side on the second-place podium. Food and medicine, third. Push comes to shove, we could sip water right from the lake and not die a horribly agonizing death from giardia or E.coli.

I threw my lightened pack over my shoulders and leaped from rock to rock.

Striker caught my hand as I windmilled for balance.

With food in his hands, Spyder walked down to the man. After the man accepted Spyder's food, Spyder pulled out his wallet and counted a stack of brightly colored shilling notes into the expectant palm.

The man, in turn, gave Spyder what I guessed was a set of keys. They shook hands.

Then the man went to sit on the rock to eat the food. Smoke and wild brush fire be damned.

I followed Spyder and Striker down to the shore.

With his hands on my waist, Striker jumped me the last little bit. There was a narrow ridge between the bank and the shore.

The boat was a distance into the water.

"Boat" might be a spectacularly optimistic name for what was in front of me. Not in terms of size—it was quite large and could probably hold more than ten maybe fifteen people—it was the condition. If ten people clambered on, would it stay afloat?

There was no pier to tie it to. A long extension ladder was roped to one of the boat cleats, and the other end rested on a boulder—shoulder height to me, but even with the deck on the craft.

With his backpack in place, Spyder seemed to float up onto the ladder.

He reached an arm down to me.

Spyder plucked me up like a child taking a flower from the garden.

Spyder's muscles were made of steel. His limbs were so long and thin, he looked as if a breeze could blow by and trip him. Though I've experienced the weird belly-dropping sensation of his doing this to me before, it had been a while, and it took me a second to gain my balance.

One foot on either side of the ladder, I took my first tentative step.

The ladder shifted up and down as the gentle waves bobbled the boat on the water. And there were things in that water that I'd rather not encounter, thank you very much. I carefully bent in two, reaching out and grabbing a rung, then bear crawled to the boat.

Finally, I scampered onboard and looked around while Spyder, agile and graceful, made his way forward without needing to stick his butt in the air.

Still on the shore, Striker lifted and shoved the ladder into the air and forward until he stood at the water's edge.

It was still dark out. I only knew what Gator taught me about gators. They liked to hunt at night and at dawn. They'd submerge at the shoreline and wait for something to come down to drink, and then it would drag them under the water and spin and spin until the quarry was dead. The alligator wouldn't eat right away; it would drag the carcass to a log in the water and stuff it underneath, leaving his supper until it rotted. That's when the alligator liked to eat it.

I gave a whole-body shudder, and both Spyder and Striker looked my way. I knew they were afraid I'd picked up something on my psychic network.

But still, my psychic network was oddly silent.

"Just thinking about alligators," I called. "How about we get you on the boat?"

"Working on it," Striker called back.

With Spyder pressing down on the ladder to keep it parallel to the shore, Striker did a kind of monkey bar climb underneath. He threw his legs over the side of the boat. Very quickly, he collapsed the lengths and laid the ladder along the port side. Striker stood and surveyed his new environment. "What's the plan?"

29

"Should I captain the boat, Spyder?" Striker asked as he secured the ladder.

I walked the boat, wondering if I thought it was sound enough to ride. Obviously, Spyder had put some action plan into effect, and that guy had been waiting for us. Surely, Spyder made that transaction sight unseen. And normally, I was fine with water. But here, there were animals that were just fine chomping on a human, and we were heading toward the fire-ringed shore, so there would be no respite to be found if this thing went down and we had to swim for the shoreline.

"Yes, I need to work with Lexicon," Spyder said. "Steer us as quickly as possible to the northwest," Spyder responded. "Lexicon and I will study the picture that Indigo drew and plot our course."

Lexicon had been in a state of utter bliss after spending the last twenty-four hours in bed orgasming, sleeping, and then waking to have another tumble. *Lexicon's* mind was dopamine mush.

My adrenaline rallied me, but that didn't mean I was on my A-game.

This was a lot.

The anchor up, with Striker at the wheel, I listened to the motor sputter and hiccough, and that didn't allay my concerns. With no chairs on board, I peeked under the lid of a wooden crate, and finding only coils of rope, I fastened the clasp again and sat cross-legged on top.

Along the shoreline to my left was a surreal orange and yellow landscape that licked out from billows of gray and black.

Flocks of birds flapped frantically above.

I tugged my tablet from my pack, checking the battery. Better to turn it off again as soon as possible. Swiping the screen, I pulled up the alien picture of what Indigo drew and tried to imagine it as a map. I covered the helicopter with my hand. We had no helicopter. Was that important?

Without the helicopter, the spider dangling from the top made no sense except that he descended straight over the queen.

Spyder swung onto the rigging box beside me; his computer was open in his hands. "If you would," Spyder said, taking the tablet from my hand, holding it in front of his computer screen, and tapping a button.

He handed my tablet back, and I pressed the button to turn it off and save power as I watched the computer screen wriggle and adjust until the outline of the lake corresponded almost perfectly with the symmetry of the blob.

"That is uncanny." Eerie, really. Goose bumps prickled my skin.

Spyder circled each of the eyes in the water with the top of a pen but drew the one around the queen thicker. "She is our priority."

The AI began populating the screen with GPS coordinates while I looked over what I could see ahead of us. The water lapped darkly against the bow. The fire gave me a sense of our proximity to the shore. Smoke rode the wind just above my head. My skin was hyper-sensitive to the tiny flicks of water sweeping back on me from our forward momentum and the first droplets of that rain that could stop the blaze.

I focused on the green box representing our boat, inching slowly across Spyder's screen toward the eyes.

"Striker, your speed?" Spyder asked.

As Striker called that out, along with other information from his dials, Spyder entered the data into the computer. In return, Spyder called out a string of GPS numbers so Striker, using his own satellite tactical computer, could head in a precise direction to the specific spot.

"The waiting should not be filled with stress," Spyder said evenly. "It is good to take the time when there is space to do so and contemplate."

"Okay, how about you throw something out there, and let's consider it." He still hadn't told me what this was about—besides not contradicting my speculations about spies in the water.

Spyder crisscrossed his legs and draped his long fingers over the bend of his knee. "'Genesis 15:17 It came to pass that, when the sun went down, and it was dark, behold, a smoking furnace and a flaming torch passed between these pieces'," Spyder recited.

I shook my head. "Speculation."

"Ah, what about Indigo's rendering isn't speculation? I was told of an event that lit the boat on fire. 'Behold, a smoking furnace.' I know that my colleague was going into the water in an attempt to save herself. I am sure she was not the only one to jump from the boat. That would make the queen true, and the eyes in the water would also be true," Spyder said. "It is our task to save them."

"How would you be so sure that the picture of the queen is a person and not the personification of the lake's name?" I asked.

"I was speaking with my colleague on the phone when the explosion took place. She is the reason we act now. Her name is Malkah Weiss. And Malkah just happens to be Hebrew for queen. Or so she tells me."

"Yeah, okay. You're probably right about that. You were on the phone at the break of dawn?"

"A group of international intelligence operatives gathered to celebrate finding a dangerous apparatus, protecting civilization. And they were determined to continue the revelry until they could watch the sunrise together. Malkah, however, called to tell me of something that needed my immediate and direct attention. It was at the point when she was ready to share the details that she found herself in this desperate situation. I gathered what intelligence I could and created this plan so that you and Striker were at a…more convenient moment, that I could ask your assistance."

Had he waited outside for our post-coital murmurs? Yeah, I didn't want to think about that.

Did I want to think about that? I mean, thank you, I guess.

"What could be of such incredible importance that she would call you at zero dark thirty and get you in motion?" My brows raised toward my hairline. "Was there a rogue nuke?"

"There was not. The unfortunate piece is that I had come to Uganda originally to speak with Malkah. We needed a new plan. When the group was celebrating, it was too soon. The apparatus had not been secured, and it rests in dangerous hands."

"But the celebrating spies don't know that?" I asked.

"No."

"So if they were all to be killed at their celebration—"

"As this is above top-secret classification, their death would leave very few with the knowledge of the apparatus's existence," Spyder said, "And only a few of us with skills and contacts to make a difference."

"Your mission is to behead The Hydra. And you're somehow one of the people who is in the know of this above-top-secret designation. You were here to tell them that they shouldn't be celebrating because they had failed, not succeeded? And yet, you were in the village."

"I waited for the cruise to conclude. Happy timing. I discovered that you and Striker would be very close and celebrating your wedding."

"From Galaxy?" I asked, coughing and tugging my T-shirt/smoke mask over my nose and mouth to take a few filtered breaths before removing it again.

"Yes, and thus, I was able to be there to witness the joyous union."

It occurred to me that Striker and I were wed by tribal law. We were a married couple in our hearts. But still, we weren't officially man and wife. We didn't get the paperwork from Grandmother Sybil and her counsel, and we had not yet presented it to the town's courts to make our marriage legally binding. Striker and I were in marital limbo.

"How do you know Malkah?" I exhaled, trying to pull my thoughts away from my personal hurdles and focus on our situation, five years in the making.

Then I heard it, that whisper at the back of my head, "*Birds of a feather flock together, and so do rats and mice.*" In my mind, the birds had good connotations, and the rats and mice had bad connotations, at least as far as this rhyme went. It could well be that the birds were the intelligence community on that boat. And knowing that Spyder was after The Hydra, The Hydra could well be represented by the rats and mice. They, too, could feel celebratory if they had rescued whatever was in play.

"You actuated a plan," I pointed out. "You have satellite intel. We're not out here acting as lone wolves."

"Indeed. I called JSOC. Their resources are required."

"Are they sending in the Teams?"

"This? No, they cannot call attention to the situation in any way. It is indeed fortuitous that we were here and available."

"Well, maybe not as much fortuitous," I countered, "as something that was put in motion five years ago. Are you going to explain this to me? Striker and I are, after all, connected to this. It was foreseen in Indigo's viewings before…well before I got tumbled into the mix."

"First, as to the passage. What do you make of this?" Spyder asked.

"If the reference is to the biblical quote, then I would puzzle it like this: the sun went down as the teams boarded their cruise boat. It was to be a nighttime party. The dark of the moon is lovely for star gazing. On these nights, the lake is at its most opaque. There is little chance that the people could spot an underwater drone and even less chance that they could thwart it. From the picture, it seems there was no time to get lifeboats into the water. Spyder, who exactly is your colleague? What's her affiliation?"

He pulled up a new screen.

And there she was, the woman with a Sephirot tattoo. I was so confused right now. "But, she's—"

"She's what, Lexicon?"

"She's black ops, probably working with the Israeli government," I said.

"And?" There was no challenge, no tip of the head. It was a word that asked for more information, that was all.

"I've had her image come up in a few cases now, just the other day, as a matter of fact. The CIA handed me a video of a party, and then Iniquus Command sent me a file of the party that they labeled different points of view." I blinked at him. "You provided me with that video."

"I did indeed." He gave me a regal nod.

"And before that, she had stumped the CIA when she used the twins as a front."

"You puzzled that case brilliantly for the CIA. That you brought her to the CIA's attention was important. And you followed through, bringing her to the attention of the FBI Joint Task Forces as well."

"Should I not have?" I felt a prickle of apprehension. Had I jammed up some cog in the wheel of international security?

"CIA John Green functions along with that FBI working group. Once you put her, Malkah Weiss, on his screen, he told John Black. John Black was in the room where you told the story of Gouverneur Morris's wayward passions."

"Black told you that?"

"He did." Spyder chuckled. "And," Spyder tapped my knee with his finger, "he said you were correct about everything that you said in that meeting. As Malkah is part of a covert group, it is within the CIA's purview to track her operations to see what is causing her concern. In nature, when a dying animal is on the plains, the vultures gather and circle. Predators watch the sky for these circles and track out to find the dying animal. The predators make the kill but do not eat all of the meat. They leave some for the birds that circled, bringing their attention to the nourishing meal. They work symbiotically. Without the predators, it would be difficult for the birds of prey to rip open the carcass."

"The dying animal in this metaphor is the bad thing that is happening?" I asked.

"It is."

"Then the vultures and predators are simply two different government entities. But Spyder, you obviously have an easy phone connection. Why didn't you just call up Black and Green and say, Vulture Malkah is circling?"

"It was my aim for you to discover the information," Spyder said, "and be the vehicle by which they learned of it. The right people would hear and act, those with disdain for the people whom they deem inferior by age and gender would disregard. And this is how I wished it."

"You could have told me," I ventured.

"No. As to hand you the answer would not have served you. I wished you to observe Malkah in action and study her as she is one of the greats in the spy world. Very few know what she really is."

I dropped my voice to a whisper. "I told the FBI Joint Task Force, Damian Prescott."

"Rowan Kennedy is on their team, and he works hand in hand with Green. Finley, too, is on that team, and his wife is working on the same questions, only from a different angle. Tell me, Lexicon, what do you know of Malkah's tattoo?"

"Little. I know that it is similar to an iconic symbol. I know that they, as a group, seem to have different spokes. Things that people are interested in. I know one of those spokes has to do with DARPA scientists."

"Not just DARPA scientists and not just *any* scientists. What specifically do you think this group is doing?"

"Thwarting apocalyptic machines of destruction, apparently."

"Exactly so. And they are not doing so with our country's best interest at heart. They focus on their own country's survival. And they will act in their country's best interest. They are our allies—until they are not."

"Yes, sir. And you needed the CIA to be aware of this party and that she was there. Casper doesn't know who she is."

"Black does. Green does," Spyder said. "Casper is of no significance to this scenario."

"But that's not what you do. You are not focused on means science as a destructive force. Your focus is on The Hydra."

"Even so."

"Is Omega involved in this?"

"One assumes. I am going after Sylanos' Cartel. And as it turns out, you may well be correct. I may be going after Sylanos himself."

I jutted forward, my hand easily reaching around to grip the incredibly thin bones above his wrist. That gesture was accepted only because he loved me. Had anyone else tried such a move, they would quickly discover their mistake.

"There is fear in your touch," Spyder said.

"Galaxy said that they had done a task for you. My niece, Cammy, drew what had been tasked. If that is Sylanos, you are in danger."

Spyder's chuckle was deep and warm. "You love me," he said, a smile still on his lips. "I know this because you see a picture and you imagine the possibility of harm coming to me, and it upsets you. Yours is but one interpretation of such a picture."

"What do you see?" I asked.

"A thread that I hoped to unravel."

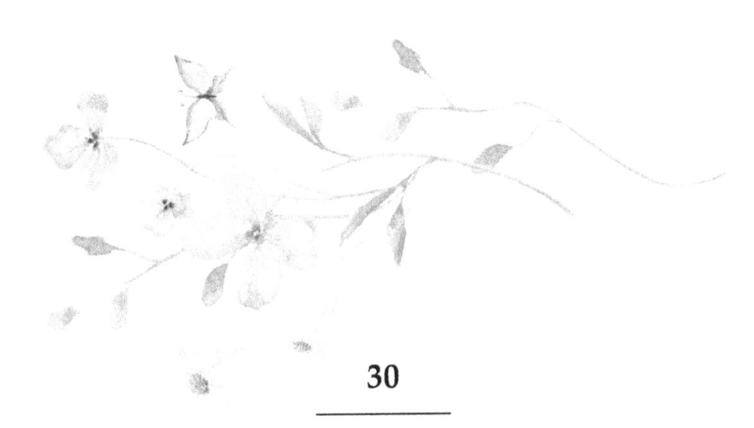

30

"FIFTEEN-MINUTE ETA TO PRIORITIZED LOCATION," STRIKER called out.

"Fifteen." Spyder and I lifted our voices so Striker knew we had both heard the information.

As I looked out over the water, the sky had lightened enough for me to see the waves rippling out from the boat as we moved faster than I had thought possible, given the sounds of the motor. We were too far from land to see anything but what looked like an alien sunrise. But then again, I had alien blobs on my mind.

And Arya.

Malkah had worked with my friend Dr. Arya Khouri as a scientist or pretending to be a scientist. The Sephirot folks as vultures seem to circle the scientific community associated with DARPA and science that was adjacent to war, like Sophia Abadi's attempt to use satellites to protect Syrian artifacts.

"How did you come across Malkah?" I asked. "Is she breaking laws in America?"

"She is not. She is going after Sylanos, as am I."

"She thinks he's alive?"

"We do not know this. We know his cartel is alive. I do believe that I will have the answer in the next day. Once I speak to a colleague, I plan to meet in Djibouti about Marcos Sylanos' present state of being."

"Someone I know?" I asked. "Another Sephirot?"

"As this is need to know, I will determine whether you need to know as we progress."

"Yes, sir. But the Sephirot are targeting DARPA scientists."

"Target? They do not wish to kill the scientists. They wish, as do all sane beings, to make sure that the science doesn't fall into the hands of those who would use the information to harm mankind."

"I'm not sure about that, Spyder." Yeah, this didn't sit right. I had too many dealings with this group to just nod at my mentor and deem his knowledge superior to mine. "They tried to kidnap my friend Zoe."

"Zoe, I will remind you, was being pressured to act unethically."

"She refused." I didn't want Spyder to defend the Sephirot. I wanted him to be on the side of my friends.

"The Sephirot, as you call them, needed her to be removed from that pressure," Spyder said simply. "Her work was entirely too close to completion, with very dire consequences."

"I guess." Okay, that was true. Though was kidnapping necessary? "What about my friend Arya when she was in France?" That whole thing with the grey lady always made me think of the Sephirot crew. I had no evidence to back it up other than my gut. And as I thought that, I heard, again, "*Birds of a feather flock together*" at the back of my head.

"The Russians were very keen to get their hands on Arya. Arya had been forced to work for them and had escaped. They kidnapped her a second time, she escaped. She needed medical help. Israel wanted to make sure there wasn't a third attempt."

A confirmation: Spyder knew exactly what I was talking about, and he knew that the grey lady was associated with Malkah. "Kidnapping, Spyder. She's an *American* citizen."

"It is probable that this working group had more information than you did at the time. Perhaps they did not wish the breadth and depth of the studies Arya undertook under scientific duress be known to the greater world."

"*Kidnapping?*" I shrilled, completely incensed.

"Protective custody, perhaps."

I could feel anger bloom in my chest. What my friend had been through was horrific. "Why are you defending their behavior?"

"Because it is the behavior of governments worldwide. Each tries to protect their citizens to the best of their ability. Sometimes, we are able to support each other's efforts, and sometimes, our efforts are in opposition. But as we pull Malkah from this lake, which I fervently hope is a happy outcome, you will see her tattoo and know who she is. I do not wish for Malkah to be treated as the enemy. At this moment, she is working with me. We are allied. How you treat her is how you would treat me."

"Yes, sir." I took a breath. Yeah, I wasn't sure I was up to live and let live in this moment. I really didn't think I would be able to do what Spyder was asking of me. "But was Malkah in France when the Sephirot went after Arya? Was an intelligence hit called against my friend? Did Panther Force thwart her assassination?"

"Giving Arya a safe place in which to regain her health was the goal," Spyder said evenly. "And also offering time for Arya to regain her memories. When Arya was kidnapped, it was because of a grant that she wanted from NASA."

"NASA. My team speculated that it had to do with the Navy because of the whales. But I know about the NASA thing. Arya had just told me about this on my last visit. Her sisters had looked through old photos Arya had sent to the family prior to her disappearance before her kidnappers used medication to wipe her memory and perform their experiments. Arya used those pictures in her therapy sessions to rebuild a basic understanding of her past."

"And?" Spyder asked.

"One of those pictures included Malkah. And that association filled me with dread. I'd held it up to her. 'Tell me about this one.' I'd smiled, but my gut had clenched."

"Go on."

"She said, 'Yes, it's very interesting. At the UN, I presented a piece of sound science I had been working on. There is a tone that I could create in the lab that puts mice into hibernate sleep. And they stayed that way until I stopped playing the sound. Thinking about it now, I believe that this could be a tool to help humanity.'"

Oh shit. I had thought this was bad during my conversation with Arya, just as I thought it now.

I had the same physical reaction—my chest tightened protectively around my heart. It was almost impossible for me to take a breath. "I told Arya that I wasn't following what she was trying to say. I'd smiled to keep her talking."

Spyder gave me a nod, telling me to continue.

I thought back to that scene. Yes, Malkah in that picture, though shorter and softer, reminded me of the gray lady who had tried to snatch Arya from Iniquus's hands. "Arya said, 'Let's take NASA, for example. They want to try to put a colony on Mars. It'll take the astronauts decades to get there.' Now, this surprised me because, as far as I knew, Arya had been working with subsonic sounds of whales and elephants, but I guess this was something she found during that research. Personally, I agree. It would be an easier task if, much of the time, the Mars-bound astronauts were asleep. Then she said that she had thought of terrestrial uses of human hibernation. She mentioned climate change, famine, and pandemics. And I guess I can see how it might be easier to cycle the population so that half of humanity sleeps and half works, and then they switch. Or to let people sleep through the event if they live in an affected area. It's the stuff of science fiction. But science fiction is imagined into a novel, and a scientific mind sees the possibility and acts on it, bringing it from fiction into reality. Hopefully, they will find ways to solve problems. And, I guess, making sure that evil minds don't exploit that technology, right?"

Knowing that the research Arya had been forced to conduct while held hostage was in the hands of Russia and used for riot control, I hoped the experiment with hibernation-inducing sound had proved fruitless. But who knew? "Questioning Arya further, she said she'd not made advances beyond the mice. It would take NASA-like funding and many years to make those sound waves at all useful." She had sounded confident, and I had let it go.

"And I see that you are applying that information to the present scenario, and now you understand the importance of this mission."

"A hibernation machine?" I shook my head. Nope, I could not wrap my head around this concept playing out in the present time. Nope, my grey matter wasn't that elastic. And yet, that picture at the UN just before Arya's abduction was five years ago.

The picture of the tree rings was right there, front and center in my mind's eye.

"If everyone in an area has gone into a hibernate state, the Russians could just walk in. Take kill shots," I said. "Take the equipment, food, and supplies and walk on out. Get some sleep and move on to the next area. It's the same outcome as that red blood cell explosion weapon George Matthews developed in a Montrim Industries lab. That hadn't succeeded. *Yet.* Was the hibernation sound wave a thing? "They can clear whole swathes of land that way. Those would be war crimes." I sucked in a shaky breath. "What have they done that wasn't a war crime?"

"Sound technology in and of itself isn't in the treaties," Spyder added. "Our treaties are not keeping up with the speed of innovation."

That makes the Russian riot suppression noise stuff look like child's play.

Striker cut the engine. "We're within range, Spyder. I'd use the night vision goggles and see if you can't find any warm bodies in the water."

31

"Got her," Spyder called out. "She's just to our left. Slowly, Striker. Slowly. Okay, there, kill the engine."

I wasn't helpful leaning over the railing, staring at the woman, clinging to what might be a side table. I tried to find ways to be proactive. I moved our equipment to the helm to avoid the risk of an accident.

Striker untied the ladder. I had wondered how they'd get her out. That made the most sense to me. I looked through the cabin for anything that would help. If Malkah was the first of about two dozen, where would we put everyone?

The rain beat down harder.

I draped a tarp, forming a make-do shelter to tend to Malkah after she was onboard. I needed to get her as dry as possible as quickly as possible.

How long had they been in the lake? Hours. How hypothermic would they be?

There was no way to heat them. I formed a plan. Wet clothes off and then under the tarp? Get them to shore as quickly as possible.

A hospital was too far away. Possibly we could find a town. Houses. People with generous hearts. But how would we get the people from the boat to respite? They had to be exhausted just keeping their heads above water. Fear sapped energy, and as I watched Spyder climbing down the ladder into the water, he, too, was in danger of his splashes calling in hungry predators.

Malkah, Spyder said, was the priority.

I wish I had brought my whole pack. The non-essential clothes cube sure would come in handy right now.

My first aid kit was bare bones minimal. I was prepared for blisters, scrapes, possibly a headache. I pulled out the mylar emergency blanket. I only had the one.

As I dug through Striker's bag to grab his first aid kit, his was tactical, so I found trauma sheers. He had a single mylar blanket.

I thought I'd look through Spyder's pack in a second, shoving the things in my thigh pocket to free my hands.

Striker had rigged some kind of ladder support out of thin air. Still, his biceps bulged as he seemed to take the whole weight of Spyder and Malkah.

It was, indeed, Malkah. I had studied her face for hours.

She looked like a drowned rat. She didn't seem to be conscious. Spyder maneuvered rung by rung. He'd pulled her hands over his shoulders and trapped her wrists between his fingers, and he pulled down, keeping her elbows locked out and her draping down his back. From the water, he probably couldn't get her into a fireman's carry. Or perhaps there was an injury that I couldn't see through the rain.

I was as wet as she was now, and that wind blew cold and sticky with soot.

As she came into reach, I grabbed at Malkah's legs, swinging them onto the boat, grabbing her around the waist, sliding in between her and Spyder to take her weight and let Spyder get on board.

As the wind rose and the rain hammered, the waves rocked us back and forth.

Anything not tied down slipped and slid, including me.

I got Malkah's legs extended out, and then, with my hands under her arms, supporting her head as best I could, I dragged her to the shelter.

Spyder and Striker worked wordlessly on getting the ladder back on the boat. Then Striker was scrambling around to take the wheel.

Things had been dangerous before. The circumstances had turned dire.

It was one thing to cling and float in a placid lake. It was a whole other scenario to do so with white-capped waves and a downpour that meant a wet inhale.

Even if it felt like Spyder and I did little as we were discussing, it was a lull—a time to regroup. Now, we were in the thick of it.

It was time for methodic action.

My headlamp set to a red glow, I cut Malkah's clothes away.

And in her semi-conscious state, she was pushing my hand away. "Spyder," she whispered with her eyes shut and drooping cheeks.

"Spyder found you. I'm his friend Lexi. I'm here to help you. First, we're getting you out of your wet clothes and try to get you a little warmer."

She gave the slightest of nods. "Only for Spyder." Then she passed out.

She had tucked a plastic tube into the waist of her pants. It slid down one of her pants legs. This might be why Spyder couldn't get her into an easier carry to get her up the ladder. Her leg was stiff with it wedged down her pants.

Obviously, she didn't want this lost in the waters.

"I need someone with the NVGs looking," Striker called. "I should be coming up on two heads about twenty yards apart."

I wrapped her in one of the mylar blankets. I squeezed her hand. "We have you. We're taking care of you."

STRIKER HAD the ladder in the water. Once again, Spyder was climbing below the smoke line, rising again with someone dangling from his shoulders.

I looked everywhere and gathered everything I could put into play to help them. They wrapped their shivering frames under tarps, anything that would keep the wind from wicking their heat away—no point in getting their clothes off. The rain still fell.

Striker called out, "I'm on the last GPS coordinate. It's just ahead."

So far, the eyes in the water had been feet, if not yards, from how they'd shown up on the alien map. And that had its own kind of mind-freak energy. I knew this was a thing, but when you see it play out in reality, yeah. It was a lot.

"There is another boat, which has reached them first." Spyder was leaning over the rail. He called out to the captain of the motorboat in a foreign language. The man responded with what sounded like a negative. Spyder began cycling through languages until he landed on one the man could understand.

The motorboat drew next to ours, with one survivor shivering on the floorboards.

It seemed to me that Spyder was haggling. He pulled out his wallet and waved it in the air.

Was he trying to buy the spy lying at the bottom of the boat or the boat itself?

The captain seemed dubious and excited as if he could not trust his luck.

Spyder turned to me. "Gather our things. Everything."

Without thought or hesitation, I did as told.

The man who curved over in the bottom of the motorboat looked like the effort of sitting upright was beyond his capacity and seemed nervous about the exchange. Spyder called, "We are lifting you onto this boat. We have about two dozen of your friends here. Your captain will take all of you across the lake to Tanzania in this boat. He has friends in a village who will warm and care for you. You are safe with him. The village is only thirty minutes by water."

Tanzania seemed to make the shivering man feel better. He raised his head ever so slightly and nodded.

The ladder lowered, and the captain helped the victim to climb.

Striker was gathering our things as I helped the newest arrival find a place and settled under a cover.

Spyder opened his wallet, pulling out a handful of shillings. He pointed to the heavens and seemed to remind the captain that he was being watched.

The man bowed. And I felt deep in my soul that this man was there to do good.

When Spyder paid him the money, the captain stared at it as if stunned.

Without another moment of hesitation, Spyder bent and lifted Malkah over his shoulders and climbed back down the ladder to the motorboat. "Come! Bring our things," he called. His words reaching my ear were wet and sloshy.

As we motored back toward where we'd left the rover, Malkah curled in the bottom of the new boat, wrapped in her Mylar emergency blanket and a plastic tarp.

I showed the plastic container to Spyder. "She had this in her pants and said it's only for you."

"I'll attend to it when we are out of this deluge," he called over the noise of the torrent and the motor. "Malkah cannot go to a hospital anywhere near here. They will be looking for her in particular. I have come to the conclusion over the last hour that the attack was focused on her. She is the torch. She was the focal point in the picture. Everything else was external to her. We must keep her safe."

Striker was in full SEAL mode.

"Striker, use your compass to aim toward your rover outside of the village. You must navigate us as close as possible."

"But—" I started.

"Lexicon." I had never heard that warning tone from Spyder

before. “Next, you and Striker will drive to where I left my car. Malkah and I will meet you there. Once you get there, we must formulate a plan. With the weather, we will not have a satellite connection. And even what small assistance we could get from JSOC, now we are on our own.”

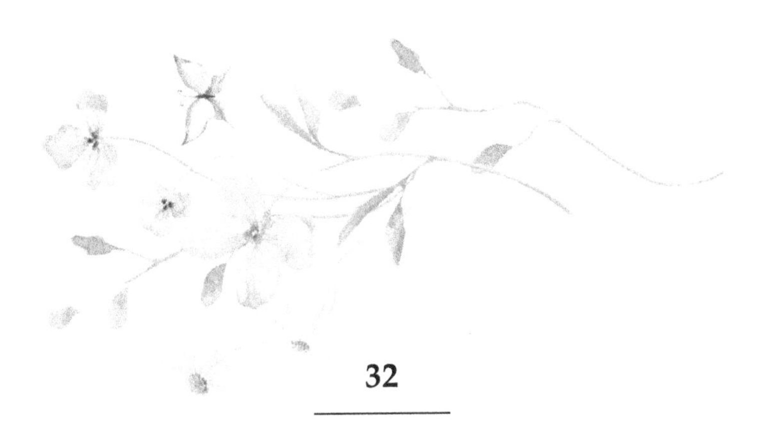

32

I PERCHED ON A ROCK, HIDING BEHIND THE WIDE BREADTH OF A TREE by the side of the road. On the boulder beside me, our packs and the electronics equipment rested. I was grateful for their waterproof material and sealed seams.

Spyder was right to have us take everything with us.

If authorities stopped him, Spyder was just a man in a motorboat who saved a drowning woman.

Striker was right to leave me here with the packs.

Without their weight and without me slowing his sprint, he could get to the rover and back much faster.

We both agreed that Malkah was in dire straits.

The rain had stopped. That was a blessing. There hadn't been any rain in Indigo's picture, no fire, no choppy waters.

But everything Indigo had drawn was accurate, and while I could despise the man, I could also feel appreciation for his talent. The eyeball map had helped us save almost two dozen souls.

Nope. That was wrong. The lake was there. The eyes were there. The queen was there—I looked down at the tube she had saved—the vibrator-looking thing was there. And the proportion was correct. In the picture, it was shaped like a dildo that was about the same length as the queen's arm. The shape, except for the cylinder, was off. The rest was correct.

The thing that wasn't correct in that picture was the helicopter.

The helicopter had been attached to the spider. I determined it was, therefore, a helper helicopter.

Not a boat. But a helicopter. Directly over the queen.

And there was one person I knew I associated with helicopters and the general area we found ourselves in, Gator's wife, D-Day.

D-Day's father owned a place out here, Davidson something-or-other. It was a fully staffed villa where Daddy Davidson and his buddies retreated from their wives and lives to drink scotch and watch the wildlife roam. What did they call that place? Range. Davidson's Range.

I pulled out Spyder's satellite phone, dialed Iniquus, moved through the codes to prove it was me, and asked them to patch me through to General Thomas. It was a matter of great urgency. I could only speak to him. And if someone had to run into the men's room and hand him the phone while he took a leak, then so be it.

Wow. I just said that. Whew.

"Lexi, I hear you've got your pants on fire." It was absolutely General Thomas's voice crackling over the Iniquus encrypted line.

"Sir, Spyder McGraw reached out to JSOC earlier today. JSOC asked that the three of us intervene."

"Were you successful?"

"I don't know to what extent, sir, we're doing our best. We need help. I need you to specifically do the following. Contact D-Day Rochambeau, who flies with Night Stalkers. Have her call her father's estate in northern Tanzania and tell them that four friends are arriving. One is ill and doing poorly. I believe D-Day is stationed in the vicinity."

"I'm pulling that up. Night Stalker Rochambeau. She's in the Indian Ocean. Northern Tanzania, you said? From the ship, that's an hour and a half. She can't fly a military bird across Tanzania. I'll talk to her. We'll figure it out. Rent her something to fly out of Dar es Salaam. It'll add time. But it makes this doable diplomatically."

"Our window is incredibly short for many reasons, sir. Have her get us at her father's place ASAP. We won't knock on that door. We need her to flash us a green light first. But this is a matter of great urgency. She needs to scramble."

"I'll get those orders issued immediately. Keep me apprised. Out."

STRIKER PULLED up in our tourist rover and helped me pile our bags into the cargo area. It occurred to me that Spyder and I had moved through a great deal of information on the boat, and Striker was in the dark about the players and the stakes. As we drove toward our rallying spot—Spyder's hidden vehicle—I filled him in.

"How far was the village from here?" I asked. "You were gone just over an hour."

"Far. Ten miles? I wasn't sprinting, but I was definitely running at my 'the terrorists are chasing your ass' speed."

Striker's expression was go-mode as we powered down the road toward Spyder.

We, of course, beat Spyder to the site. Traveling by water was farther and slower.

At Spyder's rover, Striker set out a flare in the rocks to signal Spyder in, then worked to crawl the vehicle back over the rocks and onto the road.

Our rover was out of gas.

Striker used the reservoir can to fill Spyder's tank while I made a bed on the back seat for Malkah.

Striker attached the vehicle cover to keep the wind and sun from beating us up as we drove on—hopefully—to Davidson Range. We were all exhausted by the day's events.

When Striker and I heard the motorboat coming, we made our way down to the shore.

"I cannot bring Malkah into Uganda," Spyder called. "I'm going to follow the shore until we are in Tanzania. I need you to go over the Uganda-Tanzanian border in your vehicle to remove you from suspicion of having a hand in the boat debacle. You are returning tourists. Once you are in Tanzania and out of sight of the border guards, set another flare for me."

I handed Spyder a water bottle and a towel that might help Malkah stay warmer.

After Striker and I hid our rover, we jumped into Spyder's vehicle to comply with his commands.

There, on the Tanzanian shore, Striker set out the requested flare so Spyder could find where we had parked. We waited. Trying to find something useful to do, I laid out a towel and dry clothes for Spyder over on the rock to warm, along with an MRE and another bottle of water.

Finally, we heard the churning of an outboard motor and hustled down to the water's edge.

Striker accepted Malkah from Spyder's arms and gently carried her to where we had staged. As she lay in the back of the vehicle, I dried her the best I could. As I dressed her in a set of my warmest clothes, I could see Striker standing by the tree talking to Spyder. I'm sure he was explaining the plans we'd put in motion.

As Spyder pulled his shirt down, he looked over at me. "Fortuitous." He looked back at Striker. "Very well, my concern is that it has to be this exact pilot, not just any military pilot." He scanned the horizon. "Where is your vehicle?"

"We're out of gas," Striker explained. "I calculated the distance, and one vehicle can make the trip from the reserve fuel on Spyder's vehicle. It's about an hour from here."

"Very well." He climbed into the passenger's seat. "We're moving."

Striker was behind the wheel. I was in the back, cradling

Malkah's head in my lap and trying to keep the bump and sway to a minimum as I performed Reiki. We placed warming packs at her groin and under her arms. The heat didn't seem to rouse her. I wasn't sure what was wrong, but something very obviously was.

Our conversation had turned to the logistics of the exfil.

Spyder had turned sideways in his seat as we discussed the situation.

"General Thomas hasn't reached out to us again. He said he was issuing the orders. The Davidson compound should know we're coming, and D-Day is meeting us."

"Certainly not in a US helicopter," Spyder said.

"That, I don't know. Maybe? Maybe she'll rent a plane? Maybe she'll have a copilot or medical support. I just have no idea. I did tell Thomas that there were four of us."

"We won't be able to hide Malkah," Striker said. "She will be seen. We'll need a plausible story."

"The man who is in charge of the home, he is a trusted person?" Spyder asked.

"I only know what D-Day has told me. She keeps her family at arm's length. She would do this as a military order. As to the man in charge of the compound, his tribe is small. And all of them live within the walls of the compound. Gator's in-laws treat them very well. They want for nothing, including medical help and education for their children. I believe that there is a certain pressure laid on his shoulders. He wishes to avert for his people the difficulties experienced by other small tribes. To that end, he will protect the walls and not be looking for trouble, which means I don't think, based on what I know, that he would reach out to anyone and tell them we have an injured woman with us. I wonder if the accident on Lake Victoria made it into the news, which might raise suspicions."

Spyder pulled out his phone and scrolled. "It was a story on several outlets. And they mention spies."

"I've put Malkah in long sleeves, but her tattoo makes her identifiable," I said. "As far as I know, D-Day's only been at Davidson

Range once. But her not visiting might not seem unusual to the staff. It's far out in the bush and treated like a man's—"

Malkah shifted in my lap. Her eyes sprang wide with disorientation.

I soothed my hand over her hair. "I'm Lexi. Here's Spyder."

Her hand moved to her leg, and finding nothing, her whole body quivered.

"I have the cylinder in the back. It's safe." I used the most even, practical-sounding EMT voice that I could effect. The one that told people that things were being handled professionally.

Her eyes sought out Spyder's.

He had released his safety belt and was on his knees, leaning into the back and catching her hand in his.

"Flight 173." Her voice was barely audible. "Babcock was on flight 173 to meet you with the information." She licked her lips. "He can't be found out."

"He won't. I'll help him," Spyder soothed.

That seemed to quiet her. Her eyelids flickered closed, and now she seemed to sleep.

I sent Spyder a look that asked, "Do you know what she's talking about?"

He shook his head in reply, then sat again, pulling his belt back into place.

I dug my phone from my thigh pocket and scrolled to an international news site I liked. It always seemed to have the most up-to-date information. And here it was. "A flight from New Delhi to Austria experienced engine trouble." I abridged the story, pulling out the pertinent details. "They flew south to Magadan, Russia. A small city with an airport big enough for the passenger jet. Sixteen crew, two hundred passengers, many of them are Americans. Yup, they're all stuck in Russia in a "do not travel zone."

I thought of all the US citizens charged with illegalities who were pawns in Russia's posturing toward the West.

I continued, "It's an ongoing problem. That airport is too small to have the kinds of equipment and parts that they need. They're trying to get permission to send a plane to pick up the passengers. So far, that's not going well. Nobody expected to be there, so no visas. Without a visa, they cannot leave the gym where they're housed. The official separated the crew from the passengers, and no one has seen them since the landing." I looked up to catch Spyder's eye. "Do you know who she was talking about? Did I hear correctly? Did she say Babcock? Is it the Babcock I know?"

"Griffin Babcock," Spyder said.

Striker sent a glance toward Spyder. There was tension at the corners of his mouth.

I sniffed in a quick breath.

"Please share that thought with me, Lexicon."

"Nothing, really. It's just that I was thinking about Babcock this week. It seems like a strange convergence of old players all standing up at the same time."

"Once you are in the compound, I am sure the staff has transportation. I will take this vehicle and leave you. It is crucial that I get Babcock out of Russia before they know who he is, and they insist that he share the information he has gathered." Spyder turned to Striker and then back to me. "You should know that Omega is active in this area. It is equally my task to safeguard innocents from the evils of Omega and Sylanos as it is for me to safeguard you, Lexicon. You became the enemy of Indigo, and that might still have ramifications. I wish to make sure that you can live in peace."

"Thank you, sir." I shook my head because I couldn't see how these two lines would necessarily intersect.

"We can understand why The Assembly was a powerful ally to Sylanos and Omega. Why would they align with Indigo?" he asked. Spyder was back in mentor mode.

"Because he influenced them? Because he saw something and extorted them?" I ventured.

"Or it could be simply that he presented them with information again and again about their enemies. Information to The Assembly that turned an election, perhaps. Maybe a number on a piece of paper slipped across a cocktail table with the amount that needed to be bid in order to get a defense contract. Over time, Indigo could use his abilities to convince the other three players that he was not just important but indispensable. Frith as his frontman."

I nodded.

"Now, here's something we know. There was a meeting where The Assembly discussed you. Both you and Herman Trudy attended that meeting in the ether."

"When I was in prison?" Uh-oh.

"Indeed."

"Yes, well, no, I don't remember that meeting. I was sick and hallucinating, leaving my body involuntarily. The story gets a little complicated when you know how all that works with the remote viewers. I understand that because General Elliot had an ongoing case open for me, Herman Trudy was actively looking for me. Because of the emotional pain and violence in the prison where I was held, it worked like the art in Iniquus and was doorknobbing his efforts. Trudy found me for a brief moment and followed my spirit out of my body to where I was, I guess, watching a meeting of The Assembly."

"Did Trudy tell you why your awareness might have gone to that particular meeting?" Striker asked.

"Apparently, they were talking about their remote viewer looking for me. That would have been Indigo working as Trudy's support. Iniquus was trying to find me."

"Just so. From that, you will understand that when I leave your side, Lexicon, it is in an effort to protect you—and yes, myself as well. This is why you have no indication where I am and why you can only contact me under special circumstances."

"But you got my message. Was that all right? I wanted to tell you about the picture of the rat with the tracking collar and that Striker and I were getting married and needed you there."

"'The aim of art is to represent not the outward appearance of things, but their inward significance.' Quite the clever choice of quotes." He smiled. "I, of course, recognized immediately that there was information that needed to be conveyed from Galaxy. But as you did not call me to your side with our code, I believed that because of the global significance of what I am trying to thwart, it would be best that I call Galaxy and find out about Cammy drawing a picture that was the same that Trudy drew as a viewer."

"Spooky, huh?"

"Very interesting, indeed," Spyder said. "Now, back to The Assembly meeting with you and Trudy in the ether. Trudy told me of that meeting. Understand that General Elliot had tasked Trudy with an Above-Top-Secret compartmentalized task of finding you. None of that information was, therefore, conveyed to me. However, he gave me different information. Information that I personally had tasked, and Trudy was able to gather at that site at that time, in particular the names of the people who attended. Lexicon, I did not know Iniquus was looking for you. A truth that to this day hurts my heart."

I reached out and squeezed Spyder's shoulder. "Everyone did the best they could. Everyone. So go on. There was the group that knew about me. Did that include The Assembly president who suicided?"

"It did." Spyder paused before he added, "And everyone else in that room by one means or another."

"I don't understand," Striker said.

"Everyone in that room," Spyder said clearly, "is now dead."

"Since when?" I whispered.

"Since the president suicided. He was the first of a quick succession."

"Seriously?" Striker asked. "That's…that's outside of the realm of probability."

Spyder gave a slow nod. "I would agree with your assessment."

"You had the names of the people in the meeting and the possibility that they knew of my sixth sense abilities." Oh, my heart was hammering. "You didn't take them out or anything, did you?"

"Very quickly, that concern was removed without my intervention," Spyder said.

"I'm getting the problem. Those high enough in The Assembly to know I had skills are dead. Indigo is dead. But Indigo could well have told Sylanos and possibly the owner at Omega, Dillon Cartwright, about me."

"This is indeed a possibility. And a deep concern of mine. And one of the reasons that I will continue to track down both."

"Thank you, Spyder."

"No need for thanks. However, once again, your story is at an intersection, and this time, that intersection is deadly on a mass scale."

"You're really making me reach for crumbs here," I complained.

"I'm determining how much of this story to say aloud. While you, Striker, and I practice our meditation and keep ourselves strong to prevent intrusions, the air is vulnerable."

"Yes, sir."

"Knowing that Galaxy was militarily trained," Striker said. "You can be sure that other countries did, too. A *specific* other country has retired viewers. I can imagine that they might work diligently to protect themselves and their families by continuing to provide useful information."

"Exactly," Spyder said. "So we do not do or say things which would inform them, as is possible."

For a moment, I considered what I had felt at General Thomas's SCIF. Could that have been a Russian viewer? No, it had a signature energy that was too recognizable.

"When I saw the picture that Cammy drew, I searched the Indigo files to see if there was any further information. Indigo kept asking over and over about Striker's wedding. And he had pictures of bears: a bear sleeping, a bear singing. Bear is often a symbol for Russia. I don't think it's informative in any way. Going back to the flight stalled in Russia, do you think Russia is looking for Babcock for some reason? Do you think the viewers would recognize him and flag someone?"

"Babcock isn't important to Russia. He's important to solving Sylanos and Sylanos's attempt to remain dead."

"And Sylanos' Cartel is providing a great service to Russia," Striker said. "So Russia would have every incentive to help him."

"This is why I must leave you once you've reached shelter," Spyder said. "I must act now to protect Babcock and the information he gathered."

33

Striker drove toward the broad gates that protected the Davidson Range from wild animals. And came to a stop a few yards away under a tree.

"Do we go and knock? Toot the horn?" Striker asked.

"I told General Thomas I needed a green light," I explained. "I suppose that should have been clearer. I'm used to communicating with our team, and they would know that I needed a call with an affirmation that everything was okay."

I looked down at Malkah, sleeping in my lap. Her breath was shallow and labored. Reiki wasn't having the effect I had hoped. It didn't seem to bring her any relief. "I'm not waiting." I unlatched my belt, opened my door, and was about to slip out when a man and a woman emerged from the compound. They walked to the rover with their hands open as if in greeting.

"Jumbo! Mr. Striker and Mrs. Lexi?" I was startled that they would know that I was married, then realized that D-Day would have used my Mrs. Sobado name.

Striker got out of the car. "Jumbo! I see our friend Christen was able to reach you."

"My name is Tumo. I am the caretaker." He gestured to the woman at his side in her brightly patterned dress. "My wife, Nuru."

"Jumbo! Welcome!" she said with a broad smile.

"Our apologies. Mrs. Rochambeau believed she would be able to meet you immediately, but there is a fierce wind on the east coast. She is coming to greet you herself as soon as possible."

"Thank you," Striker said. He glanced back at the car. "We have a friend who has fallen ill."

"I have prepared a room for her," Nuru said. "Please, come."

Striker went around back and pulled out our bags while Spyder moved to the driver's side.

"I love you, Spyder."

"As I love both of you. Get her safely to Djibouti. I am depending on you."

Striker now moved to my side of the vehicle. I slid out and helped to maneuver Malkah into his arms, resting her head against his chest. I reached for the cylinder and my pack with the tactical computer, the only two items that had any importance at that moment.

"Mrs. Lexi, we will put all your luggage in your rooms for you."

"Thank you," I said, but I kept these pieces with me.

We followed Nuru to a quiet room, kept dark by the shutters. A gentle breeze blew through the slats. The covers, already turned down, exposed the pristine white sheets.

Striker gently laid Malkah onto the mattress.

"If you will go just down the hallway, Mr. Striker. There is food prepared for you. I think, Mrs. Lexi, your friend would be more comfortable if we cleaned her and put her in a night dress."

Striker shot me a glance to make sure I concurred, then left as asked.

Nuru prepared a basin in the bathroom. With practiced hands that did not need my help, she rolled Malkah this way and that, undressing her top. I noticed that she stalled over Malkah's upper arm. A slightly raised scar was more prominent than one would expect, especially on the inside of her arm near her armpit. Nuru adjusted past her curiosity and pulled the gown over Malkah's head. Then she worked on Malkah's lower body, cleaning, drying, and smoothing the fabric so no wrinkle would disturb her. "She has no fever," Nuru said in a tone asking for information.

"No, that is fortunate," I offered by way of response.

"Would you like to join Mr. Striker for some food?"

"No, thank you. If my friend wakes up here, she'll be confused and probably scared, so I want a familiar face with her."

"Shall I bring you a plate?" Nuru asked.

"Not right now, thank you. If you would ask Mr. Striker to bring me one when he's done, I'd appreciate it."

Nuru offered a parting bow and pointed out a bell on the bedside table. "If you need anything, please ring."

I smiled. I was impatient. What I wanted to do was to discover what was in that cylinder. This was the thing that Malkah had been most concerned about. And I was sure it would tell me what to do next. Yes, the alien blob was, for the most part, a completed mission. But Spyder had driven off to protect Babcock. And Babcock had information about Sylanos. And Sylanos was a rat with a tracker.

Trudy said the rat and spider picture was five years in the making, and the time was now.

I came onto people's radar five years ago.

Arya was studying ways to put people into hibernation to survive famine and plagues five years ago with Malkah by her side.

What did the five years pertain to? Either? Both?

Here was Malkah, acting like all humanity—

I didn't finish that thought because a memory suddenly popped up. The first picture that Doc had handed me in Wyoming was of the queen with a pair of headphones on—not listening to music, protecting her from sound.

I thought of Spyder, wondering how he thought he could do anything to get Babcock safely out of Russia. Spyder seemed to have made a picture with all these disparate pieces where I had not. I needed time, a whiteboard, and perhaps a brain that a plethora of paradigm and reality-shifting changes hadn't kneaded.

Starting the morning when I discovered Cammy's picture, I tried to gather the puzzle pieces onto the same mental table as I worked to open the cylinder. There was no obvious seam, opening, or catch. There had to be some secret way. I believed the smooth metal surface was created with electrical discharge machining, making the joints seamless and the surface smooth.

The door opened, and like a child caught stealing cookies from the cookie jar, I hid the cylinder behind me.

"Chica, it's me."

"You're clean." He was freshly showered and in another set of clothes.

"And fed. Here's a plate for you. How about you eat and then go in the bathroom and take a shower?"

I stood. "I will if you work on opening this thing up so we can see what's inside." I handed it over. "My guess is EDM technology, so good luck."

THE FOOD WAS MANNA—THE shower heaven. But the true miracle was that Striker had put his crack engineering skills to work and found a way into the cylinder.

"What is it?" I asked, rubbing a towel over the ends of my damp hair.

"Bomb?"

I stilled. "Crap, Striker, are you serious right now?"

"Not a whole bomb, the detonator. Come here. See this."

"Actually, I do see this. This." I pointed at the odd shaped mechanism. "I've seen this. I know who knows what it's for!"

"Where?" Striker asked.

"Remember that day I went to the CIA and got the surprise invitation to the FBI meeting?"

"Yup."

"They didn't vet the slides for my being there. They had a slide up and were discussing it. And I saw that contraption in a drawing on the wall and what looked like a model or prototype. And since we think this has to do with a sound-driven neuroweapon, guess who was showing the slide."

"Calvin Hock." Striker was looking at his watch.

"The one and only."

"Midnight East Coast," Striker said.

"Like I care. I have his number. He gave it to me when he was investigating the comms issue when Scarlet had you shot at Fuller Mine. Hock wanted to make sure I could reach out immediately if I came up with anything new. I'm calling through the Iniquus switchboard." Once I had the operator on the phone, I moved once again through the questions and responses required. I told the guy the number I needed to reach and that I needed this to be a video call. He responded with, "Hold, please." A moment later. "You are on an end-to-end encrypted video line with Special Agent Calvin Hock."

"Shit, Lynx," he said. "This can't be good."

"I have something that I think you're looking for. You're still dressed. I'm glad I didn't wake you."

"We're having a bit of a stressful time. I'm at the office. And the entire Joint Task Force is in the room."

"Good, hive mind. And I'm sorry to interrupt. But me, too… stressful times. I'll try to be very fast. To orient you, I was in a meeting at Langley with you. You were giving a presentation. I was weighing in."

"Yes." It sounded like he was trying to be patient.

"There was a slide in which I saw an object. I have that object. If I show it to you, could you please tell me what it's for? I believe I know. I'm looking for verification."

The screen view pulled back, and I saw the team sitting around the table, looking tense.

Tense was the defining emotion right now.

"Okay, Lynx, let's see it," Green said.

I turned the camera to show the object.

Prescott threw his pen against the wall. "How in the hell?"

"Long story, no time," I replied. "This is my end of the bargain. Your turn."

"That's a detonator," Green said.

"Yup." Really? That's what they wanted to tell me? "More?"

"It goes to a machine that creates sound," Green said cryptically.

I didn't have time for cryptic. "Look, I know about Arya Khouri's discovery. I understand the ramifications. This is what I need to know." I focused the camera lens on the top and pointed at the insertion points for the keys. "Tell me about the two keyholes."

I spun my screen so I could see them.

On camera, I watched Hock tapping at the keyboard on his laptop. "Okay, the sound machine's technology was mutually developed by Omega and the Sylanos Cartel. Each has a key. From our intelligence gathering, it's configured this way to ensure that one team cannot use the machine against the other."

"And put everyone to sleep," I said.

Their room stilled.

"Do you know where the machine is?" I asked.

"We did up until this morning," Green said. "And then there was an event."

"The spies in Lake Victoria. Yes, I know. Are you saying you don't know where it is, but I have the only detonator?"

"Only?" Prescott asked. "We don't know how many detonators there are. We believe there is only one prototype of the machine, and they are about to test it out."

"Russia is." I threw that out, though that hadn't been verified by anything so far. "If they get their hands on it."

"Where are you, Lynx?" Prescott asked.

I ignored him. "Hock, is this set up like a nuclear bomb? What would happen if only one of the players put their key in and turned it?"

"From the schematics, there's a failsafe. If anyone twists one key, then the machine will self-destruct."

"Why would they do that?" I asked.

"This was a mutual decision between two groups who don't trust each other," Green said. "If one group attempted to use the machine without both keys, they wanted it to be abundantly apparent that the attempt was made."

"We believe that a representative from Sylanos and one from Omega are required to instigate the event," Prescott said. "Someone from Omega and someone from Sylanos would each protect one of the keys. They'd come together and decide on a target, then actuate together."

"Two equals to make the boom, right?" I asked.

"Not boom, buzz, but yes," Green said.

"You said self-destruct. Is that a surety?" Striker asked.

"By design?" Hock said. "Yes. In real world? There are no sureties. But we would hope so."

"Would it be worth the risk to destroy the machine?" Striker asked out of camera view. "They had the schematics. Another could be built."

"That's Iniquus Commander Striker Rheas, who is working this mission with me," I explained.

"The United States has the schematics," Prescott said. "We believe that the Lake Victoria attack was on a group targeted because they had successfully collected the device and all the data that went with it. That data is in the hands of the United States and no other entity. If the machine is destroyed, the problem has been contained. Without the schematics, scientists can reverse-engineer it if we fail to destroy the machine."

"The detonator and machine both went missing after we thought they were secured," Green said. "But now you turn up with the detonator. Do you happen to have the machine?"

"No." I shook my head. "Just this. Is that what you were working on when I called you, finding the machine?" I asked.

"It's what *everyone* is working on," Green replied. "Where are you?"

"If we had the opportunity to destroy that machine, would it be advisable to do so?

"Is it near a large population?"

"I don't know right now," I said.

"I can't answer that. I'm honestly not sure what mechanism they have. It might be acid, and the thing melts. It could be an explosive, and it has the potential to cause collateral damage."

"Are you going after Sylanos and Omega?" I asked.

"They haven't broken any laws," Green said. "In this regard, at least. This is perfectly legal."

"It's not considered terrorism?"

"It's a non-conventional weapon, and it is not in and of itself harmful. Perhaps kidnapping charges if it rendered people effectively held hostage? I have no idea."

"I'm asking again. If we had the opportunity to detonate that machine, is it advisable that we follow through?"

"Absolutely. Destroy the shit out of it," Prescott yelled. "And then call us back so we can congratulate you."

"Lynx," Green said, "No joking here. It is imperative that it is destroyed before it gets into the hands of the Russians."

From the corner of my eye, I could see Malkah rousing. She was watching me and listening to this conversation.

"I need to go. I'll call back if there's more." I shut the top of the computer to cut the connection. "Malkah." I leaned over her so she could see me through her slitted eyes. "I'm Lexi. Spyder, Striker," I pointed over to Striker, and he too leaned in, "and I brought you to a safe house. We have a plane on its way to take you to the American base in Djibouti and get you medical help."

She licked her lips.

"Do you need some water?" I asked.

She turned her head and gestured toward the pad and pen on the side table.

When I handed it to her, she drew a spiderweb.

"Spyder went somewhere to help get your friend out of Russia," I told her.

She licked her lips and gave the slightest of nods. Her finger barely tapped the paper. "Ship," she whispered.

"Ship?" I picked up the pad. It was almost the exact same configuration of lines as the picture that Cammy drew. The lines looked like a spiderweb. *Ship*?

I turned the pad for Striker to see.

Striker knelt so they were eye to eye. "Malkah, I know this is taxing you. Is the sound machine on the ship? We need to find it to detonate it." Not cryptic, willing to go there. Okay. I could get on that page.

"Moving ship." She pointed toward the detonator, then lifted her arm to flop over her head onto the pillow and pointed at her arm.

Striker looked at me, obviously hoping that I could make that out.

"The key?" I asked.

She pointed at her arm.

With shaking fingers, I undid the tiny buttons running from the neckline to the waist as gently as possible. I peeled the nightdress off that arm and placed her arm over her head to examine the scar. I felt it. "It's a prosthetic scar. We need some oil. I think I saw some in the bathroom toiletries basket."

Striker strode toward the door.

"And makeup wipes or tissues," I called after him.

Malkah seemed to be back asleep.

I gently removed her scar while Striker got on the phone with General Thomas. "General, what we need right now is for you to look at satellite images for any ship that is not going in a straight line from Point A to Point B but is tracing a pattern in the water. It is probably near Russia. The specific pattern we're looking for is the shape of a spiderweb."

Malkah's lips moved.

I bent low to listen.

"Trying to hide. When it leaves the configuration, *it's time*." Those last two words took on the red strobing glow of a *knowing*.

"It's time." This was the exact phrase used by Herman Trudy when he drew Sylanos and the web with the dangling spider.

"It's time" sent horror through my system.

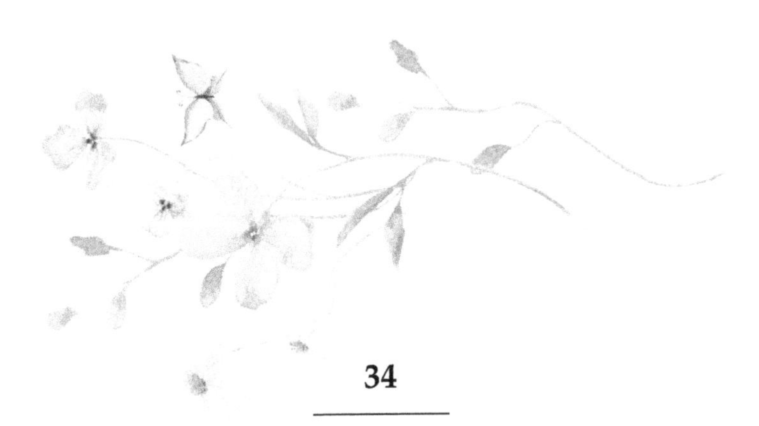

34

Overhead, the roar of a plane engine rattled the windows.

Quickly, Striker shoved everything into our bags.

After testing to make absolutely sure that the key slid into the machine, I slid the detonator into the cylinder, put the key into my phone lanyard, and hung it around my neck under my shirt.

Striker rang the bell for help with the bags.

Nuru came hustling in. “Mrs. Rochambeau is here.”

“Yes,” I said. “We don’t have time to visit with her here. Our friend seems to be getting sicker. Is it okay if we take the gown?”

“Of course, of course, and a blanket to wrap her, poor child.” Nuru bustled and shifted, swaddling Malkah comfortably in the covers.

Tumo arrived and gathered the bags as, once again, Striker scooped Malkah into his arms. Bending his legs to work as shock absorbers, he hustled out the door, across the deck, the yard, and out the gate toward the sound of the engine coming to a stop.

D-Day was hopping down, saw us racing toward her, turned, and climbed back on the private jet that would clear travel through Tanzanian airspace without any hoops to jump like a military craft would require.

We arranged Malkah on the floor, her lips turning blue.

Tumo placed the bags inside.

Nuru, perspiring and out of breath, reached a pillow toward me. "For her comfort. Our blessings travel with you."

"My orders are for Djibouti," D-Day said as the engine cranked back up.

"Yes, quickly," I called. "Do you have medical equipment?"

"I'll look for it. You fly." Striker patted D-Day's shoulder as he climbed past where Malkah lay in the aisle. I was on my knees at her head, arranging the pillow, grateful for the power of kindness.

As D-Day did her thing up front, Striker came back and opened the case of medical supplies that were stored in the galley.

I pulled the stethoscope on and listened to the erratic heartbeat. I tested for oxygenation saturation, and the number started at eighty-eight but ticked downward instead of up.

"Is there an oxygen tank or an oxygen machine anywhere?" I asked, pulling the defibrillator closer, opening the top, and reading the instructions to refresh my memory. It was a precaution, I told myself.

"Djibouti's a no-go," I whispered to Striker, "Plan B, now."

Striker moved up to talk to D-Day.

D-day was on the radio calling for orders as Striker made his way back to me. "An hour plus to get to Dar es Salaam. D-Day can't land on the carrier in this thing. We'll have to get Malkah to a hospital in the city. JSOC approved the change of route."

I had used the medical kit to the extent that I could.

Her skin lost its pigmentation, turning an ashy gray.

She took a rattling breath in.

I pulled the stethoscope into place to listen to her heart.

"Nothing." I grabbed the top of her nightgown and pulled to pop all those delicate buttons off and out of the way. They volleyed and pinged.

I listened again.

Striker leaped to her side and started mouth to mouth while I placed the pads for the defibrillator with shaking hands.

Horror washed through me as I forced myself to move methodically down the list of instructions.

The monitor pinged, CLEAR.

"Clear," I called.

Striker sat, holding his hands up to show he wasn't touching her.

I pressed the button.

Her body convulsed.

Striker had done this for me. I could feel the memory rolling off him.

The machine flashed the command, CLEAR.

"Clear," I repeated, then pressed the button.

Her body jolted.

My heart ricocheted around my ribcage. I didn't know this woman. We had exchanged a few words. But I knew her, studied her, and thought about her over many missions. She was Spyder's colleague, and he obviously cared about her.

CLEAR.

"Clear," I called out.

Suppose she didn't make it. If she didn't make it. If she didn't make it…

I waited for the next instructions from the machine, NO SHOCK ADVISED.

"I've advised the tower of a life-or-death emergency," D-Day said over the speaker. "We've been given priority landing. An ambulance is waiting on the runway—thirty-five-minute ETA. We have the winds at our back. I'm pushing this engine for all she's worth. I'll do my best to break the speed record."

"Copy," Striker called forward.

Meanwhile, I was running protocol through my brain. I listened with my stethoscope and heard nothing.

NO SHOCK. What do I do? "Okay, leave the pads in place. I'll take breath. You take compressions, three minutes, and we switch."

I remembered Meg and Rooster in Tanzania doing CPR and artificial breath. Their guide was stung by a bee and had an allergic reaction. They had four people round-robining while they waited for the rescue helicopter. It was just Striker and me, but we were motivated.

In between breaths, I set my phone to ring every 3 minutes.

I knew this effort might keep her body alive and allow her brain to die.

I wondered if I were in this position what I would want to have happen.

They told me they defibrillated me back to life. In my mind, they had applied the pads, shocked me—and other than my impact injuries—I was hunky-dory.

I didn't actually know what happened to me out there in the desert.

It could well be that my team lived through this very scenario.

"Switch."

I moved to her chest and used my body weight to push her ribs down the required two inches to be effective.

Did my team do this for me?

Should we keep doing this for her?

Striker seemed to hear my thoughts. "We keep going until we land. D-Day's a Night Stalker and Night Stalkers never quit."

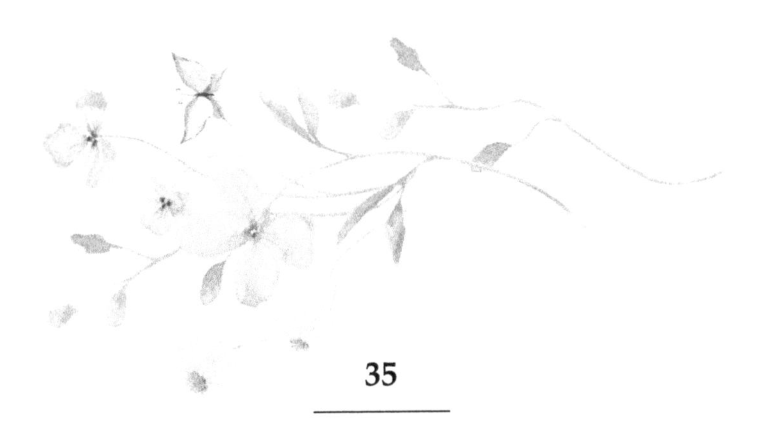

35

I SOBBED LIKE A BABY OUT OF EXHAUSTION AND GRIEF.

The EMTs swarmed the plane, attached an automatic chest compressor, and intubated Malkah. They were professional and efficient. But I had gone out for years as a volunteer EMT, and I could tell that Malkah was gone beyond the point where a miracle or a machine could bring her back.

Striker wasn't disaffected, dropping a constant string of kisses into my hair, squeezing me tightly to him. I knew he was thinking about the time he almost lost me, too.

The crew respectfully covered Malkah from foot to chin and brought her out of the plane. Out the door, I could see a black limo with Israeli flags in the front.

Obviously, JSOC had reached out to her government.

Our duty was finished, yet as they brought the gurney to the back of the ambulance, I kept thinking if I just did one thing more, she'd live.

It was irrational.

Striker pushed at me, the sat phone ringing in his ruck.

"Strike Force Actual," he said as he scrambled toward D-Day. He scooped his hand to tell me to follow. "You're on speakerphone. D-Day, Lynx, and Striker present."

"General Thomas here. When do you land?"

"We've landed, sir. Our charge has been passed to emergency personnel. We believe she is dead."

"A shit thing to happen in a storm of shit things happening," Thomas said. "I got a call from the Color Code. I'm up to date on the pressures and your activity."

"Sir," Striker said.

"We found a ship in the Aegean Sea making a spiderweb just south of Turkey. That changed while you were in the air. The south-to-north route has been extended beyond the past iterations for the first time. It will enter the Dardanelles Strait on its present course in the next ten hours. D-Day, I understand you are flying your father's private jet."

"I am, sir."

"I'm reading off a GPS coordinate in the Aegean. Plug that into your systems for me."

D-Day followed the command. "Done, sir."

"How are you fixed for fuel? As is, can you get there and get safely down?"

"I can fly right over that coordinate and land at a Turkish airport. I'm good on fuel, sir."

"Lynx and Striker will explain the circumstances on the flight," General Thomas said. "It's a long haul. But exceedingly important."

To say that time stood still was an understatement.

It felt like I was existing in a jar of cold molasses. Everything moved slowly. My muscles felt too heavy to shift my limbs.

At some point, Striker and I dozed off as adrenaline left our systems.

I roused when Striker shifted me.

"Hang on, D-Day, we're coming."

"We are fifteen minutes from the target. We have eyes in the sky monitoring this mission. You're saying that you need to send a radio wave effectively down to the ship. And you think that it will pierce the metal walls?"

"It works like a phone. If a cell phone will work where the object is, the detonator will."

"And you don't think it's down in the hold where it could not be affected?" D-Day asked.

"I think it's sitting in the poshest stateroom on the ship in plain sight," I said. "I think it's housed in something—a carved wooden box, for example—that wouldn't call attention."

"All right, well, we can only do our best here. We've been flying at an altitude of five miles above sea level. I'm going to bring the jet down as low as I can and as slow as I can."

D-Day liked to fly her helicopter a mere eight feet off the ground. I could imagine that she'd have us low enough that we were scraping the radio antennae on the ship.

"Get yourselves in place," she said.

Striker pulled the detonator from the cylinder.

I pulled the key from my lanyard.

The plane dropped its nose, and I had to put my knees on the seat in front of me to keep myself upright in my chair.

Striker got JSOC video call running on his computer, updating General Thomas.

"I'm counting you in," D-Day said. "Ten."

"General Thomas, sir, we have no idea what, if any, effect this will have."

"Nine."

"We've got you on our satellite feed," General Thomas said. "We'll be able to give you real-time feedback. You'll be able to watch it on your tactical computer."

"Eight."

"If you see nothing, how do you advise?" Striker asked.

"Seven."

General Elliot moved to a split screen, and I could see the ship.

We looked incredibly close to the water. “Head on to the airport per flight plans—”

“Six.”

“—where we have a team to meet you and take control of the detonator.”

“Five.”

“From there,” the General continued, “we’ll move on to Plan B.”

“Four.”

“Yes, sir,” Striker and I said together.

“Three.”

I inserted the key into the device.

“Two.”

“Fingers crossed,” I said as Striker held the device steady.

D-Day called, “Execute. Execute. Execute.”

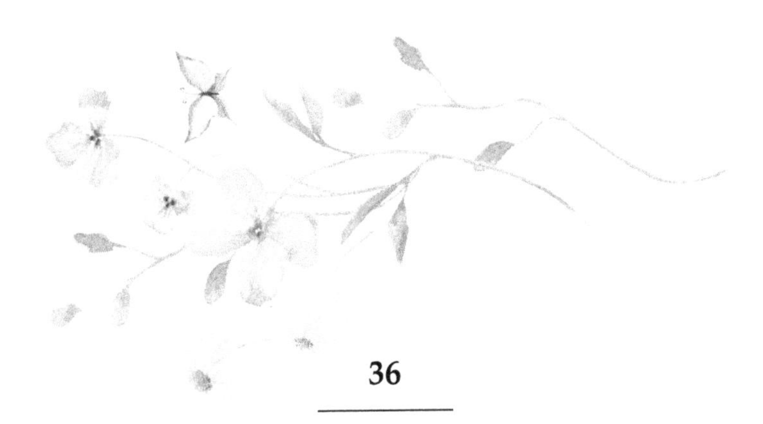

36

"Hold on back there," D-Day said into the speaker. "I'm climbing."

"I closed my eyes. It felt like I was at an amusement park, dumped back in my seat as the car clinked and clanked as it pulled to the top of a very steep rollercoaster.

I opened my eyes as I felt us even out.

"Are you seeing this?" General Thomas asked. The right half of the split screen suddenly enlarged, taking us tightly on what looked like a huge yacht or a small passenger ship. Smoke poured from the port side.

"That's toward the front, away from the engine noise. The better staterooms would be in that area."

"It's on fire," I said. "Something flammable was nearby. Holy moly! The crew."

"We redirected a naval ship in that direction at the beginning of this mission. It should arrive in time to render aid," General Thomas said. "Maydays are going out. Other boats will turn to their aid."

The screen suddenly shifted. "And there you go. A high-dollar fella is jumping ship—cigarette boat. Nope, not letting anyone else on with him. We'll keep tracking where he goes." After a moment, General Thomas added, "It looks like this mission was a success."

"I'd feel better if someone saw the device and saw the device destroyed," I whispered.

"We'll get forensics on the ship with the Navy. They know where to gather evidence. Meanwhile, the guy who made the dash for it took nothing with him."

"Sir, have you heard anything about the Israeli national?" Striker asked.

"Malkah Weiss was pronounced dead on arrival. They're running pathology now. They understand it might have been a murder. Initial findings are Malkah Weiss was poisoned. You did what you could."

It hit like a punch to the gut.

"Immediately upon arriving back in D.C., we'll do a debrief."

"Yes, sir. Out."

"We are heading straight to the airport in Izmir. I am refueling. My orders are to fly you right back to my dad's place."

"We're not staying there, but if they could give us a ride," I said. "Our rover ran out of gas, and we need to return it to the tourist company."

"Got you. Yeah, I'll make sure that's arranged when I get there. And I'm going to need a nap."

"No kidding," I said.

Striker and I were watching the satellite feed. All we knew was that there was a fire right after I turned the key. How would we be able to tell if we had succeeded? We didn't even know for sure that the device was on that boat, only that Malkah had believed that the device was on that boat.

Conveying that message was how she used her last words.

That sat like a boulder on my chest. I hoped we would be included in the need-to-know loop. Yes, I very much hoped to get some closure.

For days now, Striker and I had been in perpetual motion. And the reason for our trip still hadn't been wholly accomplished. Right now, despite our sleeping on the plane, I was wrung out.

We landed at Davidson Range, where Tumo and Nuru offered hospitality. D-Day slogged in to get some sleep. Striker and I asked for two vehicles.

Tumo was curious but asked no questions.

Then we started our crazy relay race.

I followed behind Striker as we made our way back to where Spyder had hidden his motorboat.

We used one reserve tank to fill the tank on the boat. We took another tank with us as we motored over the choppy waters to Uganda to find our vehicle hidden on the side of the fire-scorched road. Abandoning the boat, we filled our rover with gas, and I slid under the steering wheel to drive us back to Grandmother Sybil's village, where we ate a meal, offered our gratitude, and left with our paperwork.

Time at the registrar's produced our official documentation.

Back across the border, we returned to where we'd left the two Davidson rovers.

I started one up and followed Striker to the animal reserve to return their vehicle. After paying our penalty and rental payment, I drove us back to where we had parked the second Davidson rover. Once again, Striker and I split up, each of us driving a vehicle back to the Davidson's compound.

D-Day woke to fly us to Dar es Salaam, where we bought tickets for our return flight to D.C. There, D-Day retrieved the Navy helicopter she'd flown from her ship.

We hugged D-day goodbye and watched her take off as she headed back to sea.

All in a day's work for her.

Stunning activity for me.

"Was this like other missions you've been on?" I asked Striker.

"Pretty typical," he said, "except perhaps for the ritual tea." He sent me a wink. "Come on, we have a couple hours until we fly out.

Let's pick the date of our marriage ceremony, pass it by General Elliot, then get Alice and Celia on this."

"They're going to be so happy. All that work they put into planning our wedding for last June, now they can brush off those plans and put them to good purpose. The temperatures will be about the same in June as in September. We did it." I stared at him wide-eyed. "We are officially Commander and Mrs. Rheas!"

EPILOGUE

THE STREET PARTY

I STOOD ON THE STEPS AND CALLED UP TO STRIKER, "WHO WAS THAT on the phone?"

"Mimi," Striker called back. "Everyone is checked in—the folks from Miami, the Kitchen Grandmothers, Master Wang, and his grandson. They finished up breakfast, and they're loading the bus."

I jogged down the steps to look out the front window. "The party folks are here, tents are up. That noise is the fans for the blowups. Ruby and Cammy are out front with Sarah. They look like they can hardly wait."

I moved to the back of the house and was not at all surprised to find Spyder sitting at the table drinking a cup of tea, Beetle and Bella panting at his feet.

"Spyder's here," I called to Striker.

I moved toward the coffee pot as Striker came to join us, sticking out his hand toward Spyder. "Thank you for coming." He pulled out a chair for me, then sat, looking at Spyder expectantly.

"Yes, I bring news." Spyder reached a hand down to rest on Bella's head. "The ship partially submerged. They saved most of the people."

"Were *the* people saved?" I asked.

"The head of Omega is back in the Seychelles. He is the man who escaped on the fast boat."

"Figures." I made a face.

"The device?" Striker asked.

"Was found by SEAL divers and is now in the hands of the correct agencies. For now, there are at least two external people who know of the possibilities this device presents. Your friend Arya, though any amount of groundwork would show that she has little memory of her past and no ability to do further research. I believe she is safe. The pictures from her album that included Malkah were removed for Arya's safety."

I leaned forward to squeeze Spyder's arm. "I am so so sorry about Malkah."

"She lived a life where she enjoyed the risk. She was, as speculated, poisoned. Possibly on the boat, possibly before she boarded. We will never know."

"The other person who knows about the machine?" Striker asked.

"The head of Omega. But he is a tactical man, not a scientific man. He will only have understood the concept and the usefulness to his organization, not the means by which it worked. More importantly, in the same room as the device, the remains of a man were found. His DNA identifies him as Marcos Sylanos. He was considered dead, and now he is."

"For sure."

"Yes, my dear. There is but one head left on The Hydra. And it is in a weakened state."

"The gentleman who was having logistical issues with his travel plans?" I asked. "He's okay? We saw on the news that a plane was sent to collect the passengers and crew in Russia."

"He returned with me to Washington D.C. My understanding is that a plane has arrived in Russia to help others who were inconvenienced." He reached into his shirt pocket, withdrew a piece of paper, and handed it to me.

Immediately, I saw that it was a tasking sheet. I read the back to find out who had done the work: Herman Trudy.

TASK: Marriage Celebration

Friday and Saturday.

No wedding.

Celebration, other.

K9 guests.

I TURNED it over to look at the childlike drawing.

"I'm guessing these are dogs?" I looked up to Spyder for verification.

"Big for dogs," Striker said, leaning in.

"Trudy's drawing is off," Spyder explained. "He sprained his wrist in a fall and was wearing a brace. He was attempting to draw with a pencil held between two fingers."

"Ah, okay. Dogs in the water. Six of them. Beetle and Bella, Hoover, Zeus, Houston, Rory. Yes, those were the dogs we were inviting."

STRIKER and I sat on the steps to Reaper and Kate's side of the duplex. Ours had a temporary ramp installed so those who used wheelchairs for mobility could get to the facilities.

Mrs. Nelson, who used to own my home, sat on what had been her porch, looking contentedly over the neighborhood. Master Wang sat at her side, tapping a foot to the beat of the band playing at the end of the street, cordoned off with a police vehicle to keep traffic out.

Cammy and Ruby came up and sat beside us.

"Hey girls, did you just get off the bouncy house?" I asked. "You're hot and sweaty."

"Yup!"

"Fun?" Striker tugged one of Cammy's pigtails.

"Yup!"

"So I have an Auntie Kate who lives here," Cammy pointed at the door, "and a Nana Kate?"

"Yes. Nana Kate is one of my Kitchen Grandmothers."

"And I know Mrs. Sophia, who is Mr. Brian's wife, and I also have a Nonna Sophia, who is a different Kitchen Grandmother?"

"That's right," Striker said. "Most people have names that others have. Mr. Reaper and Mrs. Kate named their son Zack, and then they moved into our neighborhood, where Miss Alice has a son, Zack. There are lots of Aunt Lexis in the world. But only one Aunt Lexi who loves you deeply."

"And other Uncle Gavins?" Cammy asked.

"Yes," he said.

"What about Uncle Strikers? Because you both have two names." She held up two fingers.

"I know other people named Striker. I'm sure they have young people in their lives who are family." He pointed. "See those two people with the baby carriage? That's Mrs. Raine and Mr. Damian. But do you know what Mrs. Raine's work name was before she became a children's book artist?"

"No, what?"

"Cammy!" He tickled Cammy, making her squeal and wriggle until she was breathless.

"Her name was Cammy," I said, "but she never uses it anymore now that she has her new job."

Cammy turned to me. "If you got a new job, would your work name still be Lynx?"

"Now, what new job would I take?" I asked with a smile. I couldn't imagine working for anyone but Iniquus.

"I don't know." She shrugged. "You could be a dog walker."

"I could. It's important work. I'll tell you what, if I ever become a dog walker, I'll let you help me pick out my new work name." I smiled. "Hey, let's go back down and look and see what would be fun. I love your face paint. You girls are beautiful butterflies. And lots of sparkles, too."

Cammy held Striker's hand, and I held hands with Ruby. "We'll be back," I called over my shoulder to Mrs. Nelson and Master Wang.

In the street, the girls pulled Striker to the art tent.

I stopped at the balloon artist and asked for a sword.

With a squeaking set of twists, I was handed a long center length with two small balls on either side as a kind of hand guard.

I showed up at Striker's side brandishing it triumphantly.

Striker raised an eyebrow, and I bent over laughing.

"There's a private joke in there," Kate said, with Little Guy in front of her on the folding chair, tracing red crayon over the paper.

"Yup. Very private." I looked over where Ruby and Cammy were hard at work on their masterpieces.

Ty and Kira came up with big hugs. Rory was sopping wet. "Sorry," Ty said. "The dogs are playing in the kiddie pools you set out for them."

"As well they should. You having a good time, Rory?" He sent me a quick look and then went back to scanning my guests. "Ah, that's what he's looking for." I pointed out. "Tripwire and Dani just got here. Go say hi, for Rory's sake. We'll catch up with you later."

The music stopped. I turned when Alice asked for everyone's attention.

"Folks! Hi there. So, I wanted to show you I've set up a table on my porch." She pointed toward her house. "Lexi and Striker, I know that you asked us not to offer gifts. But, well, we couldn't help ourselves. If you two wouldn't mind coming forward for a moment."

Striker smiled at me, clasped my hand, and we walked over.

Alice handed me a black book with lemons on the front: "A Family of the Heart Cookbook—When Life Gives You Lemons."

I looked up at her.

Alice tapped the book. "These are letters and recipes from your guests. The ones Celia and I could track down in time, anyway. You put the gas peddle down, and we had to whip this thing together." She looked out over the crowd. "See what I did there?" Laughter floated over the neighborhood.

I opened the pages and looked through. "Oh, my goodness! This is precious. What a treasure." I leaned into the mic. "I can't thank you enough!"

"And to make sure you didn't get upset that we broke your no-gifts rule. Celia had them printed, so they are the wedding favors. And that, my friends, is what you will find on my porch. Please grab the gift bag with your name on it and take it home with you. Thank you!" She raised her hand, and the band took up their song again.

Alice pulled the book from my hand. "You can look at this after your marriage ceremony tomorrow. If you do it now, you'll get weepy and sentimental. I just needed to tell you about it so nobody left without their bag."

We hugged her tightly. "Thank you so much."

"Go! Go! Enjoy everyone." She shooed us back away.

"Let's check on Cammy, then talk to Abuela," I said. "She might be freaking out a bit, not knowing how this came to be. And, of course, I couldn't say anything on the phone."

"Good." Striker and I walked to the art tent, and Striker rounded the table to speak to Cammy. "Lexi?" I looked up and caught Striker in full stoic mode, standing behind Cammy.

I made my way over and took a full hit when I saw what she drew. "Hey, sweetheart, doesn't that look fun?" I asked. "Tell me about your picture."

"This is an octopus," she said.

"I see that. And what else?"

"He's sad because his arms were cut off, and he has just the one. So he can't swim in the water anymore. That's why he's on the boat."

"Did you see this in a dream?" Striker asked.

Cammy shrugged.

"Where is the boat coming from?" I forced a smile. "Do you know where the octopus is going?"

"He came from a different boat. And he's going to play on the beach, so he feels better and isn't so sad."

Striker squeezed my shoulder and was moving.

I looked up to see what he saw.

Kate grabbed her belly with her mouth open and her eyes wide with surprise.

"Kate," I called as I ran to her side of the table. "Alice, come watch Little Guy. Manny, go find Reaper." I got to her side. "Kate, you have help. Tell me what's happening."

"My water broke."

"Okay. Go time." I smiled encouragingly.

"Nope. Nope. Nope." Kate shook her head vigorously.

"Tell me, Kate. What are you saying no to?"

"Her head. I think I'm crowning."

"Striker, help me. Let's get Kate lying down."

Reaper was at our side. "Tell me."

"Baby's on her way out," I said.

"Out? No, that happens in the hospital." Reaper grabbed Kate's hand. "You okay? Hanging in there? Kate, I've got you. We've got this. We're minutes away. Talk to Indie Kate and tell her to give Daddy ten minutes. Just *ten* minutes."

Dave squatted beside us. "Reaper, get her in the police car. My guy's gonna run you lights and sirens to the hospital. Cathy ran to your house to get your bags."

Striker helped get Kate up into Reaper's arms.

She was squinching her face down tight.

Cathy ran the bags to Striker.

Striker ran the bags to the car.

The band switched to singing Ed Sheeran's 'Welcome to the World.' And the whole of Silver Lake joined in.

And I couldn't help but think of the amazing tradition of a baby's song in South Africa.

Indie Kate would be welcomed into a tribe that would love and support her, and nothing could be more beautiful than a family of the heart.

The Wedding

Gavin Michael Rheas

&

India Alexis Sobado

Joyfully invite you
to their marriage celebration

September 24 at two o'clock

The Bay House, Maryland

reception to follow

Our friends and family gathered on the benches in the glade at Striker's Bay house. He'd commissioned the creation of this spot for our wedding last June. Boulders were stacked to form a thirty-foot wall on one side. The rocks tapered off around the sides and back, creating a natural-looking hill.

A waterfall tumbled like a bridal veil from the top and went into a flowing stream that encircled the base of the slate ritual platform. In the shade of the forest trees, the floating candles glowed. In a moment, Striker and I would climb the steps and walk over the bridge to stand in front of General Elliot and Spyder.

Deep stood in the middle of the platform, singing in his rich baritone.

Ave Maria hushed the forest.

With the last note, he stepped aside.

The string quartet played Pachelbel as Deep joined us at the top of the embankment. General Elliot took his place.

"Ready?" Striker asked.

"I already ate the cake," I said. "This is the icing."

He squeezed my hand.

As the last note faded, the quartet began "A Thousand Miles." It seemed the most appropriate song to represent our journey to this moment.

My team, so handsome in their tuxedoes, started down the aisle —Blaze and Deep, Randy and Axel, Jack and Gator.

Behind them, the neighborhood kids pranced, waving wands with long, silken ribbons.

Then Cammy walked between Beetle and Bella.

And now it was time for us.

Striker let go of my hand, and I stood between Dave and Cathy, my parents' oldest friends. As we walked forward, Striker followed, flanked by Mimi and his dad.

The team had crossed the bridge, handsome in their tuxedoes. They formed a line ranging behind the General and Spyder.

With her flower wreath decorating her curls, Cammy with Beetle and Bella—wearing their wreaths around their necks—all went to stand with Gator.

With kisses from our parents, Striker took my hand again.

His beautiful architectural design meant the stairs were wide enough to accommodate us walking side by side, even with the width of my skirts.

We circled to face each other.

Today, I wore ruby red. (Or Ruby red, as I told one of my favorite little people.) It was a color that appeared in each of my Kitchen Grandmothers' weddings, whether as their dress or their flowers.

Biji hand-made this for me. She had asked Striker if he had any ideas of what he'd like me to wear, and Striker said he thought I should look like a queen and a warrior. Under the skirt, I wore sleek pants made from the same raw silk. The form-fitting, off-the-shoulder bodice and the abundance of fabric in the detachable skirt were richly embroidered with gold thread. I felt like a queen who could throw off any encumbrance with grace and beauty and do what was necessary to keep my family safe and strong.

Cammy floated forward, her fairy wings undulating in the breeze. I handed my bouquet of wildflowers to her, and she took them to Gator to hold. A whisper in her ear, and she scrambled forward to fix my skirt, making sure it was straight.

I turned back to listen to the ceremony unfold.

Striker was saying, "You are my everything, my raspberry girl. You are my springtime. You are hope and strength. You hold my soul in your hands."

The whole event felt like a dream.

I knew I was speaking.

I knew I slid my father's ring from right hand to left, making it Striker's ring as he did for me with Mom's rings, now filled with my own vows to Striker.

I knew people were cheering, and there was music.

It was a joyful, surreal, magical, gorgeous moment in time.

Striker leaned in. His kiss was tender and filled with belonging and promise.

General Elliot puffed out his chest and announced, "I present to you, Mr. and Mrs. Rheas."

Maybe there was no such thing as a happily ever after. But today, Striker

and I vowed that no matter what came our way next

we would live together happily until THE END.

READERS

THANK YOU FOR JOINING THIS HAPPY OCCASION!

While this concludes the Lynx Series,
Lynx and Striker have many more adventures in the World of Iniquus Security, with a new shared series coming soon.

A Family of the Heart Cookbook, is available for you to enjoy!
FionaQuinnBooks.com

The next book in the chronological order of the Iniquus World is,

Guardian's Instinct

with Basil St. John code name Halo, and his Malinois Max

THE WORLD of INIQUUS

Chronological Order

Ubicumque, Quoties. Quidquid

Weakest Lynx (Lynx Series)

Missing Lynx (Lynx Series)

Chain Lynx (Lynx Series)

Cuff Lynx (Lynx Series)

WASP (Uncommon Enemies)

In Too DEEP (Strike Force)

Relic (Uncommon Enemies)

Mine (Kate Hamilton Mystery)

Jack Be Quick (Strike Force)

Deadlock (Uncommon Enemies)

Instigator (Strike Force)

Yours (Kate Hamilton Mystery)

Gulf Lynx (Lynx Series)

Open Secret (FBI Joint Task Force)

Thorn (Uncommon Enemies)
Ours (Kate Hamilton Mysteries)
Cold Red (FBI Joint Task Force)
Even Odds (FBI Joint Task Force)
Survival Instinct - (Cerberus Tactical K9 Team Alpha)
Protective Instinct - (Cerberus Tactical K9 Team Alpha)
Defender's Instinct - (Cerberus Tactical K9 Team Alpha)
Danger Signs - (Delta Force Echo)
Hyper Lynx - (Lynx Series)
Danger Zone - (Delta Force Echo)
Danger Close - (Delta Force Echo)
Fear the REAPER – (Strike Force)
Warrior's Instinct - (Cerberus Tactical K9 Team Bravo)
Rescue Instinct - (Cerberus Tactical K9 Team Bravo)
Heroes Instinct - (Cerberus Tactical K9 Team Bravo)
Striker (Striker Force)
Marriage Lynx (Lynx Series)
A Family of the Heart Cookbook
Guardian's Instinct

Coming soon, more great stories from the ex-special forces security team members who live, work, and love in a tightly knit family.

Beowolf
Blaze Ahead
Sheltering Instinct
Shielding Instinct

FOR MORE INFORMATION VISIT

WWW.FIONAQUINNBOOKS.COM

ACKNOWLEDGMENTS

My great appreciation ~

To my readers who helped me plan the wedding, thank you for the fun!

To the real-world Christen Davidson, for our decades of friendship.

To my editor, Kathleen Payne
To my publicist, Margaret Daly
To my cover artist, Melody Simmons
To M. Carlon for all of her help and support.
To my Street Force, who support me and my writing with such enthusiasm.

Thank you to the real-world military, FBI, and CIA, who serve to protect us.
To all the wonderful professionals whom I called on to get the details right.
Please note: This is a work of fiction, and while I always try my best to get all the details correct, there are times when it serves the story to go slightly to the left or right of perfection. Please understand that any mistakes or discrepancies are my authorial decision-making alone and sit squarely on my shoulders.

Thank you to my family.
I send my love to my husband, and my great appreciation. T, when

my head is in a fictional world, I so appreciate your constancy, consideration, and patience as you wait for me to reemerge again, ready for our next adventure together.

And, of course, thank *YOU* for reading my stories. I'm smiling joyfully as I type this. I so appreciate you!

ABOUT THE AUTHOR

Fiona Quinn is a USA Today bestselling author, a Kindle Scout winner, and an Amazon Top 40 author.

Quinn writes action-adventure in her Iniquus World of books, including Lynx, Strike Force, Uncommon Enemies, Kate Hamilton Mysteries, FBI Joint Task Force, Cerberus Tactical K9 Teams Alpha, Bravo, and Charlie, and Delta Force Echo series, and now, a cookbook!

She writes urban fantasy as Fiona Angelica Quinn.

And, just for fun, she writes the Badge Bunny Booze Mystery Collection with her dear friend, Tina Glasneck.

Quinn is rooted in the Old Dominion, where she lives with her husband. There, she pops chocolates, devours books, and taps continuously on her laptop.

Visit www.FionaQuinnBooks.com

Find & Follow Fiona Quinn on Social Media

- facebook.com/FionaQuinn.52
- x.com/fionaquinnbooks
- instagram.com/fionaquinnbooks
- bookbub.com/authors/fiona-quinn
- goodreads.com/fionaquinnbooks

Marriage Lynx is a work of fiction. Names, characters, places, and incidents either are the product of the author's imagination or are used fictitiously, and any resemblance to actual persons, living or dead, business establishments, events, or locales is entirely coincidental.

Printed Chesterfield, VA
Paperback ISBN-13: 978-1-946661-81-4
Hardback ISBN-13: 978-1-946661-82-1

Library of Congress Control Number: 2023917418

Cover Art: Melody Simmons
Fonts used with permission from Microsoft

Printed in the USA
CPSIA information can be obtained
at www.ICGtesting.com
LVHW070933271023
761899LV00070B/1146/J